I0615834

The Prince's Angel

Legends of the Romanorum, Volume 1

Shayne Carmichael and Mychael Black

Published by Arian Derwydd Books, LLC, 2023.

Legends of the Romanorum, Book 1

In present day London, vampires exist side-by-side with mortals and live under two sets of laws. The Romanorum makes the vampire rules, helping the Princes who rule the cities, but not all vampires are thrilled with the system. A rash of rogue vampires—vampires who have killed mortals—has descended upon London, and it is up to London's vampire prince, Mael Black, to bring them under control. When he learns who is behind the rogues, however, Mael's task becomes more complicated than he would like. His only choice is to turn to a sorcerer of questionable reputation—Cian Carmichael. But Cian is more than he seems to be, and despite the dangers inherent in becoming involved with him, Mael finds he is unable to resist.

Cian Carmichael is an angel, sent to bring the rogue vampires under control. Acquiring a reputation as a vampire hunter, Cian becomes notorious in the city Mael rules. The last thing he expects is to fall in love with the prince of the London vampires.

Can these two deal with their growing attachment and save London from the threat it faces?

Arian Derwydd Books, LLC
https://arianderwyddbooks.com/
The Prince's Angel
Copyright © 2023 by Shayne Carmichael, Mychael Black
ISBN: 978-1-955467-86-5

Prologue

The Times of London
May 19, 1970

After years of negotiations with the Diocourides Society, the United States officially announced today the acceptance of US citizenship for all vampires residing there. Talks are still ongoing with Prime Minister Edward Heath concerning official status in the UK.

In 1962, the world became aware of the existence of vampires, and the ensuing battles have had a lingering effect on the populace of every country involved in the war. When a faction of vampires broke off from the Romanorum, the main governing body of the Diocourides Society, the faction attempted to take over several international cities. For over two years, the Diocourides Society and the governments involved tried to curb the problem. Through the chaos of dealing with the war, and the knowledge of the existence of vampires, many have fought to achieve equal status for them. Today, they are celebrating their achievement with their first win for the rights of vampires.

An official release has been sent to several prominent US papers detailing vampiric history. Reports have been sent to the US Congress, including the number of and names of all vampires living there. The vampire formulas were created by Titus Sennius Diocourides in 11 BC. There are six known formulas, enumerated from first to sixth. The creation of new vampires is strictly regulated by the Romanorum.

Diocourides has agreed to allow the US to help with the regulation of any new vampires created there.

First formula vampires comprise the main body of the Romanorum and rule by country. The current first formula vampire ruler of the UK is Selena Kerr. Second formulas hold the positions of princes of the cities. Currently, Prince Mael Black governs the body of vampires in London. While their status is not yet official here, there is a great deal of hope that it will change in the near future. Four hundred and eighty known vampires live in the UK, and lobbying on their behalf has been fierce in the UK and throughout Europe, where over two thousand vampires live.

Chapter One

Wales, 2005

The sun fell behind snow-capped mountains, setting the countryside ablaze and turning the grass dark gold. A brisk autumn breeze blew across the moor and whistled through the thin arrowloop windows of the tower. Inside the circular stone fortress, Cian Carmichael stood quietly, watching the remnants of the sunlight fade away. Only when the land beyond had dropped into darkness did he turn back to the quiet emptiness of his home. It was a solitude he held onto desperately.

Herbs hung from rafters, drying in the warmth provided by the fire in the hearth. He fingered a sprig of rosemary as he walked under it on the way to his bed. He knew he should be working, but, lately, his mind had been filled with premonitions that were unsettling at best. He stretched out on his bed and closed his eyes. Golden hair blanketed the rich blue silk of his pillows, creating a shimmering spider's web.

There had been a time when his days had not been so worrisome, when he had walked among others and wasn't recognized for what he was. Now he was feared, which suited him well when he wished to simply observe. A reputation was something he knew he could not avoid, and indeed, the one he had was proving to be rather interesting. He opened his eyes and stared up at the blue canopy over him. In the span of a single breath, an image formed, of himself and another man entwined in each other's arms. The man's dark hair blanketed them as they kissed. Cian shook his head, and the image disappeared. It wasn't the first time he'd seen the image. Something told him it wouldn't be the last.

He sighed and got out of bed. He had a job to do. It was why he was here to begin with. Daydreams couldn't change that, despite how pleasant they seemed. He pulled his cloak from its hook on the wall and drew it around his shoulders. Then he circled his hand in the air before him and stepped through a portal of swirling, gray smoke.

When he stepped back out, he found himself in an alleyway. He looked around, taking care that no one saw him emerge. Most people in the ordinary world wouldn't react well to seeing a man appear out of thin air. When he was sure he was alone, he started for the nearest bar. The bar was packed full of young people dancing and drinking, in varying states of undress. Cian paid them little mind as he made his way to the one empty table in the room. As soon as he sat down, a young woman came up to him.

"What can I getcha to drink?" she asked as she put a small square napkin down on the table in front of him.

He thought for a moment and smiled. It wasn't often that he indulged himself, but he had the feeling he would need it tonight. "Absolut," he told her. She nodded and turned away, moving back through the crowd toward the bar.

Cian watched her go and then scanned the throng of bodies filling the dance floor. He trusted his intuition implicitly, and tonight was no different. Rogue vampires were the bane to his — and everyone else's — existence. It was his job to eliminate them. He didn't know what tonight's quarry looked like, but when his gaze settled on a figure watching him from the opposite corner, Cian knew he had found his prey. Their gazes locked for only the briefest moment before the waitress returned with Cian's drink.

Cian handed her the money, and she flashed him a smile before walking away. When he looked back to the corner, the man was gone. Cian took a drink and closed his eyes as the vodka burned his throat. He knew his target wasn't far; he could still feel the man's energy. A few moments later, a tall figure appeared at his side. Cian took another drink and set his glass down, not bothering to look up.

"You're following me," the man said.

Cian nodded.

"Why? What have I done to garner the attention of a *sorcerer*?" The word was spoken with a distinct distaste that made Cian grin. People feared magic, no matter who wielded it.

"Preying on the weak," Cian replied without looking at him.

The man slammed both hands flat on the table and leaned down. "I'm a vampire," he growled. "What do you expect?"

Cian didn't flinch and took another drink. "You're an abomination."

"I merely do what I must to survive."

Cian looked up. The vampire's dark eyes held no remorse, and, in truth, Cian had expected none. He stood slowly and motioned toward the door. "Perhaps we should take this conversation to somewhere less populated," he said. He started for the door, and the vampire fell in behind him.

As soon as they were back in the alleyway, well out of sight, Cian turned and pinned the vampire against the brick wall.

"Do you really think you can kill us all, Carmichael?" the vampire asked with a laugh. "We're everywhere. One man cannot kill us all."

Cian raised his hand, and a blue flame flared to life in his palm. He let go, and the vampire shrieked as the flames crawled over his body. Cian watched as the creature crumpled into a pile of smoldering ashes.

"That's your mistake, my friend," he said quietly. "I am no man."

He turned and walked away without looking back. Killing was part of his job, and although his true nature did not lend itself well to such a profession, Cian's sense of duty remained strong. The protection of humanity was his concern, not the need to show mercy to a vampire. He moved quietly through the darkening streets, now hazy with a light drizzle.

Ahead of him, the gothic magnificence of St. Mary's Cathedral stood like a silent beacon to those who would heed its call. As Cian ascended the rounded steps leading up to the double oak doors, he grew more at ease, despite the incessant nagging in the back of his mind of trouble that not even he understood.

He opened one of the doors and walked in, closing it silently behind him. Beyond the entryway, he could see several people in the sanctuary, each one of them lost in their own prayer. The soft sound of someone approaching drew his attention from the sanctuary to the hall on his left. A young woman beamed at him.

"Cian! It's so wonderful to see you again."

"Is he in?" Cian asked her.

"Yes, he's here and waiting for you," she replied as they walked down a dark, stone-lined hallway. They stopped at a wooden door marked 'Employees Only,' and she unlocked it. He followed her inside, and with a press of a well-concealed button, a door opened in the back wall. She stepped aside and waved.

"Thank you, Lisa," he said. He kissed her on her cheek and stepped through the door. Once it was closed behind him, Cian started down the short hallway lit only by the track lighting hidden somewhere near the ceiling. At the end of the hall, he pushed open another door.

"Cian. Please, come in, come in."

Cian didn't see him, but he knew the man was there at his desk, facing the fireplace, the orange-red flames playing across his aging face. "Good evening, Father Shepard," Cian said as he closed the door behind him. The priest's office was blessedly warm, and Cian was finally able to relax. He shrugged his cloak off and draped it over the back of a chair.

Father Shepard turned around and smiled. "How have you been?"

"Busy," Cian said as he stretched his arms over his head and shook his hair free of its ponytail. Waves of brilliant gold cascaded over his back and shoulders. When he flexed the muscles of his shoulders and back, two wings unfurled, their azure feathers as pure as the finest sapphire and the overall wingspan twice as long as Cian himself was tall.

"Feel better?" Father Shepard asked as he leaned back in his chair with a grin.

"Much." Cian gently moved his wings, taking care not to stir up any significant breeze.

"It's always a magnificent sight to see you do that," the priest said. "Did you finally find the man you were looking for?"

Cian pulled a stool over and sat down, letting his wings dip down behind him. Their feathered ends brushed softly across the lacquered wooden floor. "I cornered him in a bar downtown."

"What's next?"

"I've been receiving reports from Rachel and Lee." Cian looked up and met Father Shepard's gaze. "It seems there's more to their problems than merely rogue vampires."

"Oh?"

Cian nodded. "I don't know any details, but I've heard enough to tell me it has something to do with the Prince of London."

Father Shepard sat back as a worried look crossed over his wrinkled face. "Cian, be careful when dealing with him."

"I will. I don't relish the idea of meeting Mael Black, but I fear I may have no choice. If it were up to me, all vampires would be destroyed. They are all abominations."

Father Shepard nodded. "As long as Black keeps his underlings under control, there shouldn't be a problem."

Cian wasn't so convinced, but he nodded and stood, folding his wings out of sight and resummoning the illusion that kept them hidden. "I should be going. Rachel and Lee are waiting for me. I must keep an eye on things, including Black. I don't trust him."

Father Shepard said nothing more, and Cian left his office. Once he was back in the main hallway, Lisa stopped him.

"Cian," she said with a noticeable touch of concern to her voice. "Are you all right? You look more distracted than normal."

Cian smiled and kissed her forehead softly. "I'm fine. My work is not easy, but it must be done. Tell your mother hello for me?"

Lisa smiled and nodded as Cian turned and left the church. Lee was waiting, and Cian had a feeling he was about to get some more news to add to his growing unease. When he reached Lee's apartment building, he took the stairs to the third floor. He stopped at apartment number five and forced his thoughts to calm. Lee would know he was troubled.

A few minutes after he knocked on the door, it opened to reveal a quite disheveled young man. He gave Cian a sheepish grin and stepped to the side, waving him into the apartment. Cian shook his head and walked in. As soon as the door was closed, Lee turned around, causing an errant feather to set a picture swaying on its hook behind him. He stopped the portrait, straightened it, and turned back to Cian.

"Do you always answer the door like that?" Cian asked him, nodding to the white wings.

"You know I don't, but I knew it was you." Lee walked into the kitchen and pulled open the refrigerator. "Want something to drink?"

"Water," Cian said as he sat down on the couch. "Where's Rachel?"

"Working."

Cian took the glass and glanced up at his younger brother. "She made you stay home, didn't she?"

Lee sank down onto the couch with a grimace. "How'd you guess?"

"Lee," Cian said, leaning forward. "What's going on? Something else is going on besides the threat of rogue vampires."

Lee sighed and leaned his head back on the couch. "Yeah. I'm not sure what's going on. I'm not particularly welcome around here."

"Why?"

Lee raised his head, his gaze deadpan. "Because I know you."

Cian nodded. "I suppose that does put a damper on things. I'm surprised they leave you alone."

"They don't mess with me because I don't do any of the killing. Rachel doesn't like to take chances, though, so she acts as a liaison. They don't know about us."

"That's surprising," Cian said. "You'd think Black would at least know."

"If he does, I haven't heard anything. Rachel hasn't heard anything in that regard either. They seem to trust her."

Cian took a drink of his water. "That helps." He set the glass down and looked over at Lee. The angel looked tired, like he hadn't slept in a while. His pale blue eyes told a much different story than his calm demeanor suggested. "What's wrong?"

"I think Rachel is growing tired of this game."

Cian sat back and crossed his arms over his chest. "Why do you say that?"

"Because she's been staying out more than she used to," Lee said quietly. "Cian, I'm beginning to think maybe my trust in her is misplaced."

"What do you mean?"

"I went out last night and found her talking to someone in the shadows. Normally, that wouldn't bother me, but a chill swept over me then that I couldn't shake. Something didn't feel right."

Cian had been worried about such a thing. It had been his fear when Lee had first met the woman. On the surface, Rachel seemed sweet and caring. Beneath the surface, however, Cian sensed something darker. He had tried to warn Lee, but as was Lee's wont, he chose not to listen, even to his own brother. Cian fought the urge to say, "I told you so."

"I know what you're going to say," Lee said with a grumble. "I've been listening to you say it over and over in my mind since that night."

"I didn't say a word," Cian countered.

Lee smirked. "You didn't have to."

"You think she might be working for Black?"

Lee shook his head slowly. "No." He drew in a deep breath then. "I fear she may be working *against* him."

No wonder Lee needed desperately to talk to him. If Rachel was working against Mael Black, then she had already signed her death warrant.

As Cian stood up, he glanced down at Lee. "I'm going to have to meet with him eventually, Lee."

"I know. Please don't mention Rachel, Cian."

"You know I won't. Promise me you'll stay out of this. In fact, I'd feel much better if you were to leave. Go back to Father Shepard."

Lee shook his head. "No. I can't leave Rachel. If she's working against Black, then she doesn't realize what danger she's put herself in."

"If she's working against Black," Cian said sternly, "then she's as good as dead, Lee." He turned and walked out of the apartment, frustrated with his brother's stubborn determination to stay in harm's way. As he stepped out into the street, Cian realized he desperately needed another drink.

He found a small, out-of-the-way-bar and slid into one of the back booths, keeping a good view of the doorway. In London, one did not turn his back on anyone. As soon as Cian's drink was in front of him, he lifted it to his lips. Just as he started to put it back down, he stopped, his attention riveted to the front door. He hated coming out at night; the vampires were everywhere, including here.

The vampire at the door looked around and ducked out once again. Cian set his glass down and followed him. The energy from this one felt different, much younger. As soon as Cian stepped around the corner of the building, a strong hand reached out and grabbed his arm, pulling him back into the shadows. He felt an arm slide around his waist, pulling him back hard against the vampire's body. When a hand descended to the front of his pants, Cian gripped the vampire's wrist tightly.

"Do you always find your victims this way?" he asked.

"I want to hear you beg for your life while I'm draining it from you," the vampire growled in his ear.

Cian sighed with annoyance. This was no rogue vampire, only a young, misguided one. Cian pushed away from him and turned around. The vampire looked surprised. Cian straightened his shirt and glanced up. "You're new to this, aren't you?" he asked. The vampire nodded slowly. "I figured as much."

"Who are you?"

"Let's just say that, if you plan on getting anywhere in this city, you'd be better off not mentioning that you even met me." Cian pulled his cloak back on the side to reveal the silver spike hanging from his belt.

The vampire's eyes widened, and he backed away, only to bump into the opposite wall.

"Don't worry," Cian said as he lowered the cloak once more. "You are not a rogue. If you need to feed, come with me."

Cian led the vampire — *quite* a young one, by his guess — back into the bar. Once they were seated, he waved over the waitress. She nodded and came back to their table, carrying two glasses — one full of dark red wine and the other empty. After she walked away, Cian drew his knife from its sheath and made a small cut on the palm of his hand. As the blood poured into the empty glass, he looked up. The young vampire's mouth was open in nothing short of disbelief. Cian grabbed a napkin and pressed it in his palm. He nodded to the glass full of blood.

"Drink."

The vampire took a slow sip of the blood and shuddered. It was obvious he was very new to this and not quite used to the taste. Cian removed the napkin and the vampire's eyes widened once more as the cut on Cian's palm faded away.

"What are you?" the vampire asked quietly.

"Don't worry about that," Cian said. "You're not from here, are you?"

"No. I arrived yesterday, from Sensey, Wales."

"What's your name?"

The vampire looked around, as if making sure no one could hear him. Then he leaned forward. "Brandon Davies."

"When were you turned?" Cian asked, taking a drink of his wine.

"Two days ago," Brandon said.

"Any idea of the vampire's name?"

Brandon shook his head. "No. Although from all that I've heard about rogue vampires, I wouldn't be surprised to find out he is one."

Cian lifted a pale eyebrow dubiously. "A rogue vampire turned you? Now that would be interesting. How old are you?"

"Twenty-two." Brandon looked around again, and Cian sensed his nervousness.

"You ran from the one who turned you, didn't you? Why?"

Brandon shuddered. "He wanted me to join him. Said he was going after a master vampire here in London. He was simply trying to boost his numbers."

Cian set his wine glass down slowly. "What master vampire?"

Brandon shrugged. "Some guy I've never heard of. Black or something like that. Don't know his first name."

"Damn," Cian said quietly. "This is getting more complicated by the minute."

"What is?"

"Nothing," Cian said. "You fall under the Prince of London's rule here. His name is Mael Black." He watched the recognition of the last name sink in. "He's the master vampire here, and I don't recommend ever crossing him in any way. Come. I'll take you somewhere safe until tomorrow night. Then you can go to Black."

He stood and ushered Brandon out the door. He would find the vampire a room and then he would go back to see Lee. Something was up, something more involved than he had originally suspected. As they started down the street, Cian stopped abruptly, causing Brandon to run into his back.

"What's wrong?" Brandon asked him.

"Shh..." Cian looked around, then pulled Brandon into the shadows.

A few seconds later, a small contingent of vampires walked by. He didn't recognize any of them, but they would know him for sure. When he was sure they had passed, he moved back out into the street, Brandon with him.

"Were they rogues?"

Cian laughed. "If they were, they'd be dead by now." He looked over just in time to see Brandon's face lose what little color it had.

* * *

As he scanned the crowd, Ashton's gaze settled on a young woman entering the bar. He watched her with growing interest as she nearly toppled the doorman over when she pushed past him. A slow grin crawled across his lips as he took in her pretty but arrogant form. There was no doubt in his mind — she was his contact. He stood and walked to her table slowly.

When the woman looked up, her gaze narrowed. With an abrupt wave of her hand, she indicated the chair near her. The gesture itself was economic in motion, as if she didn't have time to waste. She didn't look too thrilled with him, but then, she really didn't seem to care that much for vampires, from what he had heard. Ashton smirked at her as he spun a chair around and sat down hard on the wooden seat. He made no attempt to hide the lascivious gaze he raked over her body.

"Delicious." His gaze moved back up to meet with hers. "Get off your high horse, honey. What information do you have?"

"Not a damn thing unless you cut the bullshit." Her gaze met his with disdain. "And the sooner you do, the sooner I talk." She looked as if she'd as soon kill him as fuck him.

Ashton's grin widened at that. "Feisty," he said with a slide of his tongue over his lips. "I like it. But let's cut to the chase, sweetheart. Iverson doesn't like to be kept waiting."

Though a flicker of fear was barely visible in the depths of her eyes at the mention of that name, nothing else betrayed her state of mind. "Strange, neither do I. Ever hear of a sorcerer named Cian Carmichael?"

Ashton lifted an eyebrow at her. "The one who only shows up when he's not wanted?"

"Then you have heard of him." An unpleasant smirk crossed her lips. "Maybe, just maybe, one of you brilliant, intelligent vampires might be able to take care of him."

"Watch it, sweetheart," Ashton growled. "I know who he is. But how do I know you aren't lying to save your pretty ass? Just because Iverson likes you doesn't mean he won't hesitate to drain you. Or let one of us do it for him."

That look of fear returned to her eyes before it was quickly subdued. She tapped her clear varnished nails on the polished surface of the table. "Take it or leave it, *sweetheart*." Her tone stressed the last word in a sickeningly sweet way. "Iverson knows the deal, and he'll take my word."

Ashton gripped the woman's hand, almost crushing the slender fingers in his grip. He leaned forward and gripped her chin tightly with his other hand. Before she could pull away, he crushed his lips to hers, forcing his tongue into her mouth in a brutal kiss. A small, pained sound escaped her as the pressure around her fingers increased when she tried to jerk her hand back. She sharply bit at his tongue before Ashton pulled away. Her other hand lifted from the table as if to strike him, but then it slowly lowered.

"For your sake, darlin', I hope so," he drawled.

"I'm fucking Carmichael's brother. Now how valid do you think the information is, asshole?" Folding her arms over her chest, she settled back in her chair and glared at him.

He laughed. "Such a trustworthy slut you are," he said with a sneer. "I bet your boyfriend is pussy-whipped into believing you're only fucking him, isn't he?"

Her gaze slowly moved over him, and she gave him a wry smile. "What makes you think he's not the only one I'm fucking?"

"I've heard the rumors. Seems your pussy is good enough even for a vampire."

Her attitude suddenly shifted, and a deadly still calm seemed to settle over her. "The rumors are wrong, Carter."

"Oh, such coldness." Ashton leaned forward and pinned an unwavering, dark gaze on her. "No wonder Iverson likes you and fucks you every chance he gets."

"Try to get any closer, and you might just find out how cold." With an abrupt motion, she stood. "You got what you wanted. Make sure I get what I want." Staring down at him, her smile mocked him. "And nothing else is your business, is it?"

He grinned but didn't move to stand, nor did he offer any semblance of a thank you. "Later, babe."

Not bothering to say anything, she stared a bit longer before turning away from him and heading for the exit.

Chapter Two

Jake shut the door quietly as Mael studied the three young, staked vampires stretched out on the floor. Their filth-clad bodies, stained with blood, remained motionless. As Mael stepped closer to them, Jake's green gaze followed him. Carefully examining the first body, Mael ruffled through the vampire's thoughts. The vague threads of images and formed words paraded through his mind until he had what he wanted.

"James Kenner, created by Detford." It was a name Mael was fairly familiar with. The next one was a young girl, and in no more than a moment, he had what he wanted from her as well. "Sarah Severs, and her creator is Atkins."

It was the third mind that drew his full attention. This one was no more than a few days old.

"So very young. Gilbert Deckard, created by Silvers. This is the second one of his we've caught this week. Prolific bastard, isn't he?"

His comment received no answer from the other two standing guard. Sighing quietly, he crouched beside the young boy. Slender fingers reached out to lightly run over the boy's cheek. The stain marking Gilbert's aura was weak, indicating he had been created by a rogue but hadn't killed any mortal. The other two had obviously killed and would be destroyed.

"Ben, send for Neil immediately." Mael's soft voice rarely rose higher than its current tone. Glancing over to the gray-haired man leaning against the door, Mael's dark blue eyes meet the brown ones staring at him in surprise.

"But, Your Excellency, he is in retreat at Whitmore."

"Send for him anyway. I have a gift for him."

Mael's secretary left the room as Mael turned his attention back to the boy before him. He knew very well Neil still grieved the loss of his only child. He also knew the young one in front of him would, in his own way, help Neil. Intuition was something Mael never ignored. His tangible power seeped into Gilbert, drawing the boy into a peaceful haven of sleep. Slowly, Mael began untangling the thread of Gilbert's thoughts.

He took away the memory of being staked from the young vampire before he wove the replacement of those taken fragments. Wrapping his fingers to the stake embedded in Gilbert's chest, Mael yanked it out. When Gilbert awoke, he would only remember being brought here and then falling asleep. A golden light flared around Mael's hand as he passed it over the gaping hole. The pale skin beneath began to heal itself until nothing remained to show that Gilbert had been staked, except for the blood.

"The others will be brought to the throne room as tonight's feast for our guests. This one I want taken to a room. Make sure he is cleaned up and don't leave him unattended."

After instructing his enforcer, Mael straightened from his position and was out the door before Jake could say a word. The troubled state of his thoughts lingered as he left the dungeon cells. He barely paid any attention to his servants in the corridors as he headed for the central hall.

As he strode into the room, the others hovering near his throne snapped to attention. No one said a word as they parted, leaving him a path. He didn't even bother looking at any of them as he headed for his throne and then sank gracefully into it. Comforting darkness surrounded him as he leaned back, resting both hands on the arms of his throne. He was clad completely in black, even the shirt beneath the guru-style jacket. A dark blue tie almost matched the color of his eyes. Bluish tints were echoed in the fall of the thick, rich black hair that framed his face, its length ending half-way down his back. His dark gaze rested on the man who stepped forward and bowed deeply to him.

"Jensen, I don't suppose you have any good information for me, do you?" The silky, soft purr threading through the words fooled none of Mael's court.

"We've rounded up five more rogues, Your Excellency. Lancaster destroyed them as per the orders of the hunt." Raising his pale blue eyes to meet Mael's, Jensen kept his expression a calm, neutral mask. He lifted his hand and ran it nervously through his short blond hair.

"At least a small bit of good news, it seems. But I doubt if it will satisfy the Romanorum, now, will it?"

Mael knew very well the august body that governed all of his kin would not be pleased at all. They wanted names, and they wanted to know what the hell was going on. The rogue vampires could seriously jeopardize their legal status with the government of England. And once that happened, it wouldn't be long before the United States, and all other countries where they enjoyed citizenship, followed.

Somebody was freely giving out the formulas that created vampires, but he hadn't figured out who that someone was. Restraining a sigh, Mael tried to rein in his temper since it would do no good to lose it on his court.

"No, Excellency, it will not. But Savarier is waiting to see you. Perhaps she has better news." Bowing, Jensen stepped backward before returning back to his place.

Mael watched the others as they made their way to their places at the low tables to comfortably recline on the pillows. Jake and Rashid, his enforcers, entered, carrying the two staked vampires with them. They laid them both on the tables in front of the other vampires who watched with avid, hungry eyes.

"Now who deserves such delicious meals this fine night?" Mael glanced blandly at some of the others who looked his way. A faint smile hovered over his lips as he studied his court, each vampire in turn.

Lancaster entered the room as Jake and Rashid moved toward him and then stilled, one at each side of him.

"Ah, Lancaster. Just in time. I believe you have the honor of feeding from one of the rogues for destroying five of them for us. You may do with him as you please, as long as he is dead before this night is gone."

The prince's pronouncement was greeted with a great show of pleasure from the fourth formula vampire as he took his place at one of the tables. "That is very gracious of you, Excellency. I thank you for your kind gift."

"Now for the other. I think I should award her to you, Suthers." Though Mael was aware that both Lancaster and

Suthers would share the bounty with the others, it still singled out the ones the gifts were originally given to.

Almost beaming, Suthers stumbled over his words. "Thank you, Your Excellency. Unexpectedly kind of you."

Inclining his head, Mael graciously acknowledged their gratitude. When the two gave the signal, the other members of his court descended on the prone bodies laid out before them. Growls rose as the others expressed their appreciation for the delectable choices they were allowed to feed from.

Idly, Mael watched as those he had chosen to attend this night's feast grew sated from draining the two. First the male dissolved to dust, and then the female. As stray hands caressed their chosen partners, some just for the night, some far more familiar with each other, he smiled in faint satisfaction that at least two of his problems had faded away to nothing but ash.

Mael stood and left his court to their pleasures as he slipped out the huge double doors. Savarier was waiting for him when he stepped into his office. He paused, eyeing her questioningly. Garbed from head to toe in black, the petite, raven-haired woman was his assassin, and she blended very well into the darkness of night when she needed.

"What news do you have for me?"

"We intercepted two packages of formulas, Excellency. One was addressed to Prince Iverson and the other to Prince Raven."

Mael's brow rose at the mention of two very well-known second formulas. If he were mortal, he'd have a headache by now. Being very careful not to show much in his expression, he nodded slowly. "Change the contents of the vials, and then make sure the packages arrive at their destinations. I also want you to get a hold of Seymour, Avery, Jacobs, and Talbert. I want them here within the next three days."

They were four second formulas who hopefully would aid him in eliminating the other two problems. He would need their strength to take Bristol and Colchester from their respective princes.

"It will be done." Sav paused, opening her mouth to say something before closing it as if thinking better of speaking.

"What is it, Sav?"

"I hesitate to speak, Excellency, since I'm not quite sure if it means anything to our problem."

"Tell me anyway. I'll decide whether it's worth knowing or not."

"I was on the roof overlooking Gillman's Tavern. I saw somebody kill one of the rogues." Taking a deep, unneeded breath, she continued. "I swear, Your Excellency, the rogue was set on fire, but with the fucking weirdest blue flames. I've never seen anything like it." After the smallest bit of hesitation, she blurted out uneasily, "It was Cian Carmichael."

The utter stillness returned to Mael's body when he heard the name. Most of what he knew of the sorcerer was by repute, and that reputation seemed to grow with each word he heard. He just hadn't known the sorcerer was back in London. "After you round up the four I need, I want you to find and track Cian Carmichael for me, Sav. But not close enough to get yourself hurt. I only want to know about his movements."

Nodding to him, she turned for the door, heading out to obey his orders.

Mael was thoughtful as he left his office. He knew all of the rumors about the sorcerer, but sometimes it was hard to sift the truth from the exaggerations. He trusted what Sav told him to be true, so that was a piece of information that bespoke of just how powerful Cian was. It was enough to make Mael want more information on the sorcerer.

As he passed by one of the alcoves, a hand reached for him, stopping him. Quirking a brow, he stared questioningly at the young woman, wondering why she would try to attract his attention. He recognized her, but what she wanted with him, he had no clue.

"Your Excellency."

She withdrew her hand and then stepped back, keeping herself hidden from any who might look down the hallway. The distinctly shy features were delicately formed, and they momentarily held Mael's attention. As he studied her, she remained silent until his eyes met the soft, velvet green of hers. Her voice was no more than a soft whisper.

"I believe it is my Mother, Selena, who is behind the recent rash of rogues."

Her words sent a shock through him. Narrowing his eyes on her, Mael's voice grew very quiet. "Be very careful of what you say, Alissa. Selena is a first formula of the Romanorum." His words were meant to caution her and to remind her to judge if her knowledge was irrefutable or not.

"I know that, but I saw one of her letters myself, before she sealed it. And with the letter was a vial of one of the formulas, meant to be sent to Devonshire."

Remaining silent for a long moment, Mael mulled the information over as he stared unblinkingly at her. It was easy to discern there was no lie in either her voice or thoughts.

"Keep the information to yourself for now."

"She wants to see you, sometime soon. I thought I should warn you to be prepared for that."

"I will take care of everything, Allisa. For now, do not worry and say nothing to anybody else." Mael didn't look back as he continued down the hall. Everything had just become seriously more complicated.

Selena Kerr ruled the United Kingdom, and her power and right were unquestioned. He had no doubt in his mind that Allisa told him the truth, that Selena had a hand in the rash of rogue vampires. He just wasn't sure why. Or even how to stop her. This wasn't something he could just drop in the Romanorum's lap without overwhelming proof of his own.

Several investigations had been launched to find out if any of the mortals who had access to the formulas were behind this. So far, no leads had turned up. Attention would next be turned to any of the second formulas that had the power to give out the formulas, but as yet, no inquiry or even suspicion had touched Selena.

* * *

Coordinating with Ben, it took a few nights to choose and prepare the others Mael wanted to accompany the four second formulas to Bristol and Colchester. After two nights of discussion, he'd finally gotten everybody briefed and sent to join the leaders.

Settled in his office, Mael read over the report that Sav had left for him. She'd been trailing Cian Carmichael for the past couple nights, and her writing was a factual account of the events she had witnessed. His personal assassin was extremely efficient and professional. He felt somewhat relieved to note that the sorcerer had dispatched a fair number of rogues, though a small paragraph on the second page caught his attention.

Sav had witnessed the sorcerer opening a portal and then disappearing into it. From her description of the portal, it was obviously a dimensional one. That little piece of information intrigued him a great deal. In general, wizards preferred to remain on this plane and not leave this world. Only the more powerful of them talked about venturing off into unknown worlds, and only the oldest of them had the power to actually *do* so.

Mael sent out a mental message for his court magician to join him immediately. As he settled back in his chair, he read over that particular paragraph several times. Cian Carmichael had definitely become a more interesting fixation in his thoughts. The sorcerer might very well prove to be of serious use in Mael's current problems. Whether the sorcerer agreed or disagreed with that assessment mattered little to Mael. If Carmichael proved unwilling, he would just have to be made willing.

Mael's internal musing was interrupted by Cornelius entering the room. The youthful appearance of his magician fooled many. The riot of black curls on his head, the translucent quality of his dark forest green eyes, and the slender build of his body caused others to severely underestimate him. His physical appearance suggested he was a Renaissance painting come to life, and very few looked beneath that. He was clad in the robes of his status, though few paid that much useful attention to him, given the very young face. Any interest that came Cornelius' way was always lustful in nature. Not many understood just how powerful he was.

"You summoned me, Excellency?"

"Sit down, Cornelius. I need a bit of your magical help." Mael gestured to the seat in front of his desk.

"What is it you need?"

"A charm imbued with *Plagiarius Eo,* and I want it as soon as possible. I should not need to tell you to keep this between ourselves." Leaning forward, Mael rested his arms on the desk and gazed steadily at his magician.

"That is always understood, Excellency. How powerful do you want the charm to be?"

"I will talk to Garnier and ask her to supply the blood needed for it. You should have it within a few hours."

It would only take a drop of Garnier's blood to imbue the charm with the necessary power to travel to the unseen worlds. That wasn't a power Mael possessed himself, though he could travel to Barathrum within the shadows. He would need that amulet to follow Cian wherever he was going. Mael had no doubt Garnier would agree to give him the necessary blood. Though the rogue problem seemed to be confined to England, it could very well spill outward, and Europe would be next. If the mortals jumped to take action, they wouldn't care which vampires got killed. They would probably want to kill all of them.

There was a lift to Cornelius' brow with the mention of the first formula ruler of Europe, but he said nothing about that. His unquestioning obedience and remarkable skills at his crafts were what had earned Mael's respect and trust.

"I'll have it ready for you by tomorrow evening, Excellency."

* * *

The rest of the evening, Mael was deluged by demands from mortal and vampire alike to curb the growing rogue trouble. As sleep claimed him, he fell, deeply relieved, into its dark, silent arms. When he awoke the next evening, the only high point was Cornelius dropping off the needed charm.

Relaxing in his seat, Mael studied the black crystal threaded on a delicate silver chain. Light reflected off the smoothed edges of the small stone as he slowly turned it. He slipped the charm around his neck and tucked it underneath his shirt, letting the glittering stone nestle unseen at the hollow of his throat.

Within his thoughts, he quietly searched for his assassin as he stood, stepping into a pool of gathering shadows. Following the familiar thread of her presence, he emerged from the darkness and saw her leaning against the wall of a building nearby.

"*He's not that far away, Excellency. Just in that tavern over there.*"

"*Return to the palace, Sav. I will take over from here.*"

With silent movements, Mael made his way to the pub. Looking up, he caught the name painted on the sign above the door before he entered The Queen's Inn. Once inside, he blended flawlessly with the darkness as he looked around. Slowly, he surveyed the small bar, and it didn't take him long to find the one he was looking for.

The sorcerer had been described to him many times, to the point that Mael had seriously begun to wonder just how much had been exaggerated. Particularly the description of a blond god had amused him, though when his eyes settled on Cian, the words suddenly seemed a poor description at best.

Cian was watching the patrons, looking only vaguely interested as the waitress set a bottle of wine and a glass in front of him, smiling at him. Though she said something to the sorcerer, Mael wasn't close enough to hear yet. Catching sight of someone who appeared to be at least related to the wizard, Mael moved closer. He followed along the wall until he was near their table. His ability to take in the smallest of sound kept him in good stead, allowing him to catch a good portion of their conversation.

Pouring himself some wine, Cian nodded to the waitress. "Yes." After taking a sip, he looked up at her. "Keep things low-key. The last one knew me." Cian took another drink and as he lowered the glass, he looked surprised to see the young man standing beside his table. "I thought I told you to avoid me when I'm working."

The young man slid into the other booth seat and leaned forward. "We've got problems, Cian. Rachel's been talking."

Cian poured more wine, not even bothering to look up at him. "Why am I not surprised? What has she said?"

The young man leaned closer, resting his elbows on the table. "She's told Iverson about you, about what you look like, what you do. And my guesses were right, Cian. Rachel has some sort of deal with Iverson regarding Mael Black."

It required little expenditure of Mael's power to keep himself concealed from anybody's interest. His gaze traveled between the two as each spoke and then narrowed on the young man. Not really expecting to hear the Iverson's name, Mael's attention became suddenly far more intent.

Cian looked up then. "She's signing her death warrant. Black is the last one she needs to be working against." He took a drink and opened his mouth to continue but closed his eyes instead. "Lee. Get out. Go home. *Now.*" Without waiting for an answer, he stood and hurried out of the bar.

Mael felt more troubled than anything. Biting back his own growl of frustration, Mael melted deeper within the darkness to head swiftly outside. The sorcerer wasn't that far away from him. Arching his brow, Mael saw the sorcerer grab hold of a rogue's throat. The creature kicked at him and brandished a knife. Cian side-stepped the kick, but the blade slid across his belly.

As the sorcerer looked down at the wound, it began to heal. When he looked back up, he said, "You can't kill me."

As he raised his hand, a blue ball of swirling flame formed in Cian's palm. The fire flared in his hand and leapt from his palm to the rogue he held against the wall. Within seconds, the rogue's body was engulfed in blue fire. Cian let the creature's body flutter down into a pile of ash.

Only when Mael noticed another vampire creeping up behind the sorcerer did Mael move. The would-be attacker wasn't even a rogue, but obviously he had some involvement with them. Taking one step forward when the vampire passed near him, Mael's hand struck out, taking hold of the vampire's throat and suddenly stopping any forward motion.

"Sneaking up on somebody like that. What would your prince say?" Mael's quiet voice mocked the struggling vampire in his grasp. Without waiting for an answer, Mael continued, "Shall I tell you what he would say or just show you?"

The silky purr of Mael's voice had the effect of calming the wild thrashing, but the look of terror on the vampire's face told the true story. Aware that Cian had already disposed of the other and stood watching them, Mael turned his head slightly toward him and smiled faintly. He took in no more than a quick glimpse of the surprised recognition and the blue flame in the sorcerer's hand before he looked back at his captive. He'd seen little trust and a great deal of caution in Cian, but he had this other matter to attend to.

The captive vampire's mouth opened and closed like a fish as if he were trying to speak, but nothing came out with the tight pressure around his throat. As Mael stared at him, the vampire's body relaxed and even the look of fear faded from his face. The vampire moved closer to Mael after he was released. Mael lowered his hand, but only to chest level, before plunging it inside. Within the blink of an eye, his fist broke through to reach the vampire's heart. As he wrapped his hand around it, Mael savagely twisted and then yanked it out of the vampire's chest. The young vampire crumpled to the ground, motionless.

Silently, Mael watched as the body of the vampire went up in unnatural blue flames. He tossed the heart to ground where a writhing mass of shadows devoured it. When the fire had burned out, he looked back at the sorcerer who stared at him with an unreadable expression.

Smiling faintly, Mael bowed slightly, holding that gaze. Raising his hand to his lips, he licked away the blood. With the taste, hunger flared to life. He could see the flicker of darker interest before Cian started backing away from him. Slowly lowering the bloodied hand, Mael did no more than smile, taking in Cian's reaction. His mind opened just enough for Cian to feel the brush of something alien to his thoughts, seeking to learn him.

When Cian's eyes darted back up to lock with Mael's, he said. "I have no quarrel with you, Prince. Do not try to read me."

Withdrawing the mental touch, Mael said nothing, as that attempt had been deliberately blocked. His gaze slowly roamed over the sorcerer's body, carefully taking in each beautiful detail, and he felt a stirring within himself. Stray tendrils of velvet shadow uncurled, sliding through the air to brush over Mael's cheek and throat in an almost loving touch.

The sorcerer's gaze narrowed on him in warning. "I have nothing for you," Cian said dryly. The look in his eyes as his gaze traveled briefly over the prince's body suggested otherwise. "Thank you for your help." He turned abruptly away from Mael and walked out into the street, disappearing around a corner.

Mael remained where he stood and chuckled. The words didn't match what he'd seen in those enigmatic eyes.

Chapter Three

Selena lounged in her throne, legs dangling over the arm. Already having sent the summons, she waited, glancing idly around the empty room. When ebony flames erupted near her, she looked in the direction of the man emerging from the portal.

"What is it you want this time, Selena?" The demon was older than time, a fact that didn't show in the beautifully androgynous face. Leaning over, he rested slender fingers on the arm of the chair, near her legs. Looking up at him, she stared into the rich brown of his eyes and gave him a bored look.

"I need something, and I have no clue where to find it, Sagan. You will be a dear, won't you?" Her soft voice contained none of the usual seductive ability. It never worked with his sort, and she wasn't sure she'd enjoy it much if it did.

"That would depend on exactly what you want, young lady." Whenever he dealt with her, he always sounded highly amused, treating her as if she were a child just out of leading strings.

"Not a great deal. I just want the Eye of Baal."

Sagan's deep laughter rumbled from his chest. "That's all, is it? And precisely *what* do you want such an interesting bauble for?" As he stared at her, she had the feeling he could see right straight through to whatever piece of soul she had left.

"To use it. Why else would I want the stupid thing?" Even with the knowing look he directed at her, she had no intention of revealing her purpose.

"I hate to disappoint you, Selena, but that's not something I can get for you. Though I can tell you who you might be able to get it from."

"At least that's something. Who?"

"A sorcerer and vampire hunter named Cian Carmichael." A tone of ungodly amusement threaded through the name as Sagan's smirk widened.

Selena stared up at him and frowned. "Why do I get the feeling you know something I don't, Sagan?"

"Because I *always* do. You should know that by now. You'll get what you need from him; I have no doubt of that. Enjoy your adventure of a lifetime. It's just beginning."

A crease wrinkled her brow as she frowned more heavily. "I really need to find somebody else to deal with besides you."

"I wish you luck with that. Very few of my brethren will deal with you, Selena. You can't offer what you have very little left of." The amused quirk of his brow tended to infuriate her, but there was little she could do in retaliation.

"Can't you just get the damn thing from Carmichael?"

"No. That's your job, not mine. I merely provide the necessary information. I'm sure you know he's been in London lately."

"Yes, I know that." Rather than snap at him, she tried to carefully modulate her voice and subdue her own annoyance.

"Then that's all I can give you." Bowing his head to her in mock respect, Sagan stepped back, disappearing in an eruption of black fire.

* * *

"Are you mad?"

Cian watched Lee pace up and down the hallway. With every turn the tips of Lee's wings set pictures swaying on the walls. On more than one occasion, Cian had to replace a fallen portrait. Most of them were of Lee and Rachel, while others were of friends. Lee stopped pacing and glared at Cian.

"What were you thinking?" Lee asked him pointedly. "If he was created by a rogue, then he is no better than the others."

"He has not killed a mortal," Cian said calmly. "He has done nothing to warrant a death sentence."

Lee gave him a dubious look. "How do you know he has not killed a mortal?"

Cian sighed and leaned back against the wall, crushing his azure-feathered wings behind him. "He was turned a couple of days ago. Up until I ran into him, he had managed to decrease the city's population of stray cats."

"And after you met him?" The tone of Lee's voice was quieter than usual, and Cian knew his brother already had a good idea of what happened. Cian closed his eyes and waited for the inevitable.

"He fed from me."

"What!" Lee spun around and stormed back into the living room, coming to stand directly before Cian. "You fed a vampire? You're an angel!"

Cian didn't move and simply nodded. "Yes, I did." He hadn't expected Lee to really understand. Truth be told, he didn't completely understand why he had done it either.

"Cian," Lee said quietly, "they sent you here as a hunter."

"Of rogue vampires, yes. Brandon may have been created by one, but he is not one himself. An angel's blood is pure, Lee. Had Brandon been a rogue, I would've known right away." Lee was quiet for several minutes. Cian opened his eyes and saw Lee sitting on the back of the couch.

"Have you ever tasted the blood of a vampire?"

Cian laughed. "Is that what you're worried about? No. A lesser vampire would have little to no effect on me, Lee."

"What about a Master?" Lee asked him, looking up.

"A Master's blood is something entirely different, even for me." Cian shuddered at the thought. "Look, I need to get back to the hotel."

"What are you going to do with your young vampire?"

Cian sighed and shrugged. "The only thing I *can* do: take him to Black myself."

Lee didn't look entirely happy with that pronouncement, but Cian paid little mind. Lee had his duty, just as Cian had his. Cian left the apartment without saying anything more. He had every intention of keeping Brandon from falling into a rogue's hands, and as such, there was only one vampire who would know what to do with him. Cian sighed as the decision firmed in his mind. If he was going to take Brandon to Mael Black, he was going to do it with an informed opinion of the prince. As he neared the prince's mansion, his body shimmered briefly before disappearing from sight altogether.

Slipping through an open balcony door, Cian found his way into what could only be the prince's throne room. The prince himself was seated upon a throne, and for a brief moment, Cian could only admire the dark, graceful form before him. Rich sable hair cascaded over the prince's shoulders, blending effortlessly with the black of his clothing. His eyes were a deep, fathomless blue that momentarily held Cian spellbound, just as they had in the alley. In all respects, the Prince of London was the most beautiful creature Cian had ever seen.

He knew better than to argue the ethics of spying on someone unseen, yet he wanted to make sure that bringing Brandon to the prince would be a good choice. And, in truth, he couldn't deny the lingering desire to see the prince once more. Since that night in the alley, the prince's face remained with him wherever he went. Secure in his unseen state, Cian watched Prince Mael Black oversee one of his court sessions.

The prince's hand rested casually in the soft curls of a young man's hair as he relaxed on his throne. His gaze narrowed as several forms appeared in a half circle in front of him.

"What is it now, Caroline?" the prince asked, singling out one voice in an effort to still the many.

One woman before the dais politely bowed her head to the prince before she spoke. "Your Excellency, I'm still having difficulty with Malcolm. His excursions into the dock properties are costing me more than I would like."

The prince lifted a hand to silence the sudden explosion of words from a man who could have only been Malcolm. "I thought I had told you both to work out an equitable share of those properties." The prince's gaze narrowed, moving between both of them. "I will give you exactly one week to work something out. If you fail, return to me, and I will do the work. But be assured, you will lose considerably more to this throne at that time."

Cian couldn't help but smile. The prince's sense of diplomacy was surprising. The two bickering vampires stepped back and hurriedly returned to their places at one of the tables. The prince's gaze followed them before he looked to the next man who stepped forward. A young girl stepped forward as well, bobbing a quick, nervous curtsey in the prince's direction.

"Your Excellency, I wanted to introduce my daughter, Anna Marie," the man beside the young girl said.

"Bring her closer, Alan." The prince stood from his throne and walked down the steps. Pausing, he waited for both of them to approach. Anna flashed him a shy smile as she curtseyed again to him. Mael chuckled softly. "Once is enough, child." Looking toward Alan, the prince said, "A lovely new addition to our court. We look forward to seeing her more often."

Cian's gaze widened in nothing short of shock. Gone was the image of a vampire licking away the blood on his fingers. Before him stood a prince with a regal demeanor worthy of the highest court and a soft, gentle cadence to his words. Cian shook his head in confusion, unable to fathom how the prince could be so different at any given moment.

Alan definitely seemed pleased. "Thank you, Your Excellency."

"Make sure you save one of the dances at the Summer Cotillion for me, Anna." As he spoke, the prince took hold of her hand, drawing it up to his lips and brushing a soft kiss to the back. Her quiet giggle earned her a warning look from Alan, but the prince just shook his head slightly as if to say it was all right.

"I promise I will save one for you, Your Excellency," Anna said with a smile.

Turning his head so none of his court could see, the prince winked at her, and was rewarded by the soft sound of another giggle as he stepped back. He returned to his throne.

Cian's brow furrowed as he watched the prince's display. Dance? Winking? He had to suppress a chuckle of his own at the thought of the blushing young woman dancing with her prince. Then he thought of himself, pressed tightly to the prince's body as they swayed to an unheard rhythm. He shook his head quickly, forcing the image away.

Relaxing in his seat, the prince let his hand drift back to a head of chestnut hair as the young man curled at his feet nudged back against him for attention.

Another vampire stepped forward then, addressing him. "Your Excellency, we've received another report concerning Ashton Carter. He is leaving the victims to be found by mortal authorities."

The prince stilled, and there was an obvious tightening to his hand tucked within the young man's curls. As the young man pressed closer to his leg, the tension eased, and the prince smiled somewhat apologetically at him. Looking back at the man at the foot of the dais, the prince said, "Send out Sav to find him, Ben. I want that son of bitch's head before he kills again."

Ashton Carter, Cian thought to himself. He vowed to remember that one, if only to repay a debt to the prince for his help in the alley.

"I'll let her know, Your Excellency." The vampire named Ben backed up and turned on his heel to leave the throne room.

The prince watched Ben and said nothing more until another man leaned over to him, whispering in his ear. Nodding slightly, the prince lowered his voice and said, "I know, Cornelius, but I don't have the time. There's too much else that needs my attention." There was a hint of tiredness to the soft words obviously meant only for the one beside him.

For the first time, Cian took full notice of the man standing beside the prince. He stared at the raven curls and the soft lines of the man's face.

"And if you don't make the time, you're going to become useless, Excellency," Cornelius muttered under his breath. The vampire directed an odd look at the young man near the prince's feet and gestured slightly in Mael's direction.

At the more than obvious hint, the young man shifted to his knees, reaching for his prince's hand. "Why don't we retire now, Your Excellency? Everybody else can wait. You need some rest."

Cian watched and listened to the exchange between the three men and realization slowly began to dawn on him.

The concern in the young man's words touched something within Cian. Perhaps Mael Black wasn't as bad as he had thought to garner such affection and concern from so many.

Sighing quietly, the prince looked from one man to the other, and a faintly softer smile curved his lips. His free hand reached out, ruffling the young man's hair in an affectionate gesture. "I suppose I have no choice but to obey, do I?" There was warmth in his words.

Cian smiled, more than amused with the affection the prince was showing. He had not expected such a display from a man who, not long before, licked blood off of his hand. There was a stark difference between what Cian had witnessed in the alley and what he was witnessing now.

The young man ducked his head and laughed, trying to get out from under the hand messing up his hair. At the same time, Cornelius gave the prince a less than gentle kick to the side of his ankle.

"Okay, okay, I'm outnumbered." Gracefully, the prince stood from the throne, drawing the young man up with him.

Smirking over at him, Cornelius said, "I don't want to see you until after sunset tomorrow. You hear me?" Whoever the man was, he seemed to hold a high position with the prince.

The overall scene was nothing like Cian had ever imagined a vampire's court to be.

The prince looked over his shoulder at Cornelius. "Take your own advice, old man. Stay away from your workroom for once."

Just as quickly, Cornelius shot back, "If I see you before sunset, I'll stuff you in Aristotle's crystal."

Obviously giving up, the prince said nothing as the young man tucked Mael's hand into the crook of his arm and they walked out of the throne room. Cian waited for only a moment before following them. He took one glance back to Cornelius and then slipped out the door before it could close.

Silence reigned between the two men in front of him as Cian followed them up the stairs to the second floor and then down the corridor to what he assumed was Mael's room. The prince released the young man as he opened the door and walked inside. The young man followed quietly behind him before pausing in the doorway.

"Do you want me to stay with you, Your Excellency?"

Cian slipped past them, leaving only a whisper of air in his wake. Then he turned and waited. He knew he shouldn't stay, but he simply couldn't bring himself to leave.

"If you wish, Seth. I would like your company." Loosening the tie around his neck, Mael pulled it off before tossing it on one of the chairs. After closing the door, Seth moved silently up behind the prince to slide the jacket from his shoulders.

Mael turned to let Seth unbutton his shirt. Seth made quick work of it and then slipped it off, laying it on top of the jacket. A slow smile curved Mael's lips as Seth's hands returned to his chest.

Cian's breath caught as he watched Seth's fingertips glide over the prince's flesh. He closed his eyes for a moment, desperately trying control the effects on his own body.

"Who is feeding whom tonight, my little ghoul?" The soft whisper had a teasing note in it, and Cian opened his eyes to see the prince's hand curling around Seth's.

In answer, Seth tilted his head in clear invitation. Mael reached up to stroke his thumb slowly against the young man's throat. Both hands dropped then as he stepped back and sat on the edge of the bed. His leg caught behind Seth, drawing him between his parted legs.

"You need to be fed tonight, not me," Mael said quietly.

Cian wondered what the prince meant, but when Mael pulled Seth between his legs, the question was quickly forgotten. His pulse began to race as a flicker of heat traveled through his body. He shouldn't be here. Not for something so...intimate.

Glancing up at Seth, the prince chuckled at the slight trembling of the lush, full lips. One of his hands lightly caressed downward over the bare skin just beneath the opening of Seth's vest. Mael spoke softly, his eyes never leaving the form in front of him.

"Undress for me."

Slowly, Seth removed the vest and dropped it to the floor. His hands moved to unfasten the tie of his loose cotton pants, and he let them fall around his ankles. The slender, lithe body fully revealed was deeply tanned and muscular. The young man was beautiful; there was no doubt why the prince was attracted to him.

Mael licked his lips and slipped a hand around to gently cup the cheek of Seth's bare ass, kneading his fingers into the smooth skin. "So beautiful, my little ghoul."

Seth moaned softly, the sound sweet and needful. "Please, Master."

Mael quickly toed off his shoes before he stretched back onto the bed, the hand on Seth drawing him down. As the young man pressed his body more tightly to Mael's, Cian moved closer, wanting to catch every glimpse, every sigh. Long forgotten was his idea of scouting. Instead, he gave himself over to the desire that was beginning to wreak havoc within him.

Mael rolled them so Seth ended up on his back. Seth's legs quickly encircled Mael's waist. A small wound opened at the side of Mael's throat, and Seth quickly lifted his head, his mouth hungrily fastening to it. With a soft pulsing growl, the prince's body shuddered as Seth fed.

Somewhere deep within him, Cian felt an answering hunger, wanting more than anything to be in Seth's place, to feel the prince's hard body pinning him down. When Seth began to drink the prince's blood, Cian's pulse quickened. He had not suspected the young man to be a vampire, but then he remembered what the prince had called him: 'his ghoul.' He wondered what exactly that meant. The prince's growls soon gave way to a soft moan.

When Seth drew his head back, Mael very quickly got rid of his own pants. As he watched his prince, a look of unbridled lust shone in Seth's eyes before he reached for the drawer in the nightstand. With obvious long practice at this, he located the tube of lubrication and pulled it out, handing it to Mael.

Mael opened it and squeezed out a generous amount on his fingers. Then he shifted to give himself enough space to reach between Seth's legs, his fingers slicking over Seth's entrance before sliding slowly inside him.

Cian fell back against the nearest wall, breathless. His own body shuddered in turn, and he groaned, unable to stop himself before the sound became a soft murmur of air. He stilled immediately, both in fear that he had made himself known and in an effort to push back his own thoughts as he watched the prince's fingers slide in and out of the young man slowly.

"Please, Master...please...now." Seth gasped out the words as he tried to bear down onto the teasing fingers as they stroked inside him.

As his fingers withdrew, the prince's demanding kiss captured Seth's lips, silencing him. The weight of his body returned to Seth's as the head of his cock pushed against the tight opening before sliding inside. Seth wrapped his legs around Mael, forcing him deeper.

The keening cries from Seth served only to make Cian's self-inflicted torture worse. With slow, almost leisurely thrusts, the prince buried himself repeatedly in the trembling body beneath him. Mael drew back his head to stare into Seth's eyes, watching the play of needful expression in his face.

Seth begged, "Don't stop, please, Master...don't stop." His legs tightened around Mael. A hard, fast jerk suddenly buried Mael's cock deep inside him. A heated growl sounded from the prince as his hips began to push harder and quicker into the willing body of the young man beneath him.

Seth's pleas echoed Cian's silent ones. The sound of the prince's growl deepened and Seth cried out sharply, caught in the throes of his own release as his legs tightened around Mael. The vampire's head tipped back as he closed his eyes. Cian felt the tension building sharply in the air surrounding Mael and Seth with each unrestrained motion until it finally broke.

As if in perfect time, the prince growled, signaling his orgasm. Cian bit back the urge to cry out as his own raced through him, leaving him breathless and acutely aware of the warm, damp leather against his skin.

Mael's head tipped forward as a satisfied languidness stole over him. Smiling a bit, he leaned down, pressing a kiss to Seth's lips. The young man struggled to catch his breath. A caress of his hand stole slowly over Mael's back, and once his breathing became normal, a soft sound of contentment escaped him.

Cian leaned back against the wall as he struggled to catch his own breath, disbelieving of what he had just witnessed. He knew he must leave and turned away to step out onto the balcony. He looked back one last time and felt an unfamiliar ache begin within him. He shook it off and jumped off of the balcony, disappearing into the night.

By the time Cian got back to the hotel room, dawn was beginning to break. He slid the key card into the door and pushed the handle down. The room was dark, but the growing light of the sun fought to push through the blanket he had hung over the window. The room had one bed, and a thin form lay bunched up on the far side of the mattress. Cian closed the door quietly and slid his cloak off. Draping it over the back of a chair, he sat down on the edge of the bed. He smoothed his fingers down the young vampire's face, unmoved by the coolness of his flesh.

Despite not being tired, he had a distinct feeling he'd need all the sleep he could get. He stood and pulled his shirt off before lying down beside Brandon. As soon as the sun went down, he would have to take Brandon to Mael Black himself. If Brandon's sire was indeed searching for him, then the only safe haven for Brandon was within Black's care. Before long, sleep began to overtake Cian, leaving nothing but the memory of the prince and Seth to haunt him.

* * *

When Cian awoke, the sun had already set. He drew his hands down his face. When he looked to the side, he saw Brandon watching him. The look on Brandon's face was more than a simple request for feeding. Cian's mind wandered for the briefest moment as he took in the young vampire's features. Chocolate brown hair stood up in errant spikes from Brandon's head, matching the deep brown of his eyes. Despite the paleness of his skin, he still retained a handsome, boyish appeal that Cian was sure had won over many females in the past. However, judging by the look of longing in Brandon's eyes, Cian wondered if females had ever been a part of the young man's life at all.

Brandon's sleek, slender form was stretched out beside him. He was lying on his side, his head propped up on his right hand, and his other resting on his left side, conforming perfectly to the line of his body. The thin sheet did little to conceal him, and much to Cian's frustration, Brandon wore nothing to bed. When his gaze traveled back up to Brandon's face, a sweet but not wholly innocent smile greeted him.

"Are you hungry?" Cian asked, hoping to curb anything that might be looming in the vampire's thoughts.

As Brandon nodded, Cian reached over and picked his knife up off of the table. He pressed the tip to his palm, but just as he was about to make the cut, Brandon's hand stopped him. The vampire took the knife from him and dropped it to the floor. Cian's protest hung unspoken in the air as Brandon's soft lips moved slowly over his fingers, his palm, his wrist. When Brandon's mouth opened on his wrist, Cian closed his eyes, waiting.

Brandon bit down, his fangs piercing Cian's flesh slowly. As Brandon drank, Cian felt the vampire's hand slide over his smooth chest. He sucked in a breath, stifling a moan as Brandon's fingertips grazed over his right nipple. He stopped Brandon before anything could progress. Brandon released his wrist and licked the remnants of blood from his lips.

"You don't like guys, do you?" Brandon asked him. The tone of his voice was one of disappointment.

Cian reached up and stroked his cheek softly. "I never said that, Brandon," he said quietly. "However, I cannot do what you ask." He pulled the vampire down and pressed a soft kiss to his forehead. "The sun has set. I have one more job to do and then I will take you to Black."

"You mean another killing?"

Cian looked over at him as he stood. "Yes. Brandon, listen to me. I hunt rogue vampires. It's not an easy job to understand, especially when you've never had anyone to explain the laws to you."

"What laws?" Brandon asked as he slid out of bed.

"Vampires have very strict laws of their own, but they must also follow mortal laws. When we get to Black's, either he or someone else will explain them to you."

Brandon pulled his pants on and sat down to put on his shoes. "But what will happen to me once we get there?"

"Black will most likely find a Father for you. You're young and need instruction, a mentor."

"What's Black like?"

"He's the Prince of London. He isn't to be trifled with. I suggest you obey him without question. He's not an enemy you want to make," Cian said. Brandon stood and waited as Cian slid his cloak back around his shoulders. "Ready?"

Brandon shrugged. "As ready as I'll ever be, I suppose. Where are we headed to first?"

"I have to find a rogue named Ashton Carter. He's dangerously close to creating some serious problems between mortals and vampires."

Cian led the way out into the street. A light drizzle was falling, and the moonlight filtered through the rain, casting an odd silver sheen on the city. He didn't know where to start looking for Carter, but he knew what to look for. As they walked along the near-empty street, Cian kept his senses alert, wary of the slightest movement. Not only did he have Carter to look for, he had Brandon to protect.

As they neared the entrance to one of the industrial clubs, Cian stopped. He held out a hand to stop Brandon and put his finger to his lips. Brandon nodded and swallowed hard, looking around them warily. Cian closed his eyes and settled his mind to detect any darkness that might be lingering nearby. His thoughts moved past the few vampires he sensed before settling on one in particular. It wasn't Carter, but Cian knew it was one he must keep his eye on. The vampire was female, and stealth was her specialty. Seeing her as interesting but no immediate threat, he moved on.

He had just about given up when his thoughts found a familiar but unwelcome darkness. He opened his eyes and nodded toward an alleyway directly in front of them. Taking Brandon's hand in his, he moved across the street. As they moved into the alleyway, Cian pushed Brandon back against the brick wall.

"Listen to me," he said quietly. "Ashton Carter has been eluding capture for quite a while now. He's one of the more powerful rogues. I want you to stay back. Do you understand me?"

"Y-yes. What about you?"

"I'll be fine. You will see things, Brandon, that are not to be revealed to anyone."

"Okay." Brandon nodded. "What do I do if something *does* go wrong?"

Cian looked down at him. "You run."

He pulled Brandon to the end of the alley and stopped. He closed his eyes once more, searching for Carter. The rogue wasn't far from where they stood, and Cian opened his eyes. He steered Brandon into the shadows behind a garbage dumpster. Brandon wrinkled his nose at the smell.

"I'm sorry," Cian said. "I know it's not the best place in the world, but you should be safe here. Stay out of sight." Brandon nodded, and Cian moved back into the alleyway.

A few minutes later, a dark, stout figure jumped from the rooftop to land on his feet in front of Cian. The shadows did little to hide the malicious sparkle of the vampire's green eyes. His black hair was streaked with gray, and he was built like a man straight out of the military. His dark shirt showed off the muscles in his chest and arms, and had they been in the forest, his camouflage pants would have rendered him invisible. He circled around Cian, flashing a predatory grin.

"I know who you are," Carter said with a sneer. "They all talk about you, sorcerer." Carter pulled out a seven-inch knife from a halter on his thigh and twirled it deftly in his fingers. The razor-sharp blade reflected the moonlight in brilliant sparkles. "Let's see how the infamous Cian Carmichael holds up against a Marine."

Without giving Cian a chance to respond, Carter lunged for him. Cian dodged the attack, catching a brief glimpse of Brandon's terrified face in the shadows. Carter growled and spun around. As he turned, he swung his arm. The tip of his knife slid across Cian's chest, leaving a neat cut across the black fabric. Cian hissed from the sting of the cut beneath, and a look of pure shock slid over Carter's face as the cut healed. Cian stepped forward, backing Carter down the alley.

"What the fuck are you?" Carter said through his teeth. His grip tightened on the handle of his knife, and, with a determined roar, he hurled himself at Cian. When he passed through the spot where Cian had been standing, he twisted around in a circle. "Carmichael! Come out and fucking fight me!"

Cian dropped to the ground behind him, and Carter spun around. What little color there had been in Carter's face drained as wings whisked up a cloud of dirt and debris from the ground around them. The knife fell from Carter's hand seconds before Cian's stake pierced his chest. Carter remained motionless, paralyzed, and Cian raised his left hand. A blue flame sparked to life, and Cian looked back to the rogue.

"I know you can hear me," he said. "And I know you can see me. For your crimes, Ashton Carter, you have been sentenced to death. I doubt God will have mercy on your soul."

Keeping a firm grip on the stake to keep Carter's stiff body pinned to the wall, Cian lowered his other hand. The flame leapt to Carter and set him on fire. Cian held onto the stake until Carter's body fell to the ground in a mound of ash. Then he wiped the metal stake on his pants and turned in time to see Brandon step out of the shadows. The look on the young vampire's face was something between shock and disbelief.

"You're an angel."

Cian walked over to him. "Yes, I am." He looked Brandon over briefly to make sure he was unharmed. "You're not hurt, are you?" Brandon shook his head slowly. Cian smiled and stroked the fingers of one hand down Brandon's cheek.

"Does anyone else know?" Brandon asked, nodding toward Cian's wings.

Cian hid them and shook his head. "No one but my brother and a certain group of people at Saint Mary's

Cathedral. Listen to me, Brandon; no one can know of this. I'm going to have to work with Mael Black to solve this rogue problem, and Black is the last person who needs to find out."

Brandon nodded. "I gotcha. I take it we're going to meet Black now?" He shivered as he glanced over at the pile of dark ash that had once been Ashton Carter.

"Yes," Cian said. "If it were up to me, I'd keep you with me and avoid him altogether."

Brandon's gaze shot back to Cian, a glimmer of hope in the dark brown depths of his eyes. "Really? Then why don't you?"

Cian smiled and put his arm around Brandon's shoulders as they started out of the alleyway. "Because I am not a vampire, Brandon. You need a Father to teach you about what you are, what you can do, and what you cannot do. Those are lessons I can't teach you."

As soon as they were out of the city, Cian was able to relax a bit more. As they walked, Brandon slipped an arm around Cian's waist, pulling their bodies together. The closeness unnerved Cian to a small degree, but he allowed Brandon that small comfort. For himself, there was none.

When they neared the massive wrought iron gate standing guard over the entrance to the prince's home, a guard stepped out to meet them. Brandon's arm tightened around Cian's waist, and Cian hugged his shoulder in reassurance.

"Who are you, and what business do you have here?"

"My name is Cian Carmichael. This is Brandon. I found him on the street and thought maybe Prince Black might take an interest in him."

The guard's eyes widened considerably, and he backed away, nodding. A few moments later, the massive gates swung open. Brandon looked up at Cian as they started down the driveway.

"Just remember what I told you, and you'll be fine," Cian said.

As they neared the sprawling palace, Cian caught a flicker of movement out of the corner of his eye. He looked up and to his left and saw a tall figure standing on a second-floor balcony. The man was looking out over the front gardens, and as Cian got closer to the door, their gazes locked. The man's sable hair blew in a breeze, and even across the distance, the dark blue of his eyes pierced through Cian like the tip of a sword.

When the prince's hand moved, Cian's heart nearly stopped as he caught sight of a dark blue feather — *his* feather. He tried to remember when he might have lost one, and then the spying incident came back to him. A shudder stole up his spine as undeniable desire washed over him. He tore his gaze from the prince's slowly and forced the fleeting images of their bodies pressed together from his mind as he reached up to ring the doorbell.

Chapter Four

Mael stared down, catching a fleeting glimpse of a face he recognized instantly. Mael's gaze drifted slowly over the golden fall of hair. It was the color of sunlight — caught and shimmering, all the way to the sorcerer's waist. To a creature of the darkness such as himself, the sight kept Mael mesmerized. Deliberately pinpointing his senses for a split second on the sorcerer, Mael felt a tingling rush — proof of incredible yet veiled power.

Mael stepped back into his bedroom and placed the feather on a small table. He didn't know where it came from, or how it got into his room, but now his thoughts were distracted. His own response to the sight of the sorcerer disturbed him. Growling softly in annoyance, he strode across his bedroom and out into the hallway.

Ben came toward him and paused. "Excellency, there is a young man named Brandon waiting to see you in your office. Cian Carmichael brought him." It was obvious from the look on Ben's face that he still wasn't quite sure if he'd really seen what he thought he'd seen.

The words jarred Mael from his internal musing. Nodding slightly to Ben, he continued toward the stairs. When he spotted Sav heading down the hall in front of him, he said, "Sav, come here a minute. I need you to do something for me."

Turning around, she headed toward him. "Yes, Excellency?"

"I want to you find out what you can about a relative of Cian Carmichael's named Lee. And check into a girl that this Lee knows by the name of Rachel."

"I'll find out what I can. Is that all you need?"

"That's all for now. Get that to me as soon as you can." He nodded to dismiss her and then opened his office door.

Closing the door quietly behind him, Mael was careful to keep his expression neutral. As he scanned the room, a sharp disappointment rose in him at not seeing the golden-haired sorcerer. A touch of anger at himself swiftly followed on the heels of the disappointment. What did it matter to him that Carmichael wasn't here? Mael bit back the second growl of annoyance struggling to be voiced before turning his attention to the young man sitting near his desk.

From the back, he saw the spiky brown hair and the distinct discoloration of a rogue tainting the man's aura, but as the faint coloring made clear, Mael knew this one hadn't killed a mortal. It started to become a bit clearer as to why Carmichael had brought the boy here. Mael was willing to bet the vampire was very young. Moving around to the side, Mael met a dark brown gaze.

"Why don't you tell me why you're here?"

"Cian brought me here. He said you would take care of me and teach me what I needed to know. My name is Brandon."

Mael did well to hide his surprise. He wouldn't have believed the sorcerer could make the distinction between a rogue who killed and one who hadn't. Obviously, he'd been wrong about that assumption. The proof was sitting in front of him.

"He was right, Brandon. You'll be taken care of here, and nobody will harm you." Mael placed his hand gently on the young vampire's shoulder. The cadence of his voice also carried the same warmth as his smile.

Brandon stared at him for a long moment. Some of the tension in his body visibly relaxed before his gaze ran over Mael. Mael felt somewhat amused to find himself the subject of that intent focus until the boy seem to realize he was staring.

"Cian told me about you, that you'd explain the laws and find someone to help me..." Trailing off, Brandon bit his lower lip.

"You may have been created by a rogue, but you haven't killed a mortal. As long as you don't, you'll be safe." The quiet projection of Mael's power blanketed over Brandon, calming the nervousness he sensed. There was no real reason for Brandon to be nervous at all, and finally Mael felt the easing of the muscles beneath his hand. His thoughts reached out to brush over Brandon's, taking information from shallow memories.

Brandon looked back up at Mael questioningly and then shook his head slightly. "I ran away from the one who made me. I don't know who he was."

"I can easily figure that out, and I will deal with him." There were definitely places the boy didn't want him to pry, so Mael left those areas untouched. "And you lived on animals to sustain yourself. I saw that as well." He didn't bother probing any deeper than the surface of Brandon's mind. He was more intent on keeping Brandon comfortable, rather than trying to force his presence any deeper.

"For now, you will remain here with me until we can choose another who'll be suitable to guide you."

There were several of his court members who would fit the bill, but he would wait to see if Brandon chose anyone for himself. Normally, Mael would have done this for Gilbert as well; however, he already knew where it was best for Gilbert to go.

"What would it include? I mean..." Brandon shook his head, brow wrinkling in confusion.

"If you're asking me if there are intimate relations, then it depends on the parties involved," Mael explained. "Some Fathers—or Mothers—and their Children choose to become romantically involved, and some do not. That is something you would explore and discuss with whomever you pick."

Brandon gave him a quick, surprised look. "You're going to let me pick?"

"There's no reason not to let you decide for yourself who suits you the best." Mael lightly ruffled Brandon's hair.

Brandon stared up at him, bemused.

Noting the expression, the prince shook his head and laughed. "Come on, Brandon. Let's get you settled in." Stepping back, he gave Brandon room to stand and then moved toward the door.

As they walked down the hall, Brandon kept casting side glances at him. "I really didn't expect you to be this..."

"You didn't think I would welcome you, is that what you are trying to say?"

Nodding, Brandon remained silent as they continued walking across the entry way and then up the stairs.

"The situation you find yourself in isn't your fault, Brandon. I'm relieved that Cian brought you here. There is much for you to learn. It speaks in your favor that you haven't killed a mortal as well. We coexist with the mortal world, and in that, we follow their rules. We don't kill mortals, we don't drink from unwilling mortals, and we don't create another vampire from an unwilling mortal. If anyone breaks one of those laws, they are hunted down and destroyed. None of us can afford to anger the mortal populace. Because you haven't killed, you are more than welcome into our society. And for the time being, this will be your bedroom."

Stepping into the room, he turned to watch Brandon. He'd picked a room off the main hall and not far from his own. The centerpiece of the room was an oversized canopy bed of dark mahogany, draped in cream silk. It fit in well with the rest of the antiques scattered throughout the large, airy room. Judging from Brandon's expression, he'd obviously never seen anything like it.

Chuckling, Mael said, "I'll talk to Cornelius, and he'll arrange to take you shopping. I think you're going to need more clothes than what you have on right now."

"I don't know what to say. Thank you doesn't seem to be enough."

"I wouldn't worry about that, Brandon. When you get hungry, simply ring for Jenkins. For now, I think bottled blood will be best until we can test you on a mortal. Once you've proven you can control yourself, there are several mortals here who will be willing to feed you. And lately, there have been extra treats in the throne room with all of the rogues that seem to have descended on London. Now why don't you get comfortable, and I'll send Cornelius in to talk to you."

* * *

Knocking lightly on the door, Cornelius repositioned his spectacles on his nose as he waited for an answer.

"Come in."

Cornelius opened the door and paused in the doorway. "Hello, Brandon. Mael sent me to talk to you."

Brandon's gaze widened for the briefest moment. "You must be Cornelius."

"That I am." Cornelius gave the young man a reassuring smile as he closed the door behind him. "I'm Prince Mael's court magician, and he thought I could fill you in on the ropes of this place."

Brandon set his book down. "You're a magician?"

"Couldn't tell by the robe?" Cornelius chuckled and settled comfortably into the chair nearest the bed. He casually studied Brandon, taking in the youthful features. "My, but you are young, aren't you?"

Brandon sat back, propping himself up on his elbows. "I'm twenty-two. Well, I was until I was turned several days ago."

Looking at Brandon over the rim of his glasses, Cornelius didn't bother to hide his amazement. "Oh, my, you *are* very young, Brandon." Mael neglected to tell him that part. "Well, then, I suppose I'm as good an introduction as any to your new life. And before I go any further, welcome to Prince Mael's court."

"Thanks." Brandon rolled onto his side and fingered the lettering on the cover of his book.

Cornelius glanced down, finding another bit of a shock when he noted the title of the book: *The Forge and the Crucible*. "An unusual subject to interest somebody, isn't it?"

Brandon looked up at him. "Unusual subject?" Then he looked down. "Oh! The book." He opened it and flipped through the worn pages. The book was obviously well-loved. "Chemistry, alchemy, science; they've always been my favorites."

There was a gleam of interest in Cornelius, sparked by the words. "I shall have to test you, then, since you've mentioned some of my favorite subjects." He barely resisted rubbing his hands gleefully together.

Smiling, Brandon looked over at him. "I've never found anyone who shares my interests. Most people I've met are too wrapped up in materialism and other trappings of life to care about the molecular makeup of any given element, or which herbs will kill a man with a single touch, or..." He trailed off, giving Cornelius a sheepish grin. "Sorry. I haven't been able to talk about this stuff, so I'm likely to get carried away."

"My tendency is to be wrapped up in the magical side of things. The mundane is just too ordinary for me to bother with. I'm definitely going to have to show you my workroom sometime. I think you'll understand what I mean once you've seen it." Cornelius relaxed in the chair, a more animated sense coming over him as he talked to Brandon, and it brought a certain sparkle to his dark green eyes.

Brandon sat up and swung his legs off of the edge of the bed again. His chocolate-brown eyes twinkled with childlike interest. "Workroom? What's it like? I've always wanted to know more about the magical aspects, but I've never known anyone other than the fluffy bunny pagans. I mean, not all of them are like that, but the ones I've met are." His smile widened. "You have the most gorgeous green eyes I've ever seen. I hope that doesn't make you uncomfortable, but I had to say it."

Cornelius chuckled. "My workroom has no fluffy bunnies in it, just a lot of potion and ritual ingredients and one pain-in-the-ass spirit." The unexpected compliment didn't bother him at all, and actually broadened his smile. "I'm flattered that you think so, Brandon, and it doesn't make me uncomfortable."

"So, what's the deal with the court? I never really thought there *was* such a thing."

"You'll get used to it. Just remember to call Mael 'Excellency' or 'Your Excellency' in front of the vultures, treat him with the proper respect, and you'll do fine."

"I have to admit, he kinda makes me nervous, but he seems really nice."

"Mael's arrogant most times, but there's a heart in there. You just have to look for it, and once you find it, you have to remember that it's real."

Brandon sighed and looked back up at the canopy over the bed. "Yeah, I got the feeling he's a very guarded man."

"Don't worry about Mael. You'll get used to him as you get to know him."

"What all do I need to know about living here?"

"Other than being polite to the others and giving Mael the respect due to him, there's not really much else. You'll learn your way fairly easily, I suspect. And any questions you have once you've seen everything and everybody a time or two, I'll be more than happy to answer."

Brandon looked momentarily confused. "Um, there is one question I had."

"Sure, ask whatever you want."

"What about feeding?"

"Oh, that. Since you are as young as you are, and you've not had any proper training, I can have a bottle brought up to you if you would like." It suddenly occurred to Cornelius just how much he needed to take care of Brandon. "Then I suppose we can let you feed from a mortal at some time to see how you do."

"F-feed from a mortal?" Brandon stammered.

Reaching over, Cornelius lightly patted Brandon's leg in an attempt to dispel the nervousness. "I see no problem in letting you feed from either me or Mael until you feel comfortable enough to try with a mortal. Though the first time you do feed from one, I will be with you, just in case."

Brandon's eyes widened. "Feed from you or Mael?" The look of shock on his face was almost comical.

"There's no reason to be shocked."

Brandon's breath caught in his throat for a brief moment. "I don't think I could feed from the prince," he muttered.

"That would be your choice, of course." Cornelius nodded. "Then you'll have to make do with me. I really don't want trust any of the others."

"I...umm...I think I'd feel more comfortable with you."

Regarding Brandon matter-of-factly, Cornelius asked, "Are you hungry now? Which would you prefer to start out with: a bottle or me?"

"From you," Brandon replied.

"Would you prefer drinking from wrist or my throat?"

Brandon bit his lower lip. "I'm curious to know what it's like doing it from the throat. I only fed from one person before and that was Cian. I fed from his wrist."

"You fed from the sorcerer? How unusual." Cornelius stood from the chair and moved closer to the bed, offering Brandon his hand to help him up.

Brandon took his hand gingerly.

Understanding Brandon was anxious about this, Cornelius gently drew the young vampire up from the bed to stand in front of him. He tilted his head to the side, exposing his throat, simply to see if instinct would take over as he gently urged Brandon closer. Giving Brandon a reassuring smile, Cornelius waited patiently and watched as Brandon stilled for a moment, shivering.

Swallowing hard, Brandon finally leaned forward. He brushed his lips slowly across Cornelius' neck, and Cornelius felt the flick of his tongue. A shiver stole over both of them before Brandon's fangs slowly sank into him. Feeling the hungry pull at his throat, Cornelius quickly forced down his own reaction to the resulting pleasure. When he closed his eyes, Brandon's arm snaked around his waist, holding him close.

Deliberately, he kept his body completely relaxed as Brandon nestled into him. He let go of Brandon's hand and cupped the back of Brandon's head, pressing gently, encouraging him. When he felt the sensation of the pressure steadily increase, he could barely suppress his own reactive shiver. His other hand settled at the young vampire's waist, allowing Brandon to rest against him as he fed. The slow pulse of a soft growl rolled in Cornelius' chest, and he felt the shivering of the body against his before Brandon stopped feeding.

When Brandon finished, he stepped back and turned away, appearing self-conscious. "Thank you," he said quietly. "Is it normal for..." He stopped, as if he felt too embarrassed to say what was on his mind.

"Is it normal to greatly enjoy feeding? Yes, it is, as much as it's pleasurable to be fed from. Normally after feeding, you heal the wound you made by simply licking it."

Brandon laughed nervously. "I didn't know. I'm sorry if it made you uncomfortable."

Cornelius readjusted his glasses. "Why would you think I would be uncomfortable with you or letting you feed from me?"

Sighing deeply, the young vampire leaned up against the poster of his bed, his back still to Cornelius. "Because I'm gay, Cornelius. I like guys."

After a few seconds, Cornelius stepped up behind him, placing his hand on Brandon's shoulder. "And you thought that would bother me. It doesn't."

Brandon turned around slowly to face him. "It doesn't?"

Shaking his head, Cornelius chuckled. "You have to remember that our world is very different from the mortal one. Very few of us were ever stupid enough to create a child from anybody with intolerances like that. It is a highly selective breeding process, you might say. Sometimes, one slips through, but it tends to cause major annoyance to the rest of us. You might find quite a few who aren't interested in their own sex. I'm just not one of those."

A look of realization dawned on Brandon's face. "Oh." He looked off to the side, blinking several times. "You're gay?"

"Yes, I do believe I am," Cornelius said with a gentle, teasing smile.

"I've never met anyone like you before." Brandon's grin widened. "I think I'm really going to like it here."

"I hope you do enjoy your new home. It's where you belong now." The moment Brandon smiled at him, it seemed to lighten the touch of gravity. Cornelius did his best to ignore such sensations. "I think we'll both have plenty to talk about in the coming nights."

"I really need to get laid," Brandon said with a quiet laugh as he turned away once more.

"Well, now, for that, we will have to introduce you to some of the others in the court. A few of them are decent enough sorts and generally quite eager to play most times. I also need to take you shopping sometime tomorrow night. For tonight, would you care for a grand tour of the place, or would you rather settle in?"

"Actually," Brandon said, "I was looking forward to seeing your workroom."

"Well, then, come along. I'd be delighted to show it to you."

"I still can't believe I've found someone else like me."

As they walked down the hall toward the third floor, Cornelius chuckled. "I think we'll get along fine, young Master Brandon." He cast a side glance at the young man. For the first time, he'd met somebody similar to himself, and he could barely contain himself at that thought. The enthusiasm the young vampire had shown toward his mention of his workroom had him positively delighted.

* * *

"Excellency, Seymour, Avery, Jacobs, and Talbert have arrived. They are waiting for you in the central hall."

Mael nodded and continued into the throne room. The four men were standing near his throne, talking quietly amongst themselves. He'd known them for many centuries, and he'd fought beside them in several battles over the years. They each held their own cities and were uninterested in gaining territory for themselves. However, both Seymour and Avery each had a child who was ready to hold their own city, which made replacements all that much easier. Mael also knew Jacobs and Talbert would aid him once they realized why he wanted Iverson and Raven relieved of their positions.

He gestured for them to join him at the table. All four joined him without a word, though it was clear from their expressions they were curious. "Iverson and Raven have potentially become serious problems. I need the four of you to take care of them for me."

"Are you trying to expand your sphere of influence, Mael?" Avery, the eldest of the four men, asked.

Glancing over at him, Mael's gaze paused on Avery's badly scarred arms. Most of them were wounds from battles in Rome, when Avery had been a general in its army long ago. As he raised his eyes to the rugged face, shrewd, brown eyes bore into Mael's.

"Hardly, Avery. London is enough of a headache these days. Unfortunately for them, two packages containing vials of the formula were found, addressed to them."

The men's expressions ranged from disgust to shock. It spoke volumes of their trust in Mael that they accepted his word without demanding proof. All five of them lived by a code of honor few of the young ones understood anymore.

Seymour finally cut into the silence. "The rogue problem is spreading out from the confines of London then?"

"I suspect it will be soon. If Iverson and Raven are eliminated, it will be two fewer cities that have to worry. Truthfully, there are only about ten princes I trust implicitly not to be behind any of this now."

"Aye. The problem is far more serious than we first thought, Mael." Talbert's expression took on a deeply troubled cast.

Mael nodded but said nothing. He couldn't even tell them just how bad it really had gotten with Selena supplying formulas to God knows who. It would do no good to share that information, and it would only disturb them all the more. Jacobs gave him a shrewd look but chose not to voice his own questions. Seymour eyed the other three before he slowly nodded. With very little pause, each in turn nodded.

Quietly, Seymour said, "We are all in agreement in helping you, Mael."

"I'd also like to see Jared and Malcolm take their places." He glanced at Seymour and then Avery. He continued before either of them could say anything. "I will be informing the Romanorum of everything once Iverson and Raven are taken care of. Nobody will gainsay me in my recommendations of your sons. Nor can you be accused of being involved in this for your own gain. I think that's all for now. Once everybody is ready, we'll set the time for the necessary attack."

Each of them got up, and as they turned to leave, the door opened.

"Your Excellency."

Mael gestured for Sav to join them. "Sav will be helping coordinate everything between my court and all of yours. Since you've all worked with her before, I didn't think it would be a problem."

"We have no problems with her, Mael," Avery said before the four of them left, closing the door behind them.

When they were alone, Sav said, "Selena left a message saying she wants to see you Friday, and I got the information you wanted, Your Excellency. Lee Carmichael is Cian Carmichael's brother. There's nothing much on him, and the girl you mentioned is Rachel Centers. Her record is fairly clean except for a couple of bar room fights she's gotten into. Her most recent one is very interesting, though. She got into it with a vampire named Celia Keene."

"Celia Keene? Iverson's daughter?" Frowning slightly, Mael hadn't expected to hear that name. "Get somebody on Rachel Centers now, Sav. I want to know what in the hell she's up to."

"I will, Your Excellency."

The thought that Cian and his brother could be tied to all of this dismayed Mael greatly. But then, why would the sorcerer even bother killing rogues? Things just didn't add up right, and Mael didn't like any of it one bit. At least he had another night before Selena wanted to see him. Thankfully, Selena's daughter had warned him ahead of time to expect it.

* * *

The next night, Mael spent several hours with Cornelius and Brandon, shopping and getting the young vampire used to the court. With the rest of his work, Mael wasn't able to seek the peace and quiet of his chambers until long after the sun rose. He spent the time afterwards coordinating the planned attacks. Because they had to be kept away from everybody's notice, everyone had to congregate in the common room in the dungeons. Not the most pleasant of places to hold the meetings, but he really didn't have a choice. Luckily, none of them gave him too much of an argument over his requests.

Having to cut short one of the meetings to go to Selena's put him in a rather bad mood, however; the prospect wasn't all that thrilling. In fact, he downright dreaded it. Still, he had no real choice but to present himself to her as she requested. Entering her throne room, it was not a welcome sight to see only her sitting in her throne. None of her court members were present, and that was not a good sign.

"Your Eminence, it is an honor to be here." Staying strictly by protocol, Mael kept his expression to a careful mask of politeness as he moved closer to her and bowed.

"Mael, my princely treasure, come closer to me. You are late, you know." Selena's ruby lips pursed in a slight pout of disapproval, though her tone stayed soft and alluring.

Her voice had no true impact on him, but he deliberately shivered as he slowly approached her. The beautiful woman sitting so regally on her throne was not, in reality, any more powerful than he was; however, it was a facade he very carefully maintained. To most, he was known to be almost nine hundred years old, but the truth was he was almost twice that, which gave him a decided edge in dealing with Selena. His true age was something known only to a few, and he liked it that way. He had been wandering the face of the earth, growing in power, long before she was even created. As a first formula, she did have power over him, just not as much as she thought she did. Almost all worshipped the titian-haired, emerald-eyed vampire goddess. Mael just wasn't one of them.

"I really should punish you." As she held out a jewel-clad hand to him, he took it, raising it to his lips to softly kiss her fingers.

"Forgive me, Your Eminence. Unfortunately, I had to execute several more rogues before I could come to you."

Her lips twisted in another pout as she eyed him. "All right, Mael, I will forgive you this time, but next time, any rogues can wait. Everything else can wait as well. Am I understood?"

"Certainly, Your Eminence."

"You can stop with the 'Your Eminence.' I wish to hear my name on your lips." She slipped one hand up over his chest and curled her fingers to the side of his throat. A red lacquered nail dug less than gently into his skin, causing a faint flicker of pain. It was a game she greatly enjoyed playing with him.

"As you wish, Selena." The shiver that ran though his body with that faint touch of pain *wasn't* faked.

Mael remained motionless, feeling the soft brush of her lips to his. Her other hand slid slowly down the front of his shirt and then lower to his crotch. Her expert fingers firmly flexed over his cock, sending faint flickers of sensation ghosting over the skin beneath his pants. In reaction, his hips jerked into that touch as he moaned. This was the one power she did have: to cause those teasing echoes of pleasurable pain. He possessed the ability as well, but hers was far better.

As she drew away from him, a pleased smile curved her lips. "Unfortunately, I don't have the time to play with you as I would like, my pet." There was a touch of regret in her expression as she moved back to sit on her throne.

"Perhaps next time you will not be distracted by other business, Selena." He very carefully kept hidden the overwhelming relief he felt. Slowly, his gaze roamed her body, allowing a tinge of desire for her to show, though it was something he really didn't feel. She believed she owned him, and it was better just to let her keep believing that.

"I want you to get the Eye of Baal for me." She regarded him casually, as if asking for no more than a new dress.

"I think you've finally lost your mind, Selena. The Eye is only a legend," Mael said in amusement. If the damn thing still existed, anybody caught with it would be sentenced to death, and for good reason. It was rumored to gift its owner with incredible power—power of the wrong sort, since the stone was supposedly crafted by a demon.

"I know who has it, darling, but obviously I can't go get myself, now can I?"

"And who has it?"

"A sorcerer by the name of Cian Carmichael. I've heard he's been seen in London recently."

Mael really was hearing that name all too often lately. Somehow, it was no surprise Selena had managed to dig his hole just that much deeper.

Suppressing a sigh, Mael said, "I know he has been in London, but how do you expect me to get the Eye of Baal? If he really does have it, which I seriously doubt."

"Use your imagination, my pet. I have the greatest faith in your skill to get me what I want. I expect you to have that stone in your possession within the next two months. Now go." With a casual wave of her hand, she dismissed him from her presence.

Bowing to her, he murmured, "My only wish is to serve you." His thoughts, however, were muttering an entirely different sentiment. His only real wish was to get the hell out of there.

Chapter Five

Several days passed before Cian had any need to return to Black's mansion. Although he had promised Brandon he would visit, this was not a social call. He needed to speak with the prince himself. Lee had pleaded with him not to say anything, but Cian knew better than to keep this much a secret. The prince had a right to know, and if he was lucky, Cian hoped to talk the prince into granting Rachel amnesty, against his own better judgment. He watched Ben walk away, leaving him standing at Prince Black's office door. He knocked on it and then waited, wondering just how well this meeting was going to go. When the door opened, Cian took a deep breath before stepping inside.

"Good evening, Your Excellency."

A flicker of surprise shone in the prince's eyes. The prince gestured toward the chair in front of the desk before he settled back, relaxing in his own chair. "Good evening. I must say I'm surprised to see you here."

"Thank you," Cian said as he sat down. "I haven't come here to visit Brandon. I came here to speak with you specifically about an issue that concerns me greatly."

The prince leaned back, one leg crossed the other, and he folded his hands over his knee. "Then what is it you want to talk about?"

Cian shifted in his chair, feeling the prince's dark gaze rake over him like a caress. It was an unnerving feeling. "A close friend of mine has become inadvertently involved with Prince Iverson. My friend's girlfriend has become misguided and is working with Iverson. While I do not particularly trust the woman, my friend is another matter."

"Iverson is a very dangerous vampire to even be seen with now." The prince appeared to choose his words carefully, and they came out slowly, containing their own subtle warning. "If your friend can remove his girlfriend from that undue influence, she might live longer."

Cian sighed. "What I'm about to tell you cannot go beyond this room, Prince Black. The friend I am referring to is my brother. His name is Lee, and his girlfriend is Rachel Centers, a mortal woman who apparently has close enough ties to have spoken with Iverson in person. I do not trust her, and Lee has informed me that she has revealed my identity as a rogue hunter to Iverson and those who follow him. If Iverson were to be...removed, I would want full amnesty for Rachel, if at all possible."

Mael's expression became deeply thoughtful as he listened in silence. "Iverson will soon be taken care of, Cian. If you wish, there are a number of ways I can remove her from his influence until the danger has passed. I'm not sure I can guarantee her safety if she's caught anywhere near him when the shit does hit the fan."

"I would be indebted to you." Cian paused for a moment more, his gaze taking in the prince. Mael's dark eyes keep him riveted, and he longed to reach out, to slip his fingers through the prince's ebony hair. He shook his head briefly before continuing. "What rumors have you heard from Iverson's camp?"

"I will take care of the matter of your brother's girlfriend, though you might not want to consider yourself indebted until she is safely out of it," Mael said with a shrug. The dark eyes that held Cian's gaze had a knowing look to them, as if the prince knew of his own effect on Cian. "As far as the rumors go, Iverson seriously overstepped himself."

"Are you aware there is a plot on your life?"

"Not the first and probably not the last."

"You take such a threat lightly?"

"I never said that. I simply stated it's not the first."

Cian stood and began to pace. "Did Ashton Carter have any direct connection to Iverson?"

"He had an indirect one through another prince, but since Iverson is working with the other prince, they could be considered somewhat of a connection."

"Damn. He was more intent on toying with me than anything else. I didn't get much out of him." Cian stopped pacing. "Who is the other prince?"

"The Prince of Colchester, Raven McDonald. Any reason you are asking?" Mael paused, frowning slightly. "If Carter said anything to you, then it's entirely possible he had dealings with Iverson. My network, while huge, is not entirely foolproof."

"The most I got out of Carter was the not-so-subtle mention of killing you. He seemed to be rather proud that Iverson had even called on him to start things in motion. I'm afraid Rachel is part of their plot, even though she has no clue what she's getting into." Cian leaned back against the wall, shoving his hands into the pockets of his leather pants. "I'm trying to figure out what's going on. There's more to this than a simple rogue problem; I just don't know what."

"Then there is more than even I know. I was unaware of any link at all there. Though I can't say I'm entirely surprised Iverson wishes to kill me. He's in the thick of the problems with the rogues, even supplies his own for the cause. Whatever cause that might be." Mael stood and rounded the desk to settle at the edge of it.

"What other reason would two princes have to kill you?"

"Aside from London being a great prize? I'm not fully sure. I am interested in your stake in all this, sorcerer. Why are you so deeply involved?" Folding his hands, the prince rested them on his thigh.

Cian's lips curled into a wry smile. "It's my job. I was sent here to deal with the rogue situation. My brother has been my London contact. If there's more than a rogue problem, then my job is jeopardized thanks to Rachel." He pushed off from the wall and walked slowly to stand before Mael, crossing his arms over his chest.

Mael straightened just slightly, a half-lidded look drifting slowly over Cian. "I don't think your job is jeopardized just yet. You need not worry."

"Good." Cian turned around and started for the door. He paused with his hand on the door handle. "Oh, and don't worry about Iverson. I'm sure he and I will cross paths soon."

"Leaving so soon?" The words and soft, sultry tone carried a hint of regret.

Cian stopped before stepping out the door. He turned slowly to face the prince, closing the door behind him once more. "Why would you want me to stay?"

"To talk with you for a while." The inflection remained an almost seductive rhythm.

"Talk?" Cian pulled the chair over to sit closer to the desk. He leaned back until he had to look up to see the prince's dark eyes. "What would a vampire prince want to talk about with a simple hunter?"

"How about that simple hunter? Especially when I think he's not quite as simple as he says." Mael's hand slid slowly downward, closer to his knee and more in the direction of Cian.

Cian watched him intently, and the memory of that hand sliding over a young man's naked flesh came back to haunt him. He swallowed hard and forced himself to look up into the prince's eyes again. "I am no different from any other man."

A slow smile curved to the prince's lips, his expression vaguely disbelieving. "You are trying to tell me you are like any other man? Allow me to doubt that, if you will." A dark glimmer in those eyes met Cian's unwavering gaze. "No. Somehow, I don't think you would be as interesting if I thought you an ordinary man."

Cian chuckled. "You find me interesting? Now that's a new one. Most vampires I've encountered wanted nothing more than to kill me or get me into bed," he said with an amused grin.

The prince's gaze raked slowly over Cian. "I can see why some would want to get you into bed. You smell of sunshine, sorcerer, and the color of your hair would fascinate the darkest of us."

Cian smiled, more than pleasantly surprised at the compliments. "And you, prince, you are rather intriguing to me." He made no attempt to hide the hungry gaze as it traveled over the prince's body. "Tell me: which do you prefer to get into bed?"

The prince shifted slightly, as if something were a touch too tight. "I prefer men, though I've been known to enjoy women. While you're asking such intimately personal questions, I might ask the same."

Cian settled back in the chair, stretching his arms and locking his fingers behind his head. "I'm not known for being coy, prince. I only have eyes for men."

"I'm coming to understand that little fact about you. Any men in particular?"

Cian remained silent for a moment, too entranced with the prince's dark hair and the dark blue depths of his eyes to speak. "I'm inexplicably drawn to the darkness, more than I should be, I think."

A more satisfied cast settled over the prince's expression. He twisted slightly on the edge of the desk, his legs angled toward Cian. "I believe I am drawn to the light myself. Even with the thought that it might burn me."

Cian's gaze drifted from the prince's eyes, down his body. "The light does indeed burn, prince." He grinned and raised a hand, bringing a small blue flame to life. He rolled it over his palm and then turned his hand over, letting the flame dance across his knuckles. "Do you always play with fire?"

"Given that a certain amount of pain can entrance me at times, what do you think, sorcerer?" Mael's gaze followed the dance of the flame.

"Really?" The flame slid up Cian's arm and across his shoulder to caress his neck as he tilted his head back. When he lowered his head once more, he smirked. "I'll remember that."

"We'll have to see if it does you any good."

Cian snapped his fingers, and the flame flickered out. He stood, bringing their faces within inches of each other. "What makes you think I would act on anything?"

The prince shifted, his thighs bracketing Cian's legs. "What makes you think you won't?"

Cian made no attempt to move. "Arrogance suits you, prince."

The barest touch of Mael's fingers smoothed slowly over Cian's hair. His fingers fanned the golden strands out to the front of the Cian's black shirt. "And lust suits you perfectly."

Cian gripped the prince's hand and stopped it before it could move any farther. He brought it to his lips and slid his tongue along the length of two fingers before sucking them into his mouth. The soft sound from Mael became an audible growl. Mael's other hand moved to Cian's hip, drawing him in tighter, against the definite hardness of his cock.

A light knock sounded at the office door.

Cian grinned and pulled away. "Thank you for seeing me, Your Excellency." He leaned forward and slid his tongue lightly across Mael's lips. "*Tan y tro nesaf...*"

"Thank me when I've seen more of you."

Cian moved to the door and opened it, brushing past the man on the other side as he made his way out. As he walked away, the prince's last words lingered in his mind.

* * *

By late afternoon of the next day, Cian had finally admitted to himself that his attraction to Mael Black was deeper than he really liked. A passing fancy would not have bothered him, but something in the prince's eyes drew him in. Truth be told, one night with the prince would never be enough. He arrived at St. Mary's just as the sun was beginning to set. He had spent most of the day wandering the city in a daze, the events of the night before haunting him relentlessly. He walked through the sanctuary and pulled back the curtain of the confessional. He knelt down and spoke softly.

"Bless me, Father, for I have sinned. It's been a long time since my last confession. I desire another man."

"While there are those within the Church who do not agree with such things, God does not discriminate, my son."

"But the man I desire is a vampire."

The priest sighed. "Vampires are dangerous."

"And Mael Black is the most dangerous in the city."

"Yes, he is," the priest said. "But what has Mael Black to do with you, my son?"

"Because it is the Prince of London I desire." Cian slid the curtain back.

The priest's face lost all its color. "Cian..."

"Good evening, Father Shepard."

"Is it true?"

Cian nodded. "It is." He looked down and took a deep breath. "I found a young one. He was newly turned, and if my suspicions are correct, his sire is a rogue." Father Shepard's eyes widened in horror, but Cian raised a hand, stopping the priest before he could speak. "Brandon has not killed a mortal, Father. I took him to Mael Black; he's the only one in this city who can help."

"And that's when you met Black?"

Cian shook his head. "No, I didn't stay long enough for any introduction."

"Then how can you desire a man you have not seen?" Father Shepard asked him.

"I have seen him. The first time was when he unexpectedly helped me with a kill. Then I went to him last night to discuss business," Cian said. He tilted his head back and closed his eyes. "Father," he said quietly, almost as much to Heaven as to the priest beside him, "I've never felt such a strong desire in all my existence."

"Mael Black is a powerful, dangerous man, Cian," the priest said.

"Yes, I know." Cian stood and left the confessional.

A few moments later, Father Shepard stepped out as well. "How is the hunt?" the priest asked as they walked through the cavernous gothic sanctuary.

The waning sunlight filtered through the stained glass windows flanking the sanctuary. Worshipers sat scattered in the wooden pews, most of them in quiet contemplation and prayer. A few looked up as Cian passed them, unsure what to make of him. Although he could hide his wings, he couldn't hide his aura, and while they were few in number, some people knew him for what he was.

"The hunt," he said, pausing for a moment as he searched for the right words, "is going as well as it could be. I finally managed to corner Ashton Carter." He looked over, noting the combined look of shock and awe on the priest's face. "Carter will no longer be a problem to anyone."

"Did he give you a tremendous amount of trouble?" Father Shepard asked, leaning closer and lowering his voice.

Cian stopped walking and turned to face him. He slid a finger through the slit in the front of his shirt. The flesh beneath was smooth and pristine, showing no sign of ever having been cut. "Just enough," he said. "I need to go now. I want to check on Brandon."

Father Shepard lifted a salt-and-pepper eyebrow but said nothing. Cian smiled, silently grateful the aging priest didn't argue his reasons. Cian placed a soft kiss to his friend's forehead and left. He had every intention of checking on Brandon, but he also couldn't deny the desire to see Black once more.

The cathedral was only a few blocks from Black's mansion, and as he neared it, Cian felt a strange sense of nervousness and hope well up within him. The guard at the gate let him through without a word. Cian figured he must have become a regular sight to the occupants of Black's court.

He paused halfway along the walkway to the mansion, watching the balcony closely. When no movement came, he took in a deep breath and continued to the door. A few minutes after he knocked, it opened. He stepped into the foyer and couldn't help but admire the grand sweeping staircase that dominated the room. Suits of armor lined the walls, and hallways disappeared behind the staircase. It was indeed a grand entrance, suitable for a prince.

"Good evening," a man to his left said.

"Good evening. I'm here to see Brandon. He's the young vampire I brought here."

"One moment." The man disappeared into a room off to the left. A few minutes later, Ben appeared.

"Good evening," Ben said. "You are here to see Brandon, I assume." Cian nodded. "Very well, follow me please."

Ben started up a flight of stairs, Cian following closely behind him. When they reached the top, they went down a lengthy hallway. Ben stopped in front of a door and stepped aside.

"If you need anything, please call."

Cian watched Ben walk away and then knocked on the door. He heard the rustle of someone getting out of a chair or a bed, and then the door opened. Brandon's face lit up, and he graced Cian with a broad smile.

"Cian!" Brandon stepped to the side and grabbed Cian's arm, nearly dragging him into the room. He closed the door and threw his arms around Cian. "I was wondering if you'd come to see me."

Cian smiled and hugged him. "Of course, I would. How are they treating you?"

Brandon stepped back and waved his arm around. "See for yourself! Mael Black is actually quite nice. They took me shopping for new clothes and everything."

Cian looked around the room and was relieved to see that Brandon wasn't lacking in anything. Brandon went over to the bed and dropped down onto the cream-colored bedspread, propping himself up on one arm. A book lay beside him, turned upside down to hold his place. Cian walked over to a chair and sank down into its plush cushions. Brandon looked to be quite happy.

"I'm glad they're good to you. What about feeding?"

Brandon rolled over onto his back and put his hands behind his head. "Mael said they want me to start on bottled for right now. They'll test me with a mortal later. I never knew vampires had such strict laws."

"They aren't so much vampire laws as they are mortal laws imposed on vampires. I suppose it's a small price to pay for being allowed to exist without much trouble from hunters."

Brandon sighed. "Yeah, I guess you're right." He rolled his head slightly and looked over at Cian. "What about you? How have *you* been?"

Cian knew it would do no good to tell Brandon of his desire for Mael Black. Instead, he smiled and stuck with neutral topics. "I'm well. I paid a visit to an old friend this evening — Father Shepard, of Saint Mary's."

"I know him! My family is Catholic, and we went to Saint Mary's a few times when I was a kid."

Cian fought the urge to remind Brandon that he was *still* a kid, no matter how old he was in years. His soul was young. "Father Shepard is a dear friend. I've known him for quite a long time. I still need to visit my brother."

Brandon's expression changed to one of surprise. "You have a brother? Is he...you know...like you?"

Cian laughed. "Yes, he is. He lives with a mortal woman."

"Does she know what he is?"

"No. No one knows about either one of us," Cian said, casting a cautionary look at Brandon. "And it needs to stay that way. I have to work directly with Mael Black, and my identity cannot be known."

"I gotcha, I gotcha," Brandon said with a laugh.

"I need to go now, however. Lee is expecting me." Cian stood, and Brandon sat up on the edge of the bed.

"Cian," he said quietly, "can I ask a favor?"

"Anything," Cian said. When Brandon looked up at him, however, he began to regret his answer. He could read Brandon's wish without the need for words.

"Just one kiss," Brandon said quietly as he stood. "That's all I want." Cian sighed. "Please, Cian. Just one."

Before Cian could say a word, Brandon was standing before him, pressing his body close to Cian's. Cian started to protest, but Brandon's arms slid around his neck and the young vampire's lips descended on his, silencing him quickly. He returned the kiss, taking care to not put anything more behind it. Then an image flitted through his mind, of Mael Black's lips on his, the prince's tongue sliding across his own, their bodies pressed tightly together. He forced his heart to slow down its furious beating, and he gently pulled Brandon away, breaking their kiss.

"Thank you," Brandon said with a smile.

"I'm sorry I can't give you what you want," Cian said as he stroked the young vampire's face. "But don't take it as me not caring. Quite the contrary." He pressed his lips gently to Brandon's forehead and went to the door.

The moment Cian stepped into the hallway and closed the door behind him, he froze. He sensed a strong presence, one he could not have missed even if he had wanted to.

His heart began to race in his chest, and he turned slowly, meeting the dark blue gaze of the prince.

"Cian." The prince approached Cian slowly, extending his hand.

"Your Excellency," Cian said with a slight bow of his head. He took Mael's hand and resisted the urge to lace his fingers through Mael's. When a fleeting image of those hands on his body came to his mind, Cian's heart skipped a beat. He pulled his hand slowly from Mael's grasp, sharply aware of reluctance...on both their parts.

"I take it you're here to see Brandon."

Cian fought another surge of desire as a distinct spark of lust glittered in Mael's dark eyes. No one had *ever* had such an effect on him. "Yes, I am. I want to thank you for taking him in. Considering he's never killed a mortal, I knew you'd be the one to help him."

"He'll be perfectly fine here," Mael said. "There are several suitable in the court to take on the role of teaching him, and he'll make his own choice."

"I'm pleased to know that. I trust he has behaved himself."

Considering Brandon's infatuation with him, Cian wondered if maybe the young vampire had expressed similar interests in Mael Black. As he took in Mael's muscular form once again, Cian couldn't imagine someone *not* desiring the vampire prince. Wary of the man and the power that simmered just beneath the surface, Cian pushed away all wayward thoughts. Here was someone who was more than he seemed to be, stronger in body and will than his calm, collected manner suggested. The soft cadence of Black's voice settled around Cian, as if it were trying to draw him in, like a beacon in a tempest. Cian fought the near-overwhelming urge to pull the prince into a kiss.

Mael lifted a dark eyebrow. "If you mean what I think you do, he's been behaving perfectly well. Feel free to visit him here anytime you wish," the prince said. "Since you are fond of the boy, I'm sure you'll want to check in on him from time to time."

"Thank you. He seems to have taken an interest in me, one that I cannot reciprocate. However, I do care for him and wish only the best for him."

"Unfortunately, an attachment to you is extremely unsuitable. Hopefully, he'll realize that when he becomes better acclimated to his new life."

"I would have to agree. I don't think he truly understands what I am."

A low growl rumbled in the prince's chest, and he reached out. He slid his fingers through Cian's hair, catching a golden strand and wrapping it around his fingers before letting it slip between them. "And I don't think you truly understand what he could be," Black said. "But he will be very well taken care of; you have my word on that, Cian." He released Cian's hair suddenly, pulling his hand away as if he had been burnt.

Cian stepped forward. "I've been around long enough to understand more than you think I do," he said under his breath. The air between their bodies was stifling, heated and charged. The closeness made Cian's pulse race.

"But you've not been around long enough to understand what you should." The prince moved closer still, until they were inches from touching.

Cian bristled. The prince seemed to be baiting him, and a flare of heat flooded through Cian's body. The prince's arrogance served to both annoy him and entice him further. "You have no idea how long I've been around, prince."

Without another word, Mael closed the distance between them and pressed his lips softly to Cian's. He threaded his fingers through Cian's hair, entangling them in the golden strands and increasing the pressure of his chaste kiss.

A soft groan escaped Cian's lips, and he opened them on the prince's, giving into his desires. He slid his tongue slowly across Mael's lips, seeking entrance. The prince opened for him, and Cian was granted his first taste of Mael Black.

His heart thundered, and Mael's hand fell to his hip, pulling him closer until their bodies were pressed together. Cian slid his fingers through Mael's dark hair, deepening their kiss. A wash of pure heat rushed through him, creating an ache that he knew only the prince of London could assuage.

Mael pulled him slowly into the bedroom, never breaking their kiss and guiding him by the hand on his hip. When his tongue slid across one of Mael's fangs, however, Cian pulled away quickly. He felt the tiny prick from the tip of the sharply-pointed tooth and was sorely reminded of what Mael Black truly was.

"I must go," he said as he backed away.

The heated desire darkened the prince's eyes, and Cian watched as Mael's tongue licked a stray drop of blood. Cian groaned inwardly, knowing the prince would sense a very distinct—powerful—difference. An angel's blood was nothing like a mortal's.

With the sound of voices coming up the stairs, Cian backed out into the hallway, never taking his gaze from the prince standing beside an immaculate bed. Cian knew without a doubt that, had he not pulled away, they would be in that bed now, their bodies entwined just as he had seen in his mind. He bowed his head briefly.

"Thank you again." He turned and hurried down the stairs, paying little mind to the vampires coming up.

As soon as he was out of the house, he flattened himself against the outer wall, desperately trying to catch his breath. Images of Mael invaded his mind, and he groaned. He pushed away and hurried down the path. He had to put more distance between them. He was dangerously close to giving in to his desires. What would his boss say?

As he hurried to Lee's apartment, Cian tried to force all thoughts of Mael Black from his mind. His efforts were proving to be fruitless as more time passed. He thought for a moment about avoiding the prince completely, but with the increasing rogue problems and the connections between Rachel, Iverson, and Carter, he knew that wasn't possible. By the time he reached Lee's front door, only his outward appearance suggested calmness. Inside, he was anything but.

The moment the door opened, Cian saw the dubious look on his brother's face. Lee was too smart to not notice the change in Cian's demeanor. As he walked into the apartment, Cian figured it was best to get the initial question out of the way.

"I kissed him," he said before Lee could even open his mouth. Lee said nothing but went into the kitchen to get them both something to drink.

Cian collapsed onto the couch, his thoughts still in a whirlwind. Lee set a glass of ice water on the table in front of him a few minutes later, and even with his eyes closed, Cian knew his brother was staring at him. Had he been a mortal, Cian would've asked for something much stronger than water. He opened his eyes and met Lee's steady blue gaze. He didn't have to ask what was going through Lee's mind; he could read it on his brother's face.

"I'm not going to ask what possessed you to kiss a vampire," Lee said quietly as he sat down in the chair across from Cian.

"Good," Cian said. "Because even I don't know. I only went there to check on Brandon."

"So how did you run into Black?"

"Brandon's room is right next door to Black's. Black and I came out of the rooms at the same time."

"Coincidence, huh?" Lee asked. He didn't sound entirely convinced.

Cian sighed and reached for his water. He prayed the ice-cold liquid would quench the fire raging inside him. He had desired humans before, but never like this. He drank half the water in one swallow and cradled the glass in his hands, letting the cool dampness on the outside seep into his fingers.

"Black was as surprised as I was," he said finally. "The kiss was far from expected."

"Who initiated it?"

"He did." Cian raised a hand to stop Lee before he could say anything. "But his kiss was chaste, Lee."

Lee's eyes widened as the weight of what Cian had said sank in. "You turned it into something more?" Cian nodded. Lee jumped to his feet and began to pace the room. "Have you lost your mind? You're an angel, Cian! You're one of Michael's top enforcers, not to mention one of his closest friends. You can't feel things like this for a vampire."

"You think I don't know that?" Cian asked him. "But I cannot change what I feel, Lee, any more than you can change your love for Rachel."

Lee shot him a cold look. "Don't compare your...lust...for a vampire to my love for Rachel."

Cian groaned. He hadn't expected Lee to understand any of this. Despite his time on Earth, Lee had not changed. He was still the same intensely pious angel he had always been. Cian was still pious, yes, but the time spent moving between his own plane and this one had served to humble him a bit, to the point where he was better able to handle the usual oddities of the human race. He was not beyond lust, and he felt it to be a side effect of working so close with humans. He set the glass down and stood. He gripped Lee's shoulder, putting an end to his infernal pacing.

"I am not comparing anything," he said, "but I have spent enough time with humans to allow myself the ability to effectively blend in."

Lee raised an eyebrow dubiously.

"Make no mistake, Lee. I'm fully aware of the dangers of desiring Mael Black. I will not cave in completely to them."

"Yet you keep them," Lee said with a dejected sigh.

"I told you: I cannot change what I feel." Cian placed a kiss to Lee's brow. "I must go. I need to return to my tower. It's the only place I have that I know Mael Black cannot follow me to."

Lee wrinkled his brow at that. "Follow you? You think Black would follow you?"

"He feels the same desire, Lee, and..." He stopped before saying too much. Telling Lee that Mael had tasted his blood would only make things worse.

"And?"

Cian shook his head. "Nothing. Lost my train of thought, I suppose. I'll be back later."

He closed the door to Lee's apartment and sighed, leaning back against it. He didn't like to argue, but contrary to what most humans believed, angels had the same range of emotions a human would have.

His tower. Yes, he needed to return to his tower. In another plane of existence, it was the one place he could go to escape the constant pull back to the prince.

It only took him stepping out into the street to curb his thoughts on returning to the tower. The desire to see the prince again was burning through him. He walked the city streets until the desire became unbearable. As he started for the mansion, his body shimmered from sight. He found the balcony to Mael's room and rose into the air. As soon as he touched down, his wings descended, and he stepped into Mael's chambers. The room was empty, but Cian had a feeling the prince would show up soon. Dawn was not far off.

Then the bedroom door opened, and Prince Black walked in. As he shut the door, a quiet sigh escaped him. The smooth imperturbable mask of his features eased into more worried lines. It was clear he was completely lost in thought.

Cian watched in silence as the prince undressed and neatly folded his clothes, placing them on the dresser. His head tipped back as he closed his eyes, stretching his arms upwards. Each muscle in his body tightened and then relaxed, and Cian's breath stilled. The prince lowered his arms, and his hand came to rest on his chest. When Mael opened his eyes, he seemed to catch sight of himself in the mirror near him. A frown marred the smooth lines of his lips. What he saw in front of him seemed to displease him.

The prince touched his lips, absentmindedly brushing against them as if in remembrance of something else. His cock began to harden, and he growled, turning away from the mirror. Cian's breath hitched as his gaze slid down to take in the full sight of Mael's arousal. His own lips remembered their kiss, and Cian closed his eyes for the briefest second, remembering the taste, the insistent darting of Black's tongue. Cian shook his head and opened his eyes, feeling his own arousal at the memory.

Mael silently padded to the bed and stretched out on the covers. No more than a moment passed before a soft knock sounded at the door. When it opened, Seth stepped inside, closing the door behind him.

"Master, do you wish to be fed?"

Cian's eyes widened at the thought of witnessing this yet again. His timing when it came to the prince seemed to be intent on tormenting him. He took even, silent breaths in an attempt to calm himself.

Turning his head in Seth's direction, the prince answered him with a small nod. "Come here, Seth."

Obediently, Seth walked toward the bed to slide in next to Mael. Half hovering over him, Seth bared his throat in clear invitation. A faintly enticing smile drifted over Seth's lips as his hand moved to rest on the prince's chest.

Cian swallowed, unable to take his gaze from the two men. It was a place Cian wished he could be. He stifled a groan before it could escape. What possessed him to torture himself like this?

Raising his hand, Mael caressed the nape of Seth's neck and drew the man down toward him. As Mael's fangs pierced his flesh, Seth cried out softly with the pleasure clearly enrapturing his trembling body. Mael drank deeply from him, a soft pulsing growl sounding.

Cian's own neck throbbed, teasing him with phantom sensations of Mael's mouth closed over his flesh. The cry that escaped Seth mirrored the silent cry in Cian's mind, and the prince's growls were doing damnable things to his insides.

Seth's hand caressed slowly down in random patterns against Mael's skin, drawing the faint upward arch of the body beneath it. Mael's hand slipped from his hair to slide down Seth's back, resting on the curve of his ass. Cian bit at his lower lip, wishing more than anything that he could take Seth's place. He imagined the feel of the prince's hand, gliding down his spine. He watched Seth's hand as it traveled downward, and Mael's body arched again. Oh, how he longed to be the one to incite such a response from the prince.

The prince's fingers kneaded gently to the soft flesh beneath them as he drew back his head, resting it to the pillow. When Seth's hand wrapped to his cock, a reactionary growl erupted from Mael as he stared unblinkingly into the young man's eyes. The heat was there within the dark glittering depths as the prince's hand covered the one stroking slowly over him. But then it abruptly faltered for some reason, and he carefully removed Seth's hand.

"No, Seth, not now."

Seth let him remove his hand with a look of disappointment. "I no longer please you, my Prince?"

Cian let out a silent sigh of relief as he relaxed against the wall. He fought to slow his heart down, as he had been certain he was going to see the prince come yet again. That would have been a test of his own will to remain hidden.

A slow smile of reassurance curved Mael's lips. "No, it's not you, my lovely little one. You are far too pleasing at times. But my mind is not here with you. I will not take you, imagining you to be someone else."

Seth seemed momentarily confused by Mael's refusal. "I do not mind. I would be whoever you wish me to be." There was a small movement as his hand tried to return to its prior place, but Mael stopped him.

"No, it's time for you to seek your own bed, Seth. And leave me to mine."

Reluctantly Seth crawled from the bed, and a moment later, the door shut behind him, leaving the prince alone.

Cian wondered at Mael's words, feeling Seth's disappointment sharply.

Mael stared upward into the canopy. The tone of his voice was rather frustrated as he muttered to himself. "You are such a fool, Mael. To think of the sorcerer in this way is complete foolishness."

The slow drift of his hand roamed over hardened flesh, and he groaned softly. His fingers smoothed over his chest, lowering to the taut muscles of his stomach as he closed his eyes. Cian watched Mael's hand descend, and he licked his lips. The prince's hand came to rest at his hip, his fingers brushing once over his hard length. The sun was now up, though, and Mael stretched once before settling, becoming totally motionless.

Cian peeled himself from the wall, half relieved the prince did not relieve his arousal and half wishing he had. He moved to the bed when he was certain Mael was asleep. His gaze traveled down the hard, muscular lines of Mael's body. The prince's cock was still hard, and Cian resisted the near-damning urge to reach out and stroke his fingers down its length. Instead, he imagined that body over his, that cock buried inside him, Mael's tongue sliding along his own.

With a frustrated sigh, he moved away. He opened a portal and cast a last glance back to the sleeping prince. To touch the man would be his undoing; that much Cian knew. He shook his head and stepped through the portal.

Chapter Six

The unexpected encounter with the sorcerer left Mael shaken. He'd wanted to follow after Cian and stop him from leaving the house. He could still feel the hunger of the man's mouth on his. When he moved out into the corridor with the intention of following Cian, the sound of Jensen and Savarier coming up the main staircase stopped him. Sav gave Mael a curious look, and Mael watched the realization dawn in her expression. He couldn't hide his hunger quickly enough from her sharp, dark gaze.

"A moment of your time, Excellency?"

He answered her with a short nod before he turned in the direction of Cornelius' tower.

"Give me a few minutes, Jensen. I'll catch up with you in the main hall," Sav said before she followed Mael. "Your Excellency, is something wrong?"

Giving her a side glance, he saw the curiosity, and he could read the thoughts behind it. "Other than our rogue problem, everything is fine, Sav. The four I sent for are in place, and I need you and Ben to coordinate sending out twenty of my enforcers to aid them."

"It will be done."

As he stilled in front of Cornelius' door, her hand curled to his arm, drawing his attention back to her. The deep concern in her eyes touched him. His hand covered hers as he smiled at her. "It's all right, Sav. Don't worry so much about me."

Shaking her head, she said, "Just be very careful, please."

She started to say more, but he lifted his hand and pressed a finger lightly to her lips. Then he nodded. She stared at him silently and then turned, walking away.

Upon entering Cornelius' workshop, Mael saw the magician in the midst of working an incantation. A darkish purple mist, coming from the small bubbling cauldron on the floor, surrounded the mage. His normally pristine attire was distinctly disheveled, which meant he was in the middle of working on something important. Turning, he gave Mael a quick smile.

"Something I can help you with, Excellency?"

"Can we talk?" Moving toward the work desk, Mael picked up one of the stools and set it closer to the magician.

"Officially or unofficially?"

"Unofficially."

"Good, because I really don't have time for the pompous nonsense right now, Mael. Tell me what's on your mind." Perching on his own stool, Cornelius carefully measured out several of the ingredients strewn on the table near him.

"Selena is behind the rogue vampires."

The only person he would share that information with was his magician. For one, he knew it wouldn't unduly worry Cornelius; and two, he really did need some help. He also trusted Cornelius with his life. He'd been friends with the vampire mage for almost his entire existence.

"Not surprised. Not surprised at all. She's always been a bitch who wanted more than her fair share." She may have fooled a great deal of their society, but deadly red-headed bitches really weren't Cornelius' thing. Mael pretty much shared that opinion.

"If you could tell me how to kill her, I would be ever so grateful, Cornelius." Not that he thought his magician really could, but it never hurt to hope his mage could come up with an idea.

Cornelius shot him an irritated "don't fuck with me" look. "Are you completely out of your mind?" Then the annoyed expression changed rapidly, and a tinge of excitement lit his green eyes. "Now wait a minute. I just..." His words trailed off, and he quickly stood and went to the bookcase at the back wall.

Mael watched the agitated movements with a quirk of his brow. Sometimes it was very hard to follow Cornelius, and his habit of rapidly changing expressions didn't make it any easier.

"Now, which book is it in? I know I have it here somewhere." Muttering to himself, the mage quickly scanned a row of books, running his finger across the bindings.

Since Mael still had no clue what the man was going on about, he remained silent, sitting on the uncomfortably hard chair.

"Aha! I knew I had it!"

He eagerly pulled the book from the shelf then turned, heading back to his work desk. Rapidly thumbing through it, he found what he wanted and set the book down on the desk, turning it to face Mael.

"See? There." A stained finger pointed excitedly at a passage in the book.

Mael looked down and noted the title of the paragraph. "The Sword of Michael?"

"Without a doubt, the most powerful weapon against us, Mael. It was supposedly made for the Archangel Michael himself."

"Do you expect me to ask the Archangel Michael for it?" Mael's lips twitched, but he tried to suppress the smile. There wasn't a doubt in his mind that Cornelius actually would expect him to do just that.

Shooting Mael another irritated look, Cornelius continued as if he hadn't been stupidly interrupted. "Damn legends always get it wrong. I said it was *supposedly* made for him, not that it *was* made for him. Now let's see." He pulled the book back toward him, quickly reading over the passage. "It was last owned by Louis XIV, but it disappeared shortly after his death in 1715. Not surprising there. As I remember, the French king was positively paranoid about vampires — for good reason, though, as the Prince of Paris kept trying to kill him. That's why the king moved from Paris to Versailles. When Louis acquired the sword in 1693, Alistair left him alone."

"Any idea where it disappeared to?"

"Unfortunately, no." The magician shut the book.

Sighing, Mael shook his head, lost in thought. First the Eye of Baal, and now the Sword of Michael. Given that choice, he knew exactly which one he would corner Cian Carmichael for. Thoughts of the sorcerer brought a tingling sensation to his body, and he shifted in his seat. The unique flavor of the blood he'd caught the smallest taste of only whetted his appetite for more. The thought brought out a strange overwhelming craving for it, something he seriously wasn't expecting.

"What in the hell is wrong with you, Mael?"

"I've unexpectedly found myself interested in somebody." Saying he felt interested had to be the worst understatement of the last century. Every time he closed his eyes, images of Cian played though his thoughts, and he could feel the intensity of that kiss.

"I really hope you haven't gone over the deep end for Selena. I'd have to kill you myself." Cornelius' eyes narrowed on him, fixing a disagreeable look on Mael.

"No. Not Selena. It's Cian Carmichael who interests me." A wry smile twisted Mael's lips.

Cornelius' eyes widened in shock. "Don't you have enough problems with the rogues and Selena? Not to mention the Romanorum breathing down your neck. You really do need to get your head of out of your ass and rearrange your priorities."

Mael's wry smile turned distinctly wolfish. "But what better way to relieve the tension, wouldn't you say?"

"You are completely out of your mind, Mael." The intial vehemence in the magician's voice faded. Shaking his head, Cornelius turned his attention back to measuring ingredients. "At least it's not me this time. I'm not the one who wants to stick my dick in a sorcerer who kills vampires."

"He only kills rogues, Cornelius." Mael watched idly as a shadowy form flitted across the room and hovered near Cornelius' bookcase.

Rolling his eyes at that piece of flummery, Cornelius said, "Like he wouldn't kill the rest of us if he could get away with it."

Mael chuckled. "I think Aristotle is about to abscond with one of your books." The spirit of Cornelius' crystal ball already had a shadowy hand outstretched, reaching for a book. Far easier for him to let Aristotle amuse him than to have to dwell on the truth of Cornelius' words.

"Don't even think about it, Aristotle! I'll bottle you in a beer keg if you touch anything!" The magician never even looked up from his work.

Not at all abashed at getting caught, the spirit merely flashed a grin at both of them before crossing the room to hover in a corner.

"I really would like you to return that sapphire tie pin you borrowed last week, Aristotle," Mael said. Cornelius wasn't the only one who had a hard time keeping the wayward spirit out of his things. Mael stood and headed toward the door.

"If you manage to get that sword, let me know, Mael. I want to draw an illustration of it." With that parting shot, Cornelius went back to work.

As he made his way downstairs to his throne room, Mael had a lot more on his mind than he really wanted. Something about the sorcerer spurred a great deal of lust within him, and his ability to control that came into question. He had yet to get some semblance of restraint on himself. His fingers ran through his hair distractedly before he entered the central hall and made his way toward the throne. Surveying the others as he settled into the chair, he remained silent. The mild bickering that rose from the nearby tables neither bothered nor intruded on his inner thoughts.

When Brandon entered the central hall, Mael stood and held his hand out to the boy. The invitation for Brandon to join him didn't bother the rest of the court members. None felt threatened in their own positions by the youth. When the young vampire moved up the steps of the dais, Mael settled back in his throne, gesturing for Brandon to sit in the chair at his right.

"Welcome to my court, Brandon."

"Thank you for treating me so kindly, Your Excellency."

Mael smiled wryly. "I see Cornelius has been teaching you court behavior. I hope he also mentioned that it's all well and good for public, but in private, you don't have to be so formal. At least not with me."

"No, he didn't mention that."

Mael lightly patted Brandon's hand. His voice lowered as he said, "There are several in my court who I wouldn't care to have any informal moments with, but you aren't one of them. Feel free to speak as you wish and keep the formality for public."

"I was hoping I didn't have to act like a stiff all of the time." Brandon flashed him a quick grin before looking toward the rest of the court lazily stretched out on their pillows. None seemed at all interested in anything outside their own little conversations.

"Why don't we take a walk in the garden so we can talk more easily." Standing from his throne, Mael waited for Brandon. He wanted to discuss a certain topic, and he preferred no other ears hear it. No matter how uninterested the others seemed, that wasn't always the case.

"Sure." Brandon walked with him toward the huge glass double doors leading to the gardens outside. A servant opened one of the doors for them and then closed it behind them.

Mael took a breath of the fragrant night air perfumed by the roses that grew nearby. They continued walking deeper into the gardens before he spoke. "I heard Cian Carmichael came to see you."

"Yeah, he did. I was really hoping he would, but I wasn't sure when." Brandon glanced at Mael, and the sparkle in the young vampire's dark brown eyes was apparent.

"That's something I wanted to talk to you about, Brandon. I realize you are very interested in him." Staring at the sweet, youthful face, Mael lifted his hand, cupping it gently to Brandon's cheek. He felt the slight press of Brandon's face toward the comforting touch before Brandon lowered his eyes, not answering him.

"In your lifetime, you will love many, and not necessarily your own kind. There is nothing wrong with that. But you have to understand there will be many who won't understand what you are, and at times, you will be judged for your very nature. We are vampires, Brandon. I don't believe Cian would ever feel love for any of our kind."

Brandon completely stilled with Mael's words, staring unblinkingly up at him. "But he brought me here. Doesn't that mean he understands a vampire's nature?"

"No. He has preconceived notions that we are not natural. Some people think we are very unnatural and evil creatures who are only bound by the laws they place on us. They don't seem to understand we're as human as they are."

"But Cian isn't..." Brandon stopped abruptly as if realizing he shouldn't say anything, but he quickly recovered. "He isn't like that. He even fed me."

The pronouncement startled Mael, and it brought back memories of his own small taste. "He accepts us to a degree because he has to live with us, and he's not the only creature you'll ever meet with that same problem. Humans, weres, fae, and other sorcerers sometimes don't see us as something they want to seriously get close to. We deal with them, but most times not in very intimate ways."

From the hint of tears in his eyes, Mael could tell Brandon was struggling with this.

With a quiet sigh, Brandon said, "I do love him, but kinda like a father more than anything else. He's older than me, a *lot* older, and he makes me feel safe and protected."

"Obviously, Cian is concerned with you. To have brought you here and to have fed you means he cares. Feeding you is very unusual, I will admit. But it's good to have him as a friend."

"I understand, but why would it be unusual for him to feed me?"

"It just shocked me." Mael gave him an amused smile. "A vampire hunter normally wouldn't feed a vampire. It's a rule in the hunter's handbook, I'm sure."

"But he doesn't hunt just any vampires. He hunts rogues."

"He hunts rogues because to hunt and kill a normal vampire is a death sentence, Brandon. As long as we don't kill a mortal, we're tolerated."

"I see." Without further comment, Brandon pulled away.

Mael stepped back, but he had the feeling there was more the boy wanted to say. "I'm not sure you do, and I get the feeling you want to say more. Don't be afraid to speak to me, Brandon."

"I..." Taking a deep breath, Brandon quickly looked down at the ground. He shifted from foot to foot as he fidgeted with his hands. "Will you promise not to say anything to Cian?"

Arching a brow, Mael stared silently at Brandon, wondering what on earth was making him so nervous. "I won't say a word about anything you tell me."

Turning away, Brandon walked over to a patch of flowers. "Cian made me promise I wouldn't say anything. He isn't a mortal."

Mael's gaze followed Brandon's movements, and he took in what the young man said. He frowned, not fully understanding. However, he didn't push Brandon for anything else, nor did he try to read his mind. Brandon gave him a great deal to think over. It very well fit, with the remembered taste of the sorcerer's blood, that Cian wasn't all he appeared to be. "I won't tell him you told me anything. He is somewhat unusual for what he is supposed to be, so I suppose that would explain things. Still, it doesn't change the fact that I believe he doesn't have a great deal of liking for our kind."

Brandon turned around to face Mael, his smile one of relief. "Thank you. I don't want him to be mad at me." His brow wrinkled as if he was lost in thought before he added, "I think he might have a liking for someone besides me anyway."

"Someone besides you?"

Brandon cleared his throat and blushed slightly. "I think he...umm...likes you."

Mael didn't bother hiding the disbelief that rippled through him. It took him a long moment before he composed himself to say anything. "You might be right to a degree, Brandon, but you're probably wrong that it would mean anything. I'm a vampire, and in the end, that's all that will matter."

Brandon opened his mouth to say something, and then shut it, clearly thinking better of it. Shrugging, he asked, "Is there anything else you wanted to talk about? I'm getting hungry. Cian didn't feed me when he came by."

"No, go ahead and see Cornelius. He's probably in his workroom right now, but he'll take care of that."

As the young vampire wandered back into the central hall, Mael became lost in thought once more. Both he and the sorcerer were aware of some pull of attraction between them; he just wasn't sure himself what to make of the intensity that seemed to flare each time he saw Cian. Or that, apparently from Brandon's words, Cian had said something to the boy about his own feelings.

* * *

For two weeks, other matters kept Mael occupied, and he didn't have the time to try to find out more about the sorcerer himself. Each time he tried, somebody or something needed his attention. Thoughts of Cian held Mael captive until he was able to sneak away from his court one night.

Leaving Cornelius in charge, he only told his magician there was something he needed to attend to without the distraction and knowledge of the court members. After Cornelius leveled a piercing green gaze on him and one eyebrow almost disappeared into his hair line, the mage waved him off.

Mael made his way to his bedroom. After moments of fierce concentration, he gained no sense of the sorcerer at all. Frowning, he drew the crystal out from under his collar and opened a gateway.

As he stepped through, a strong fluctuation of his power poured outward, searching for the smallest hint of the blood he'd tasted. He paid no real attention to the shimmering kaleidoscope of colors that made up the room surrounding him, not until a small black space began to open nearby. All it had taken to find the sorcerer whenever he wished was that small amount of blood he'd tasted. His power could pinpoint Cian's presence anywhere. From what Sav had told him, he already knew Cian traveled outside their normal plane of existence.

He exited the portal into a stone-walled room. A veil of shadows immediately covered him to keep him from the sorcerer's sight, and his power ensured that no sense of him could be detected.

The room had a comfortable, rustic, well-lived feeling to it. The polished wooden floor reflected the flames of the crackling fire in the stone fireplace. A large, rough wooden table sat against a wall with two chairs made of the same material. Another longer, thinner table lined another wall, with shelving above it that contained myriad colorful jars.

There was a short set of wooden stairs to the left that lead up to a hatch.

Mael knew the sorcerer was nearby; he could hear the sound of a shower running, coming from somewhere near him. He leaned against the wall furthest from the fireplace and waited. The darkness that draped around him seemed no more than the ordinary shadowing of the room.

When Cian stepped into the room, Mael's gaze drifted slowly over the towel-clad body. Sparkling diamonds of water glistened over the sorcerer's smooth skin. It figured the one time Mael decided to spy on the sorcerer unaware, the man would be almost naked. Mael wasn't sure if that was good luck or the worst luck possible. The urge to reach out and touch a golden strand of hair hit him, but Mael forced himself to remain immobile.

Cian took a deep breath and stretched his arms over his head, locking his fingers together to stretch the muscles of his back. As he moved, Mael looked his fill, gaze running slowly over the sun-kissed skin. The smooth glide of muscle fascinated him.

The crackle and hiss of the fire drew Cian's attention momentarily, and he went over to it, slipping his fingers into the flames. When he pulled his hand away, a single flame rolled over his palm. He twisted his hand, and the flame danced across his knuckles. With a snap of his fingers, the flame flickered out.

Mael watched Cian's command over the flame with a faint appreciative smile. Cian reached up to the mantle and took a jar down. After pouring what looked like wine into a golden chalice, the sorcerer went over to the bed and dropped his towel, revealing the smooth, slick lines of the sorcerer's hip and curve of his ass. He settled back against the headboard and sipped on his wine slowly.

If Mael had a heartbeat, it would have been racing. With the chalice still in his right hand, Cian traced the fingertips of his other hand slowly over his chest. As a fingertip grazed across his nipple, he sucked in a quick breath and then rolled his palm over the small bit of flesh before giving it a single, sharp twist. He hissed and set the glass down.

Mael found himself unable to look away, even though he knew he really should leave. His gaze followed the descent of Cian's hand over the sorcerer's taut stomach, and lower, reaching for a swollen cock. As the sorcerer took it firmly in his hand and gave it a single, slow stroke, Mael felt an answering stir at his crotch. He had to bite firmly on his lower lip to stifle any sound struggling to come out.

This was torture in its purest form.

Cian slid down in the bed and pulled his legs up, resting his feet firmly on the mattress, spreading his legs. His strokes on his cock increased in speed and pressure, and he sucked two fingers into his mouth. He moaned around them softly and shifted, burying both fingers to the knuckles inside himself.

Mael could barely still the restless shift of his body as he watched in rapt attention. Struggling against the sudden awakening of his own lust, it took a considerable amount of willpower not to go to that bed and join Cian. Mael wanted nothing more than to taste the arousal that filled his senses.

Mael's gaze dropped to the slide of Cian's fingers in and out of his body, matching the rhythm of his fist. As Cian arched his back and neck, Mael's gaze drifted back up. When Cian's cock erupted in his hand, Mael's name slipped from the sorcerer's lips in the tortured, hungry cry. The sorcerer collapsed onto the bed, one arm falling limply over his chest and the other hand still wrapped around his cock.

The sound of his own name staggered Mael. It would be foolish to be caught here, yet Mael couldn't help the pleased feeling that descended over him, knowing Cian sought his own release while fantasizing about him.

As Cian reached down and grabbed the towel off the floor, wiping off the mess in his hand, Mael could smell the arousing scent from his position.

When Cian was done, he stood and ascended the stairs. A few moments later, he emerged and slid between the silk sheets of his bed. The fire in the hearth died out, dropping the room into total darkness, save for the silvered moonlight shining through the window.

Several long moments passed, and still Mael hadn't left as he should. Only when the quiet, steady rhythm of Cian's heartbeat and breathing indicated that he'd fallen asleep, did Mael finally step from the shadows. He walked across the room toward the bed and stilled, gazing down at sorcerer's face. Resting his hand on the poster of the bed, he felt the smooth wood before looking at one of the angels carved into it. Something in its expression oddly matched that of the sleeping sorcerer.

Very careful not to awaken him, Mael studied the man in silence. He ignored the painful constriction of his pants and focused his attention intently on Cian. The sleeping innocence of Cian's face, relaxed from the worries of his life, tugged at Mael. Part of him remained very aware of his own need, but something else was there as well. He reached out and ran one finger along a stray wisp of Cian's hair.

The gold seemed to be filled with sunshine, and it beckoned his touch. He wanted to speak, but he was afraid he'd wake the slumbering purity that so enraptured him. This infatuation was slipping out of his control. As his fingers traced the soft features of Cian's face, his voice came out in no more than the softest of whispers.

"It would be best if I left you alone, my angelic sorcerer."

Knowing everything to be complete and utter foolishness on his part, Mael shook his head. He stood and returned to the darkness, opening the portal to step back into his own world. Back in his own chambers, he undressed. Before the sun rose, he lay in his bed, the darkness surrounding him within a loving shield. He felt its soft tendrils curl to his form, brushing in a light caress to his skin. The quiet enveloped him like a welcoming lover as he reflected on his conversation with Brandon.

At the time, he knew he'd been talking to himself as much as to the boy, trying to remind himself just why the attraction to the sorcerer would do him no good. The instant chemistry between the two of them was something he hadn't felt in ages. Lust he was familiar with, and had felt times uncounted, but what filled him with the sorcerer near was uncontrollable. If they hadn't been interrupted during that first kiss, he would have had Cian in his bed now. And if he gave into his desire, he knew he would want more.

For the first time, he acknowledged the deep flicker of pain he'd felt when Cian pulled so abruptly away from him.

He'd caught the horrified ripple of that thought when Cian accidentally cut himself against his fang. The addition of seeing him in the act of masturbation had only worsened things.

As he lay there, Mael wished he could keep a huge distance between them. It just wasn't an option he could afford. He needed Cian's help before the problems in his city spread even further outward and before Selena tried to follow through with her threat to kill him. He even wondered if that had become an excuse simply to see the sorcerer again.

Focusing within to the source of his power, Mael whispered, "Cian."

A heavy flow of his signature energy twined with the sound, giving the word potency. He'd tasted the sorcerer's blood and had known in that instant the powerful strength within it. Whatever rumors were spoken about Cian weren't anywhere near the truth, and Mael wanted to test just how strong the man was. Nothing felt certain.

Wherever he was, Cian would hear the call, and there was no way he could deny it. As Mael's mind slowly slipped into the blanketing peace of sleep, he felt the memory of the press of Cian's lips to his. It was his last conscious thought.

* * *

When the sudden oppressive sense of her Father's presence drenched over her, Selena found it near impossible to keep the casual, relaxed pose. She turned her head to look at him and gave him a bored look.

"Hello, Father. What brings you out from your hellhole tonight?"

Memnet circled her, walking around the back of her chair and trailing a single fingertip over the contoured back. The finger slipped down to caress over her shoulder and down her arm, leaving a lasting impression with such a simple touch.

"I have come to check on your progress, my child."

The last word carried a touch of tangible pain and a single flicker of thought, reminding Selena just how much she belonged to him. The pain and its promise of more to come distracted her. Biting at her lip, she nodded and very carefully kept down the instinct to not let him out of her sight.

"Both Raven and Iverson are doling out your packages. The rogues are starting to appear in London in heavier numbers. It's keeping everybody busy."

Memnet stopped before her, gripping her chin between his thumb and forefinger to lift her head. A fathomless gaze settled on her, as if he were peering deep within her soul. "And what of *you*, my child? What have you been doing while my orders are carried out by others?" He waited for her to answer but didn't release her chin.

She knew better than to struggle against the painful pressure of his fingers on her face. "I have been scouting for a few others for you. I do have to be careful to whom I propose this."

A satisfied yet malicious smile settled on his lips, and she felt the tightening of his grip on her chin. He moved his thumb up to stroke her bottom lip, leaving a searing trail of sharp pain in its wake.

"I want more formulas distributed."

She tried hard not to react, but she couldn't resist the sensations that pulsed through her. Increased pressure radiated over her skin, and her lower lip trembled under his touch. She needed a few seconds to gather her scattered senses before she could answer him.

"But, Father, too much of it will bring the mortal authorities at our throats. I don't mean to argue, but that wouldn't be good for any of us." She felt helpless and knew he could see it in her. The veil of her lashes tried to conceal her fear and longing, and, most of all, her hatred.

He released her chin and traced a slow line down her throat, pausing at a vein. He inhaled deeply, applying pressure with nothing more than a fingertip. "Ah, yes, the mortals. My child, the mortals are not my problem; they are yours. Or have you forgotten your duty already?"

Her head tipped back, the arch of her throat following the path of his touch, keeping that contact. The swift pulse of pain blossomed in her mind, drawing a shudder from her body. Before she could even answer, the second wave ran through her, the moan torn from her throat her only answer. She wanted to get away from his touch, but she couldn't. It promised its own form of fulfillment. Finally, she nodded as she opened her eyes.

"I haven't forgotten. I will do what you want, Memnet."

Pausing for the briefest moment, the smile faded slowly from his face. His gaze narrowed as his mind began to reach within her, slipping through her thoughts like a spirit slid through time. Feeling the intrusive demand of his mind, her eyes widened as she stared up at him. She quickly threw up a barrier of static to try to stop him as she struggled to sit upright. Shadows came from the corners of the room, drifting across the floor toward them.

"You dare fight me?" He stood up straight and watched as the tendrils of darkness curled to her ankles and wrists, pulling her to her feet and out into the middle of the room. She didn't dare struggle anymore as she was dragged from her place by the binding shadows.

Memnet circled her, his words particularly vicious. "Perhaps more is needed to...open you up to me." He stopped behind her and trailed a fingertip down her spine, leaving a stinging, lingering pain in its wake. With the rush of pain, he penetrated the barrier in her mind, and she couldn't stop him from seeing what he wanted.

"The Eye of Baal, is it?"

Not knowing what to say, she remained completely silent.

"Such a powerful tool in the hands of an unruly child," he purred in her ear. "Perhaps it is time, my child, to remind you." He slipped a hand around to the front of her throat as the shadows gathered around them.

"No, Father...please." She still pleaded with him, knowing it would do no good and that she was truly fucked. As the shadows clung to them, she could still see his face and feel his touch. The softness of his tone didn't fool her, and the anger burning in his eyes left her incapable of looking away from him.

When the shadows faded once more, tendrils curled around Selena's wrists and ankles once more, forcing her to remain standing. When Memnet turned, he had a small silver dagger in his hand. Using the tip of its sharp blade, he drew the knife down Selena's body, cutting her dress and leaving it to fall to the floor in pieces. She remained absolutely still, but the kiss of the blade to her skin made her body tremble as it fed her its distinct pleasure.

"Tell me, my child," Memnet said as he began to circle her nude form. "Why would you want the Eye?"

She could tell he knew exactly why, but he wanted to hear it for himself. As he moved from her side to her back, a thin line followed on her skin from the blade pulled across it. Droplets of blood pearled at the edges of the cut before running down her right thigh. She felt it tickling her skin as Memnet licked his finger. He then traced the line of the cut. The wound burned as if set on fire by acid, causing her to squirm. As he moved around her back, he did the same to her other side. If she lied to him, it would be worse for her; there was no doubt about that. It could get very much worse.

"I wanted to get rid of you, Father," she whispered to him.

"Ah, yes," he said with a distinct purr to his words. With a flick of his hand, the dagger disappeared. He knelt to slide his tongue over the cut on her left side, savoring the taste of her blood and the burst of pain through her body. "To get rid of me," he echoed her, as he moved to lick the cut on the other side. He drew his fingers up from her knees to her inner thighs, leaving fresh cuts to bleed with just his touch.

It felt more painful when he made the cuts himself, without the dagger, and they didn't heal because she wasn't allowed to heal them. The touch of his tongue followed the sting of the blade, increasing that burn. Lowering her head to stare down at him, she felt the betraying shiver of need that kept her body within his reach. Her words carried no small part of the anger she held for him.

"I want you gone from my life. To never see you again."

He stood slowly, sliding his tongue up her body, from her navel to the hollow of her throat, leaving yet another deep cut to drip blood to the floor. "Oh, but my child," he whispered. "You cannot be rid of me." He slid the tip of his tongue along her lips. "You *crave* me. You crave what only I can give you."

She couldn't deny that because only at his hand could she even touch the feeling of pleasure. She didn't struggle against him. Each cut in her skin kept that sensation slowly pulsing through her body and into her mind. The arch of her body strained against the ties, trying to reach him.

Memnet smiled before capturing her in an enslaving kiss, every stroke of his tongue creating a pulse through her. Without pulling away, he undressed and then gripped her sides, his palms pressing into the cuts. He pulled her to him, coating them both in her blood as it streamed out of the cut down her torso. When she felt the nudge of his thigh between hers, his skin grazed along the cuts, sending fresh bolts of pain through her.

"You need me, my child. Only I can give you what you so desperately crave."

Her awareness only encompassed the slide of her own body and mind, captured by him with the pain that he gave her. A shudder betrayed her sharpening arousal. Part of her wanted to fight, but it never did any good, and this was just the beginning of what he had planned for her. This whisper of those echoes touched to the innate struggle, the need to fight him.

He pulled away from her lips and stroked her cheek, streaking it with her blood. He lifted his finger to his mouth to taste and then slid his tongue over her cheek.

"I believe it is time, my child." The words were softly spoken but hardly comforting as he looked to the side, toward the bed. "When I've had my pleasure, I will open you, exposing every inch of your body, to taste, to touch, to control." He stepped away from her, and the shadows released her as he pointed to the bed.

His darkness smothered her, trying to steal the very last part of her left, and she barely restrained the scream that wanted out in her mind. Following his direction, she moved obediently to the bed. To do otherwise would only make it worse.

Chapter Seven

For two days, Cian managed to ignore Mael's calls. They came as whispers, his name spoken by the vampire prince. The more he ignored it, the stronger the pull became. He paced the floor of his chambers in the tower until he was sure the wooden beams would give way beneath his feet. At the end of the second day, he finally decided to give in. He opened a portal and stepped through.

He stepped out in a garden. As he looked around, he spotted the path that led to the front. He knocked on the front door, and a few minutes later, it opened. The same servant as before ushered Cian inside.

"I'm here to see the prince."

The man nodded, and Cian followed him upstairs. They stopped before Mael's bedroom door, and the servant opened it. Cian didn't bother questioning why here and not Mael's office.

"Wait here," the servant said. "His Excellency will be with you soon."

Cian watched the servant leave and closed the door behind him. He turned and looked around Mael's bedroom. He hadn't gotten a good look at it before, and now that he could, he mused it resembled a room at Napolean's Fontainebleau. With its gilt woods and rich cream fabrics, it had a decadent, old world charm. He was so busy admiring the scrollwork of the wood that he didn't hear anyone come in until he heard Mael's soft-spoken voice.

"I"m glad you could make it, Cian."

Cian turned around and saw the prince standing near a tapestry on the wall. The prince remained still, his demeanor taking on a strange formality. Cian had been trying to avoid him for days, and all he wanted was to get this meeting over with. The longer he stayed, the more the prince became a dangerous temptation.

"Why have you called me here?"

"Couldn't I have called you here just for the pleasure of your company?" Mael asked as he started toward Cian.

Cian's eyes darkened from their pristine gray-blue to a fathomless coal black. He eyed the prince warily. "My company? Why would a vampire want the company of a hunter?"

Mael stilled suddenly before him, visibly startled. "I had thought your eyes were blue, sorcerer. So the rumors are true. Your eyes do change."

"They do." Cian was tiring of this game and simply wanted to get out.

"What causes it?"

The air between them became heated, and Cian watched the prince's dark, smoldering gaze slide over his body. The energy overrode Cian's senses, and he backed Mael up against the nearest wall.

"Anger," he whispered. He leaned forward and placed a hand on either side of the prince's head, palms flat against the wall. "Fear." He closed the distance between them and brushed his lips softly and slowly across Mael's. "Passion."

The look on Mael's face was a pleased one, and he hooked his fingers in the waistband of Cian's leather pants, pulling him closer until their bodies touched. He whispered against Cian's lips, "So are you angry with me, afraid of me, or do you want me?"

Instead of answering Mael's question, Cian crushed his mouth to the prince's, his tongue demanding entrance. A low growl rumbled through the prince's chest. Cian's tongue darted inside, and he pressed his body tightly to Mael's, groaning at the friction between their bodies. The prince's hand slid to Cian's hip, pulling him tighter against the hard body.

It had been ages since Cian had been with another man, and the moist heat of Mael's mouth sent a shudder down his spine. It was a drugging, heady heat that seared Cian from the inside out. The thought of that mouth, wrapped around him, drew a groan from his lips. Cian broke the kiss.

"You called me here for this, prince."

A mixture of lust and hunger burned in the dark depths of Mael's eyes. Before Cian realized what happened, Mael shoved him against a wall, pinning Cian to it with his body. He struck with no warning, his fangs sinking deep into Cian's neck. Cian hissed and shoved him away. He touched his hand to his neck and scowled at Mael. He reached out and gripped the prince's throat tightly, pulling him close again.

"So that's it," he growled. "A test of wills, is it?" Keeing a firm grip on Mael's throat, Cian threw him onto the bed and straddled him, effectively pinning him down. "Well, prince, looks like you're in a bit of a quandary, don't you think?"

Mael smiled, but Cian sensed more behind it. "Let's see if you can stop me, sorcerer." With a strength that would make most cower away in fear, Mael threw Cian off of him and rolled to the edge of the bed.

Cian straightened himself. "A challenge?" He circled around the bed, stalking Mael slowly. "You are testing me? You're bolder than I gave you credit for, Black."

"And here I thought summoning you here to me would prove just how bold I am." Mael remained utterly still, body tense like a cobra ready to strike as he watched Cian closely. He didn't seem to be unnerved as Cian drew closer. "I'm testing you, and you are testing me."

Beneath the prince's calm veneer Cian became aware of a surge of power. It drew him to Mael like a moth to a flame. He stopped within inches of the prince and slid his fingers through Mael's hair. He jerked the prince's head back roughly, and their gazes locked.

"Why are you testing me, prince? You know *nothing* about me."

"But I want to know. Isn't that enough?" Mael asked with a mocking grin.

He wrapped his hand in Cian's hair and pulled him forward, his mouth opening in silent invitation. Before Cian could protest, he shuddered as a wash of intense power surged through him, radiating from the prince. The moment their lips met, Cian growled as his tongue darted into Mael's mouth, drinking in the moist warmth. He fumbled with Mael's pants until they slid to the floor. Seconds later, his own pants joined them. As he stepped out of them, Mael's shirt landed on the floor. The prince pulled Cian's shirt over his head and then moved back to his lips to continue their kiss.

Another heated rush shot through Cian, and he gasped, losing his senses. He felt Mael push him back toward the bed, but he offered no resistance. Mael followed him, pinning him down on his back. Cian was vaguely aware of his arms above his head, but when Mael whispered in his ear, he no longer cared.

"I want to know everything."

Cian groaned and arched his back, responding to the friction between their bodies. "You don't want to know everything, prince," he whispered.

"Let me decide that, Cian." Mael stared down at him with a dark, intense gaze. Within those depths, Cian saw the prince's need clearly: the obsession to possess him, to claim him.

A whisper breezed through Cian's mind, confirming what he had already figured out. He spread his legs, allowing the prince to settle between them. This was madness, but he could no more resist than he could deny what he was.

"*Fwcia fi.*" He strained against Mael's hold on his arms, desperate to touch him.

Mael shifted slightly away from him long enough to slick himself up with saliva, and then he rubbed the head of his cock over Cian's entrance. He lowered his face to Cian's and whispered, "Say my name, Cian. I want to hear my name on your lips."

Cian lifted his hips, his body aching to feel Mael inside him. Like a crushing weight to his will, he breathed the prince's name. "Mael. Please. I need you."

"*Come li ho bisogno.*"

The prince descended on Cian's lips, silencing them both. At the same moment, he thrust forward, impaling Cian on the entire length of his cock. Cian clawed at his back and wrapped his legs around Mael's waist, holding him tight and pulling him deeper. Mael began to move, slowly at first. When Cian grew impatient, he gripped Mael's hips and pulled him down hard. Mael's fingers slid down Cian's arm and over his chest. When Cian gasped as a nipple was twisted painfully, Mael's tongue darted into his mouth.

As Mael's thrusts grew in intensity, Cian felt pleasure swell inside him. The prince's body began to shake with his own release as Cian arched his back. Cian moaned into Mael's mouth as his own body began to shudder with his impending orgasm. Seconds later, Mael descended on his throat, his fangs sinking into Cian's flesh to drink deeply. Cian dug his fingers into the prince's back as he came. With every pull of Mael's lips at his throat, another rush hit Cian, dragging his orgasm out for what seemed like ages. A strangled cry escaped him, and he dug his fingers into Mael's shoulders, the unending surge of power and pleasure engulfing him.

When his lips brushed Mael's skin, he opened his mouth. His intent was nothing more than a small lovebite, but when another rush hit him, he growled and pierced Mael's skin with his teeth. The rush of blood over his tongue startled him, but with the taste of it, he could not pull away.

Mael's body stiffened immediately, yet he continued to drink. Cian shuddered beneath him. Mael released his throat and placed a soft kiss on the wound. A small slit appeared on his neck, and he guided Cian to it. The moment Cian's lips touched it, the tears began to fall.

His mind screamed at the act, yet the rich taste of Mael's blood washed through him, easing the hunger he felt. He closed his eyes, saying a silent prayer. The weight of things he should not feel for the prince stole over him, forming an ache within his chest.

As Mael stroked his face gently, a soothing wave of energy washed through Cian, calming him. Cian swallowed and forced himself to open his eyes, meeting the prince's gaze.

"That should never have happened."

"I know," Mael said quietly. Cian detected a trace of pain in the prince's eyes as Mael shifted off of him and collapsed onto the bed.

Cian rolled over, propping his head up on his hand. His gaze traveled down Mael's body, and his hand followed suit. He wanted to memorize every line, every curve. He leaned over and pressed a soft kiss to Mael's shoulder. "*Rwy'n dy garu di.*"

Mael closed his eyes, and a tremor ran through him under Cian's touch. A wry grin crossed his lips. "I never learned to speak Welsh."

Cian laughed softly and brushed his lips over his ear. "Probably the best for both of us, my prince."

Though his eyes opened quickly at Cian's words, Mael remained silent for a few seconds. His own soft laughter soon joined Cian's. "I take it you won't translate that for me."

Cian traced his fingertips over Mael's chest, up to his throat. With the only the slightest pressure, he turned Mael's head to face him. "Perhaps later," he whispered softly on Mael's lips.

As they met in a kiss, Cian sensed an urgency within the prince, echoed in his kiss. Sighing into Mael's mouth, Cian slipped his hand beneath Mael's head and simply focused on the feel of their kiss. From the fevered dance of Mael's tongue on his and the desperation in the prince's claiming of his mouth, Cian began to wonder if perhaps Mael felt something more than attraction between them as well.

Mael pulled slowly away from their kiss and turned his head from Cian. "I won't call you like that again."

Cian felt the words as a blow to his heart. He stroked his fingers down Mael's face one last time before sliding out of bed. Once his clothes were on, he stopped with his hand on the door, his back to the bed. Without another word, he pulled the door open, then closed it between them. There was no victor in this game. Not this time.

* * *

For a Thursday night, the bar was busier than usual. Couples, singles, men on the prowl — they were all there. Cian had already turned down several advances, many of them from gorgeous men. The only man he wanted was the one he could not have. To make matters worse, he felt a craving — an unholy craving — and every time he thought of Mael, it flared. He took another swallow of wine and fought back another surge of hunger. It had been three days since he had seen Mael, and things were only getting worse. He had fallen head over heels for the vampire prince, and now he was trying desperately to avoid him.

He was so lost in his own brooding thoughts that he didn't realize anyone was standing beside his table until a shimmering blue feather floated down to the tabletop in front of him. He shook his head quickly and looked up. Brandon stared back at him, his dark, soulful eyes full of surprise and worry.

"I didn't know you drank," Brandon said with a subtle hint of amusement and a nod to the glass cradled in Cian's hands.

Cian smirked and downed the last of his wine. He closed his eyes slowly, taking his refuge in the steady burn. "I can't get drunk, if that's what you mean." He lowered the glass and glanced up at Brandon. "Have you fed yet?"

Brandon shook his head. "Not yet. I needed to get out of the mansion for a while, but I was on my way back there when I found this." He picked up the feather and twirled it in his fingers.

Cian plucked the feather from Brandon's fingers and smoothed his fingers down the shimmering length of it. The dim lamp hanging down above their heads set the blue on fire, bringing out the silver tones within it. He stroked it slowly, concentrating on the color as it faded from blue to silver. When he pulled his hand away, Brandon's eyes widened as Cian turned the knife around, letting the light from above spark off the steel blade.

"How the fuck did you do that?"

Cian lifted a blond eyebrow and smiled for the first time since Mael had made love to him. He drew the blade down his palm and let the blood spill into the empty wine glass. As he pushed the glass to Brandon, the cut healed. "I'm a sorcerer, remember?" No sooner than the words left his lips did his heart threaten to cease beating. He shuddered as the scent of Mael wafted through him from his blood.

His blood.

He squeezed his eyes shut in a desperate attempt to quell the surge that threatened to overwhelm him. He refused to return to Mael. He was determined to fight it.

Brandon lifted the cup to his lips and began to drink. Within seconds, he set the half-emptied cup down. "What happened?"

"What do you mean?"

Brandon's hands began to tremble as he held the cup between them. "There's a scent to this blood that I recognize, but it's not just yours. Cian, I *know* Mael's scent. There's only one way it could be in your blood."

Cian sighed and sat back in the seat. He shook the knife, and the form of a feather returned. "Finish your drink," he said with a nod to the glass still in Brandon's hands. When Brandon began to drink once more, Cian continued. "Yes, you smell Mael Black in my blood." Brandon eyed him cautiously but said nothing. "For several days, Mael called to me. When I could no longer ignore it, I went to him. I knew what was going to happen before I ever stepped foot into that house. I was determined to resist the temptation Black presents to me. When he approached me in his chambers, however, I found I couldn't resist him."

Brandon set the glass down slowly. Cian watched with a throbbing hunger as Brandon's tongue slid across his lips, licking away a trace of blood. It wasn't the kid he wanted; it was the blood that held a promise to the end of his torment.

"Couldn't resist him," Brandon echoed. "In other words, you fucked him." Cian nodded slowly. Brandon drew his hands down his face. "You're an angel, Cian."

Cian let out a deep sigh. "He bit me. The pleasure I felt while he fed was beyond anything I've ever known, and I got carried away. I bit too hard on his shoulder, breaking the skin. The second his blood touched my tongue, it was too late."

"Oh, my God."

"Believe me, God's heard that many times since."

Cian waved over the waitress. She brought another wine bottle to the table and took the empty one. Brandon watched with wide eyes as Cian popped the cork and tipped the bottle up, drinking the wine straight out of it. When he set the bottle back down, Cian lifted an eyebrow at him.

"You're addicted," Brandon said matter-of-factly.

Cian laughed. "Am I that obvious?"

Brandon sat back and gave him a dubious look. "Just a bit. You drink like a wino, Cian."

"I can't get drunk," Cian reminded him.

"Uh-huh. But you're addicted to wine anyway. Why? What is it about wine?"

Cian sighed, knowing he wasn't going to win this one. Brandon was entirely too persistent. "Yes," he conceded. "I'm addicted to red wine. I suppose because it burns my throat enough to block out whatever's on my mind. For the most part." He took another drink and stilled. "Go back to the palace, Brandon."

Without waiting for an answer, Cian stood and left the bar. He could feel Brandon's confused and concerned gaze on him, but the presence of rogues overrode any other thought. He stepped into a pocket of shadows and waited.

A few minutes later, a small group of vampires walked by. Their laughter penetrated the darkness of the street, and they turned, heading for one of the lesser-known bars. From the shadows, Cian watched them closely. He moved when they did and stopped when they stopped. He had always been able to evade vampires, but since drinking Mael's blood, his ability seemed to have doubled. For that, he was grateful.

As they neared the club, two of the vampires broke away from the group, leaving the other four to enter alone. The four did not concern him. It was the couple that split off that held Cian's attention. As they stepped into the alleyway, he moved, taking to the air.

A gust of wind blew up around the couple, breaking their kiss abruptly. The one with his back against the wall looked around quickly. The female he held pressed harder against his body.

"Who's there?" the man asked.

The wind died down, and Cian stepped out of the shadows. His wings spread out behind him, blocking their escape out of the alley. The woman's eyes widened, and she hissed. She pulled away from the man and started to run. Cian held up his right hand and hurled a ball of blue fire at her. She shrieked and crumpled to the ground, rolling and slapping her clothes in an attempt to put out the flames. Cian exhaled from where he stood, and the fire flared, engulfing the woman. Seconds later, the fire extinguished itself, leaving nothing more than a pile of blackened ash. He turned to the man who stood plastered to the brick wall.

"Wh-who are you?"

Cian reached out and gripped the man's throat. He lifted the vampire up, leaving his feet dangling several inches off of the ground. The vampire clawed at his hand, breaking the skin. The moment the smell of the blood reached Cian, he squeezed the vampire's throat tighter. The surge rushed through him, dragging a hungry growl from his throat. A flame sparked to life immediately in his other hand, and he shoved his fist through the vampire's stomach. The creature shook violently against the wall, then shrieked once before the flames consumed him, turning him to a smoldering pile of ash. Cian stepped away and stared down at the ground for a moment before walking away, brushing his hands on his pants as he stepped out into the street, his wings descending unseen.

* * *

Brandon sat down on the stool and looked around the workroom. "Damn."

Glancing over at him, Cornelius smiled. "Damn what?"

"I still can't believe I'm here. Since I was eight years old, I've dreamed about stuff like this. It's just hard to believe." Brandon looked over at Cornelius. "So what do you want me to do?"

Cornelius chuckled softly and shook his head. "Calm down, my boy. This room has been here for many years, and it isn't going anywhere anytime soon." He slid one of his books over to Brandon and reached for one of the extra pens and pad. "Why don't you look through what I've written on that pad and find the corresponding pages in the book. Then write down the listed ingredients for me. Make sure your writing is neat and that you accurately copy what is necessary."

"Gotcha." Brandon opened the book and set to his task. Unlike many young men his age, his penmanship was highly legible and very neat. He immersed himself in the book, losing track of everything else.

"I've never had anybody willing to sit beside me doing this," Cornelius said after a while. "I must say it's very pleasant change for me."

Without looking up from his work, Brandon said, "Really? How could anyone *not* want to do this? Maybe it's just me, I guess. I'm just weird. I was always the nerd in school, the guy with his nose stuck in some science book."

"Mine used to be stuck in science scrolls. This tends to be the tedious part of the work. Cross-referencing books, writing down the rituals and ingredients. Attention to detail is very important."

Brandon nodded and looked up briefly. "Same goes for chemistry. I remember the first time I experienced chemistry in school. It was in seventh grade, and the class was a physical science class." He laughed as he continued to work. "My best friend and I were partners, but he had no clue what he was doing. He went to throw something away when I wasn't watching, and a few seconds later, a huge blue flame burst out of the garbage can. They had to evacuate the entire damn school."

Settling back slightly from the table, Cornelius broke out into laughter and had to pull back at his spectacles to wipe a tear from his eye. "At least it wasn't your fault. I recall one time when my Father's hair fell out because I accidentally copied the wrong section of the ritual for him. He really wasn't happy with me until after the next night when it grew back." An unholy amusement lit his eyes. "He did look rather funny with no hair, eyebrows, or lashes, though. I won't even say anything about the rest of his body."

Brandon's eyes widened. "At least it grew back! My brother managed to singe his eyebrows off while stoned. Don't ask me how he did it; I wasn't there. I just remember coming home one night after a date, and there was my little brother, with half of his eyebrows gone." He shook his head as he laughed.

Cornelius laid his pen aside for the moment, eyeing Brandon with a laugh. "I would like to know how that one happened."

"What? My brother?" Brandon chuckled. "I have no idea. He was still lit when I got home. Hell, I wondered if he even realized he had done it. I asked him what happened and never got a straight answer out of him. He was too far gone. By the next morning, he couldn't remember a damn thing. Knowing him, though, he probably tried to use part of my chem set as a bong and something got mixed up by mistake."

"I certainly hope he never goes into chemistry. Frightening thought that is." Turning slightly in his seat, Cornelius leaned his elbow on the table, facing Brandon. "And those stories are why, until you know what you are doing, you don't play with this stuff."

"No kidding. Last I heard, he wanted to go into the medical field. Still a frightening idea as far as I'm concerned." Brandon looked up from his work once more and cocked his head to the side, noting the look Cornelius was giving him. "What is it?"

Cornelius shook his head slightly. "Enthusiasm and a brain in the same body. You remind me of myself when I was a great deal younger, and you've surprised me, I think."

"Surprised you? How?" Brandon set down his pen and leaned on the table, propping his head up on his hand.

"You are a very unusual young man. Or don't you realize that?" Cornelius pulled off his glasses again, not really needing them to see, and laid them on top of his open book.

For the briefest moment, Brandon found himself at a loss for words. The mage's eyes were mesmerizing, to say the least, and Brandon found himself caught, unable to break away from such a gaze. "I, well, I'm just me, really. I've always been the odd one, whether it was because I was gay or because I cared more about science and ancient alchemy texts than sports."

Cornelius smiled at him. "Well, Just Me, I'm delighted to have your enthusiasm beside me. You're not so very odd here."

"What about you?" Brandon asked.

"What do you want to know about me?"

Brandon shrugged. "Where are you from? How did you get started in science and magic? You know, those kinds of questions."

"Ah, those questions. To answer, I was born in ancient Rome, more birthdays ago than I care to count. When I was mortal, I studied magic in the Temple of Hera. The science was a great deal different back then." Relaxing against the edge of the table, Cornelius' tone had a musing sense to it, and his gaze seemed a touch distant. "Though keep the Temple of Hera to yourself," he added as an afterthought.

Brandon lifted a dark eyebrow. "Not a word." He turned and leaned back against the table, stretching his legs out for the first time in a few hours. "Ancient Rome, huh? That explains your looks."

"I probably shouldn't have mentioned it, and I'm not quite sure why I did. And, yes, it was *very* ancient Rome. Very little of it is left except for a few tourist traps, which would be why I'll never go back."

Brandon stilled as something began to dawn on him. "Wait a minute. The last true Roman emperor was Romulus Augustus, in 476. You can't mean that ancient Rome."

"I was most definitely born before him." Cornelius nodded slightly. "The year I was born, Tiberius was still on the throne. My father hated him."

Brandon's mouth dropped open. "Oh, my God." He shook his head. "It definitely explains your looks, though. You remind me of a Renaissance master's painting."

"I knew some of those painters. Really wish I didn't, though. Most of them were an infatuated lot." Grimacing slightly, Cornelius started to laugh. "I think there are a few paintings of me hanging about somewhere. You'd have to ask Mael. He'd remember better than I do."

"I can see why someone would want to paint you."

"Some of them used to follow me around all of the time. It got damned annoying. Every time I looked up, one or another would be staring at me."

Brandon stood and slipped his hand under Cornelius' chin, turning the mage's head gently as if he were a painter himself. Cornelius seemed vaguely surprised, and his gaze held Brandon's. Brandon smiled and released him.

"I imagine it probably did get annoying. But with inspiration like yourself, it's no wonder such wonderful art came from that time."

"It would have been nicer if they'd found inspiration elsewhere. I only remember being annoyed. A lot. I know I'm not ugly, but still I found them to be a silly bunch."

Brandon simply grinned. "I wish I was an artist," he mused as he straddled his stool. "I'd love to be able to paint you, and I would promise not to annoy you. As it is, however, I can barely draw a stick figure. Ask me to draw a molecule of one element or another, and I can do it. Ask me to paint a masterpiece, and all you get is a glob of paint on a canvas."

"Not everybody is born to be that annoying. Thank the gods. I prefer you just the way you are, Brandon, believe me. Magic is more infinitely fascinating than paint jars.

Brandon felt his face warming and turned away slightly. "Maybe one day I can learn the magic side of things as well."

"Now that, my boy, I can teach you," Cornelius said.

Holding out his hand, several colored sparks lit in his palm. The graceful sway of color danced in the air above his hand before it spun outward and then slowly settled to the floor. Where the tiny beads of sparkle landed, two figures suddenly appeared. A man and woman, dressed in the clothing of an era gone by, slowly twirled in a waltz to unheard music. Their translucent quality made them seem like ghosts.

As Brandon watched the display, his eyes grew wide with awe. "It's beautiful," he whispered. He reached out, sliding his fingers over Cornelius' palm slowly. "How did you do that?"

Smiling, Cornelius curled his hand to Brandon's fingers. "It's no more than a memory, stolen from time and caught by my magic. It's part of what I can teach you, if you have the mind to learn it." The dancing couple slowly faded back into the air.

A quiet catch of breath escaped Brandon's lips with the mage's fingers curled around his. For a fleeting moment, visions of those hands on his body flitted through his mind. "I do have the mind to learn it," he said as he pulled his hand slowly away.

Gently, Cornelius squeezed Brandon's hand before he could draw it back completely. "You would give me the ability to see an old world through your eyes. You've already given me a chance to touch the sense of wonder you felt at what I just showed you. I would be more than happy to teach you."

Brandon remained silent, unable to form words. The heat from the mage's hand lingered, and he suddenly longed to touch Cornelius. He licked his lips and simply nodded.

Cornelius smiled and reached for his spectacles, setting them back in place. "Shall we go back to the tedious work at hand, or would you prefer to learn more history?"

"What would you like to do? I'm game for whatever you want."

"We should probably get the work out of the way and then we can entertain ourselves with conversation." Turning to face his work again, Cornelius picked up his pen.

Brandon turned back around on his stool and returned to his own work, once again losing himself in the words that he copied down.

* * *

Selena stayed in her bed for several days and nights, falling back in and out of sleep. Healing the damage done to her took every ounce of the energy she had left. She knew Memnet had brought her back and laid her out in her bed when he was done with her. At first, he had held out the promise of everything as he fucked her. But before she could touch that fulfillment, he had snatched it from her, just as he always did. The overwhelming pain scattered her mind, leaving her bereft of any release.

Afterwards, he tore her apart, physically and mentally. He had laid her body open, reminding her that nothing of her was free. Not even her mind had been left untouched. His darkness had invaded every space with excruciating pain and the brand of his ownership. She couldn't fight at all by then. There'd been a point when the agonizing pain he gave her held no pleasurable element. Nothing but unrelenting waves of pain beyond endurance shattered her into millions of fragments.

No mark remained on her body to even show what had happened to her. She wasn't sure if that was a curse or not anymore. Had she been human, she would have died at some point during that torture. But death seemed to be a luxury of escape she had no access to. For a brief time, the idea of simply giving up the Eye ran through her mind. It was then she started to cry, silent tears of blood slipping down her cheeks. Now there was nothing left in her but the blood tears as she lay there, barely able to move.

Closing her eyes tightly, she refused to give into that. She couldn't escape Memnet, and it had to be either him or her. That lone thought possessed her, driving out the black despair that threatened to overtake her. The next time he visited her, he would realize that she hadn't given up on obtaining the Eye of Baal. Either she had to get her hands on it, or she would die anyway because he would kill her. Or even worse, he would take away everything she owned and force her back to him, for an eternity of imprisonment in his hands.

As one of her servants entered her chambers, Selena gestured her toward the bed. She had to feed and get what was needed before her Father's next visit. Time was running out.

Chapter Eight

When he dismissed his court from the throne room, Mael motioned for Ben and Sav to stay with him. For the last week, the phrase Cian had spoken haunted him. When Cian inadvertently bit him, Mael tried to stop his own feeding, but he knew it was already too late. His senses tracked the power of his blood as it was absorbed into the sorcerer's system, and he felt the mental connection forming between them. He kept that link closed, however, because he simply couldn't take advantage of so easily reading Cian without his knowledge.

The moment Cian paused in front of his bedroom door, Mael had been aware of something trying to reach out to his mind, but before he could take it in, the sensation was gone. Since then, he'd kept his distance, but in the back of his mind was the understanding that sooner or later, he would have to explain to Cian that he was now a ghoul. That alone brought out a possessive tinge to Mael's thoughts. Cian was his blood now.

"Ben, do I have a Welsh translator in my court?"

Giving him a startled look, Ben shook his head. "No, Your Excellency, we don't."

"Then find me one, dammit!" Generally, Mael's tone never held such a demanding, impatient quality with his secretary.

"Certainly, Your Excellency. I will find one."

Casting a glance at Sav, Mael said, "What news do you have for me?"

Deliberately he kept his mind off of anything but the business he needed to take care of. He couldn't afford to allow any of the personal chaos within him to show. Nor could he let himself focus on it.

"Ashton Carter has been taken care of, Excellency. I regret not being able to inform you sooner, but the last time I spoke to you, I had forgotten in the rush to get your enforcers to Bristol and Colchester."

Mael smiled for the first time in a while. "In light of that excellent news, I'll forgive you for the lapse in time. I was beginning to think I would have to go out and hunt the bastard myself. Who took care of him? Whoever it was deserves a very good reward."

"It was Cian Carmichael. I had been following Carter, but before I could get to him, Carmichael cornered him in an alleyway. By the time I managed to get to one of the rooftops overlooking the alley, Carter was a pile of ash."

Somehow, Mael felt no surprise hearing the name, nor by a flicker of a lash did he show the turmoil the mere mention of the sorcerer brought to his thoughts. "I am most pleased. This court owes Cian Carmichael a great deal of gratitude. Make sure Scotland Yard is notified that Carter has been executed for his crimes. That should calm them down for now."

Ben nodded. "I'll tell Deputy Commissioner Bent when he calls me tonight. He's been calling me every night since Carter went on his killing spree."

"And what of Colchester and Bristol, Sav?" Mael's gaze returned to his assassin.

"Everyone is in place and awaiting your order, Excellency. Neither Iverson nor Raven suspect they are being watched. Both have a small nest of rogues, and none have been hunting as yet."

"I want the matter taken care of before those young ones start killing. I've already informed Escoban in Rome of the situation, and Diocourides has handed down the ruling allowing me to do as I see fit. Make sure the mortal population is kept away from their places of court and tell the others to coordinate to take Bristol and Colchester tonight. I want no mortal casualties; we have enough problems as it is. Both Iverson and Raven are to be taken alive, if possible, and brought here."

"What of their children?" Sav asked quietly.

"If any aren't in the court compounds, I want them rounded up and brought here as well. From there we can determine what they know, if anything, of their Fathers' dealings."

Both of them bowed their heads to him as Mael waved his hand slightly, dismissing them.

A minute later, Jensen opened the throne room doors. "Your Excellency, Her Eminence, Selena, is here to see you."

Selena breezed into the room behind him. "Enough, Jensen. You've done your duty, now go away."

Jensen, Sav, and Ben were smart enough to exit very quickly, leaving him alone with the pain in the ass making her way toward him.

Standing from his throne, Mael repressed a sigh as he moved to greet her. "Your Eminence, a great pleasure to see you. What brings you to my court?"

"I am not happy with you, Mael. Especially since you haven't brought me my gift yet." As she came to a stop in front of him, her hand went to his chest, running her long red nails down the silky material of his shirt.

"You gave me until the end of the month, Selena. Remember?"

"I grow impatient for it. You should know me by now. I also wanted to discuss the sorcerer with you."

"What about him?" Remaining completely still beneath the scratching of her nails, Mael watched her calmly.

"I heard he came to see you last week. He was shown to your chambers, and I understand both of you remained closeted there for quite a while. Are you playing with him, my pet?" The seductively soft tone of her voice didn't fool him. Within her words, he caught the hint of anger.

Arching his brow, Mael's expression took on a mildly amused edge. "Really, Selena, I'd think your spies could do better than that and simply tell you whether I am or not."

A thin cut suddenly appeared, slashing his cheek, as she stared at him. He felt the faint stinging pain worsen when she raised her hand to take hold of his chin. The grip drew his face down to hers.

"It would be worse for you if I really believed you were, Mael. I will not allow you to have him as a toy, or anything else." Her tongue darted out, delicately licking at the blood trickling from the cut.

"You have decided to take it upon yourself to decide who I do and do not sleep with now, Selena?" While he felt relieved she believed him about Cian, anger stirred at her attempt to order him in such a way. The cut to his cheek quickly healed as she drew back.

"No, but if I find that you are in league with him, darling, I'm really going to hate to have to fill your position after I kill you."

Unfazed by her threat, he remained calm. "I suggest you allow me to handle the sorcerer as I see fit, Selena."

"If I don't have my gift soon, I will be handling *you* as I see fit, my little pet. Don't forget that." She released him before she moved slowly for the door.

Watching her silently, Mael knew he didn't have much of a choice. He had to see Cian before Selena tried to follow through with her threat. There was no doubt that she had the undisputed power to do it.

* * *

As the reports began to come in from Bristol and Colchester over the next few weeks, Mael busily handled the night-to-night concerns of keeping those courts calm in preparation for their new princes. Thankfully, neither court resisted once the charges against Iverson and Raven became known.

Raven had been captured and locked in the palace's dungeons, awaiting the punishment verdict from the Romanorum. So far as any could tell, none of his children or his court were involved in the rogue situation. Iverson and his daughter, Celia, had eluded capture. Three of his children, brought in for interrogation, were found innocent of any dealings and set free to return to their homes.

Sav and several of Mael's enforcers were on the hunt for Iverson and Celia, but thus far, they'd had no success in running them to ground. Once the situation settled, Mael knew he needed to go see Cian. Although the rogue trouble and the problem with the vampire formulas had been taken care of, he still had to deal with Selena. And for that, he needed the Sword of Michael.

Stepping through the black portal that would lead him to Cian, he glanced quickly around, spotting the sorcerer before he was even noticed. "So this is where you hide from me." The light within the room had no effect on him, though he would be very careful to avoid the stream of sunlight coming in from the one window of the room.

Cian spun around, dropping the jar in his hands and spilling a mass of dried leaves onto the floor. "How did you get here?"

"Fairy dust." The words were no more than faintly teasing as Mael's gaze traveled slowly over Cian before lifting back his face. His expression altered into slightly more sober lines. "We need to talk."

The sorcerer stooped down to scoop the leaves into his hands. "Normally I'd say there's nothing I have to say to you. However, I believe you are correct."

Mael caught the familiar echo of his own blood within Cian's. His more bestial nature stretched slowly within him, roused by that scent. He moved toward Cian, crouching down to help him clean the mess.

"I know we do. That's why I finally decided to come here and talk to you. More importantly, it's about the fact that you drank my blood."

The fact that his life was potentially on the line right now might have been considered more important, but he needed to deal with this and explain it to Cian first. Cian stilled immediately. Mael could hear the sound of Cian's heart racing, and he knew Cian was fighting his own hunger.

"What's happening to me, Black?" Cian stood, dumping the handful of leaves onto the table. He placed both hands on the top and bowed his head slightly, taking a deep breath. "You don't understand. Because of my nature, drinking your blood will cause serious trouble for me."

Mael straightened to place the leaves on the table as well. It pained him to watch the sorcerer, hearing the confusion in his voice. He laid his hand over Cian's. "You're hungry, Cian. Your body needs my blood now because you are my ghoul. Without my blood, that hunger will grow worse."

Cian slowly turned to face him. "What?" He pulled his hand out from under Mael's and backed away, shaking his head. "I can't."

Mael's features took on a very neutral, smooth mask. He tilted his head slightly and allowed a small wound to appear at the side of his throat. A thin line of blood welled at the edges. The scent alone would draw Cian to him. Cian's fists clenched and then he spun back around, shoving Mael hard against the wall, his mouth closing over the cut as he started to feed.

Mael tangled his fingers tightly in the blond hair, feeling the draw at his throat. The pleasure caused a soft, pulsing growl to rise within him. Quickly, he opened the thread of their connection, but only to allow a quiet, comforting feeling to blanket over the sorcerer's distress and anger, to help him calm. As Cian's body molded tightly to his, Mael could feel relaxation setting in. The only sound around them was the hungry pulse from Cian and Mael's own growl of pleasure.

When Cian finally stopped feeding, the slide of his fingers ran through Mael's hair as he pulled away slowly. Before Mael could speak, Cian descended on his lips, thrusting his tongue in, moaning softly into Mael's mouth.

Mael's arms encircled Cian's waist, keeping Cian tight against him. The feel of the sorcerer's lips was irresistible.

Cian pulled slowly away from their kiss, but not from Mael's arms. "We still need to talk." He tilted his head to the side, toward the table. "Would you like some wine? Or is that pointless to ask?"

Another pulse of growl came from Mael, this one lower and fainter. He knew the only thing that kept the sorcerer calm was his own power in soothing him. "I know, otherwise I would have you on that bed right now." He knew he shouldn't say that, but how in hell could he help it? "I can drink wine as well as any other alcohol, though it has no effect on me." He relinquished the hold he had on Cian and sat down.

Cian retrieved a jar from the mantle. "Red good for you?" Without waiting for an answer, he set the jar down on the table, along with two metal goblets. He poured wine into both and sat down across from Mael. "Now, what do you want to talk about? I have the feeling it wasn't solely the need to tell me about drinking your blood."

"It was the most important to me because I didn't want you to suffer in not understanding what was happening to you. You also need to know that you now share a connection with me, Cian. Our minds are linked in such a way that I can read your thoughts, and you can read mine — unless we block them from one another. As to any other reason why I'm here, I happen to need an artifact that you might be able to get for me. Well, two, actually, but if you can get the first, I won't need the second one."

Cian lifted an eyebrow dubiously. "Thank you for the concern." He took a drink of his wine. "What artifacts?"

Mael took a small sip of the wine before setting the glass back down. "The first would be the Sword of Michael. It disappeared a few centuries ago, and I've been told you have the Eye of Baal."

Cian choked on another swallow of wine. "Have you lost your mind?"

Mael calmly drank another sip of his own before answering. The tone of his voice was distinctly dry. "I've been hearing that a lot lately, and, no, I'm not. If I can get the sword, I'll be able to deal with a very huge problem of mine, and I won't even need the Eye. I only need the sword for a short time. One night, and I promise I'll return it to you."

Sighing, Cian drained his glass. He stood and went to the window, staring out at the mountainside beyond. "I don't have the sword, although I know where to find it." He turned and cast a crystal blue gaze on Mael. "But I do have the Eye. Why do you want them?"

Giving him a calm, measured look, Mael's expression smoothed to a bland edge. "Because I need to remove someone. I'd rather not say who because it's my problem to deal with. As far as the Eye goes, I don't want it. Somebody else does, but if I remove that somebody, then they won't get the Eye."

"Do you have any idea what the Eye does? Have you any concept of the power behind it?"

"It boosts power, as far as I've heard," Mael said with a nonchalant shrug.

"Boosts power?" Cian shook his head and laughed. He headed for the wooden stairs. "Don't move. We have much to discuss."

Cian returned a few minutes later carrying a wooden box. Setting the box on the table, he opened it, the lid toward Mael so he couldn't see inside. A few seconds later, Cian held up the Eye, cradling it in his left palm.

"This is the Eye of Baal." He took Mael's hand and turned it up, placing the Eye in Mael's palm. "Perhaps less will need to be said if you were to hold it for yourself."

Mael eyed the small crystal sphere, no bigger than a golf ball. Within it was a single red gem suspended in a gray, murky substance. When he looked back up at Cian, he didn't feel too terribly impressed. But a split second later, he felt the almost overwhelming rush of its power. The energy poured through him, tapping into depths it took him a moment to understand. He stared at Cian with understanding, horrified.

"She can't have this. It's doubly important I have the Sword of Michael. I *must* have it."

Cian took the Eye from Mael and placed it back in the box. "Who can't have it?"

It took a minute for the power to ebb. Mael shook his head. "That is a problem that I must deal with, Cian. All I ask for is the sword for one night."

Cian set the box on the mantle with a sigh. "So you will feed me and lie in bed with me, yet you will not be open about this. Very well. Yes, I can get the sword."

"No, Cian. That's not it. The less you know, the better off you will be. The problem with the formulas and the rogues has been dealt with, though Iverson and his daughter, Celia, escaped the taking of Bristol. They are being hunted now."

Even Mael had his own doubts about being able to take care of Selena without that sword. He really didn't want Cian getting into the middle of it and possibly getting hurt. He'd already been a great deal of help with every other problem; there was no reason to risk him as well at this point.

"The better off I will be." Cian laughed, the words muttered to himself. He turned to face Mael. "I will get the sword. Where and when do you want me to deliver it?"

Mael stood and slowly approached him. His expression softened. "Within the next week or so. Two at the very most. You can bring it to my home. I'm sorry you drank my blood. I would have stopped you if I could have."

Cian's tense stance relaxed. "Yes," he whispered breathlessly, but he shook his head as if trying to rid himself of something. "I can have it in a week. It will take some convincing on my part, but I will get it. And you honestly think drinking your blood is my biggest issue here?"

Regarding Cian steadily, Mael took in his expression, trying in his own way to understand. A faintly bitter smile curled the corners of his lips. "What could be worse than to be a vampire's ghoul, Cian? To need his blood for the rest of your existence. Whatever could be worse than that?"

Cian reached out and slid the fingers of his right hand through Mael's hair as he smiled wistfully. "To be in love with one."

Mael froze. Closing his eyes, he tried to block the hurt that burned at him. His voice came out hoarse. "Dear God, no, Cian. It is only the blood within you talking." Unable to help himself, he wrapped his arms tightly around Cian's waist, not allowing him to go anywhere. The sorcerer's arms circled his neck, keeping him just as close.

"*Rwy'n dy garu di.*" The soft whisper accompanied the gentle kiss of Cian's lips across Mael's cheek. "I want you, my prince." The tip of his tongue flicked over Mael's ear, and Cian slid his fingers through Mael's hair, tilting his head back.

Mael shivered, and a soft groan escaped him. The slow tracing of Cian's tongue from the hollow of his throat to his lips left a wet trail tingling against his skin. He was completely helpless to whatever the sorcerer wanted to do. His own hands slid slowly downward from Cian's back before slipping up under his shirt. The feel of that bare skin drew the caress of his fingers.

"Then take me," he murmured.

Cian pulled away. He stripped Mael quickly and then himself, a hungry gaze sliding over Mael. Pushing him backward, toward the bed, Cian pinned Mael with a black, predatory gaze. As Cian dropped to his knees by the bed, a gentle push of his hand shoved Mael to his back. Slipping his hands under Mael's legs, Cian pushed them up and apart before he leaned down and licked a slow line up Mael's cock. The quicksilver sensation spread like wildfire through Mael with the upward movement of that tongue and the press of the sorcerer's lips back down his shaft with soft kisses, until Cian reached his ass.

Mael hissed with the teasing feel of the sorcerer's tongue probing him. Cian sucked two fingers into his mouth, then pushed them slowly inside, twisting them. A shudder ran through Mael, and Cian moved his lips up to swallow Mael's cock in one breath. It had been much too long since Mael had felt anything like it.

Another groan escaped him. "Cian." His fingers snagged within the blond hair as he lifted his head to look down. The sight alone was enough to drive him even more toward the edge. He tried to keep his body still for a moment, just to calm himself. As he felt the hot slide of that mouth, his hips jerked in reaction. When Cian slowly removed his fingers, disappointment ran through Mael.

"Stay there."

Cian stood, walked over to the mantle above the fireplace, and picked up one of the jars. He returned to the bed and stroked his own cock, slicking it with the oil from the jar. Mael watched, and the tip of his tongue darted out to wet his suddenly dry lips, feeling the ache of his own body. He needed to feel his sorcerer, and nothing else intruded on that one thought. His eyes never left Cian's, watching as Cian knelt back on the bed between his legs. As Cian leaned slowly over him, Mael could feel the teasing of the sorcerer's cock over his hole.

"Say my name again, prince."

Feeling the barest brush of lips lingering over his own, Mael slowly caressed Cian's arms. When he tilted his head slightly, Cian whispered in his ear.

"Say my name as I make you mine."

With the slow push of the sorcerer's hips, Mael felt the entire length of Cian's cock sliding deep inside him. He cried out Cian's name softly as his body opened. A hungry kiss quickly silenced him.

The sound of the distinctly possessive growl from Cian played over Mael's senses as he felt the slow but forceful rhythm of the body taking his own. With the slide of the sorcerer's hand downward, gripping his hip tightly, Mael arched up. The languid thrusts took on a sharper rhythm as his arms snaked around Cian's neck, matching each quickening movement. The dig of the nails at his hip radiated their own faint pain. Mael dragged his nails downward over the sorcerer's back, leaving red marks in their wake. It pleased him to feel the trembling response from the sorcerer. Breaking off the kiss, Mael laid his head back against the pillow, letting his senses drink in the sound of his lover's ragged breathing and the sweet scent of pure arousal between them.

"Please...I need you.

The urgent sound of the words drew Mael's attention upward to see Cian tilting his head in offer to feed him. He lifted his head to Cian's throat, fangs sinking deep to draw at the river of life beneath the surface. The sudden, more desperate thrust of the sorcerer's body sharply increased the friction over Mael's cock. It brought him too close to losing all control, and a violent shudder ran through him suddenly as his come slicked their bodies. He heard a loud, deep growl above him and felt the straining pressure of the cock inside him, filling his body with that release.

The flavor of the blood he drank took on the sweetness of Cian's orgasm, and Mael drank hungrily. He kept his lover locked in the arms of that exquisite world until he knew he couldn't take anymore of Cian's blood.

When he stopped feeding, the feel of a tongue at his throat caused him to reopen the earlier wound. Cian latched on and drank deeply. Moments later, he pulled away and collapsed onto Mael's chest, panting. Mael's arms encircled the sorcerer, keeping him there for the moment as he savored the scent of their intimacy.

"My blood is your life, my sweet sorcerer. It will always be yours."

"As is mine to you, my prince. Perhaps one day you will learn just how true that is. For both of us."

Gently touching his face, Mael's fingers slowly drifted to the outline of Cian's jaw. "You are a part of me now, Cian. God help both of us." A bit of a smile curved his lips. "I think we'll need it."

"I don't think God saw this coming." Cian leaned into the touch, closing his eyes slowly. "I certainly did not."

"Nobody could have predicted this, Cian. And I can't find it in myself to regret a moment."

As Cian pulled out of him slowly and rolled onto his side, Mael moved with him, keeping the contact.

"Despite my fears, I can't say that I regret it. And you never did tell me how you got here."

A carefully study of Cian revealed what wasn't being said, and Mael's lips twisted slightly in a bittersweet smile. He reached for the black crystal dangling at his throat. "This allows me to travel to other worlds. All I need to pinpoint you exactly is a taste of your blood."

"Well, there's no escaping you then," Cian teased. "I still want to know who you intend to use the sword on, but I suppose you'll tell me in time."

Mael eyed Cian steadily in silence, considering the words, and it took him a moment to say anything. "Will you promise to let me handle it, Cian?"

Cian lifted an eyebrow before he sighed dejectedly and nodded. "I promise." His gaze narrowed on Mael as he added, "But if anyone lays so much as a finger on you, they will answer to me."

"It is Selena, one of the first formula members of the Romanorum. She rules England, and she wants the Eye. She is also behind every problem I am currently having."

"Doesn't sound like an entirely pleasant situation. However, if the sword will help, then I will get it for you."

"No, Selena is not pleasant at all. Not by any stretch of the imagination. I will only need the sword for one night. Then I promise you, on my honor, I will return it to you."

"Good, because I'm not sure how long I'm going to be able to get it for you. It's not an easy thing to acquire."

"Somehow I didn't think it would be." Mael pulled reluctantly away and sat on the edge of the bed for a moment. "I need to leave now. Unfortunately, my kingdom does not run itself."

As Cian sat up, Mael felt the run of his fingertips down his spine. "I know. By all means, don't hesitate to come see me whenever you wish."

Cian kissed his shoulder softly and then turned Mael's head slowly toward him. Mael returned the brief, fleeting kiss before the sorcerer pulled away.

"I must be going myself. I have..." Cian paused for a moment, as if weighing his words. "Work to do."

"Work? I won't ask further about it." He had the feeling Cian was going to hunt, and he wasn't about to prompt for details. Standing from the bed, Mael gathered his clothes and quickly dressed as Cian silently dressed beside him.

When he was done, he activated the crystal at his throat and opened the portal to his own world. There was nothing said, but the look that passed between them said more than either of them had the words for before each went his own way.

* * *

Reopening the book, Cornelius focused his attention back on it to avoid the questions and internal reverie nagging at him. Stretching in his position on the bed, he resettled, propped up against the headboard.

"Whatcha reading?" Brandon asked as he stepped into the open doorway.

Glancing up from the book, Cornelius grimaced slightly. "Marcus' treatise on the official properties of black sand. In Latin. A boring but necessary read." He closed the book and set it beside him.

Chuckling, Brandon walked over to the bed, stretching himself along the end of it and propping his head on his hand. "Latin? Good God, I bombed it bad in school."

Cornelius' gaze followed him, and he stifled a sigh, reining in any additional images that popped into his thoughts at seeing the young vampire lazing on his bed. Sometimes, his thoughts were a bit hard to control. "You'll be studying it anyway. Many of the works on magic are in Latin. Dead language it might be, just not to the minds of the idiots who wrote this stuff."

Brandon grinned at him. "That's fine with me. I taught myself how to read Egyptian hieroglyphics a few years ago."

"Very few works exist in hieroglyphics. The fools who burned down the Alexandrian library can be thanked for that."

Brandon rolled onto his back, stretching his arms above his head and arching his back. "Yeah, no kidding. But I've always found languages interesting, so I try to learn as much as I can. I think I just bombed Latin in school because we had a new crop of freshmen, and there were too many cute, new guys that kept my attention diverted."

Cornelius' gaze roamed over him, taking in the planes of the young vampire's body and the contraction of flexing and relaxing muscles. A second later, he forced his eyes back on the book near him. "If you enjoy languages, you should have no problem then, Brandon. Hopefully your attention will remain intact."

Brandon turned back onto his stomach and rested his chin on his hands. "Somehow I doubt that."

"Why do you say that?" Cornelius' gaze returned to Brandon, unable to stop the slow perusal over the form laid out on his bed.

Brandon let out a soft, musing moan and turned his head. He smiled softly at Cornelius. "Because the scenery is nice here, too."

Cornelius chuckled quietly. "At times, I have that problem as well, though not very often. Magic tends to take my mind away from much else." He looked up to meet Brandon's gaze.

"The scenery here has distracted you before?"

"Once or twice. I have been here since 1775..." Cornelius paused, frowning to himself before continuing, "or was it 1675. I remember the Stuarts had the English throne at the time, though I didn't pay much attention to the politics back then."

Brandon laughed. "I love talking to you."

"You do?" Cornelius was both flattered and pleased. "I enjoy talking to you as well. Though I probably do say too much at times."

"You're so laid back and honest. You don't bullshit people. I respect that. A lot. I don't think you talk too much."

"I didn't mean that I talk too much. It was more that I probably say too much, as in things I really shouldn't. Some things will have to stay between us. Such as the Temple of Hera."

"You know you can trust me, right?" Brandon looked up at him. "I think you're perfect the way you are, Cornelius, no matter if you say things you shouldn't."

Smiling slowly at him, Cornelius nodded. "I trust you, or I would have never felt comfortable enough in just rambling. I'm far from perfect, but I thank you for the compliment. Just remember it when you're annoyed at me for making you translate Latin."

Brandon chuckled. "No one is truly perfect, but you're special just the way you are." He grinned and reached over to grab the book, pulling it toward him.

Unaccountable warmth seeped through Cornelius, and he studied the boy intently. Brandon's face and form were as appealing as his mind and thoughts, and Cornelius was having increasing difficulty keeping any form of interest from becoming noticeable. "I'm thinking you have the same type of perfection yourself."

Brandon looked up from the book, looking momentarily surprised. A flush of light pink colored his face before he lowered his gaze quickly. "I..." He cleared his throat and tried to continue. "Um, thank you." He quickly seemed to find a sort of escape in the book in front of him. "Wow, maybe I remember more Latin than I thought."

Catching the flicker kindling briefly in Brandon's eyes, a feeling akin to shock rippled through Cornelius. He knew then that the young vampire was as interested as he was. Without thought, he reached out to gently lift Brandon's face so he could see his eyes again.

"You're welcome. I'm not sure which of us is luckier, since we both are a rare breed." He heard the slight catch of a breath in Brandon's throat as the beautiful brown eyes closed. With a rueful smile, Cornelius released him, pulling his hand back to his lap. Brandon groaned and buried his face in the blanket.

Sighing quietly, Cornelius recognized the sound for what it was, but there was little he could do about it. The way things stood, there was no way in hell he could even show the slightest amount of that kind of interest. It would piss off Mael to no end.

"You're killing me, Cornelius," Brandon mumbled into the blanket, the words laced with playful frustration.

"I am?"

"Figuratively speaking. It never fails. I get interested in someone who doesn't share the interest."

"I wouldn't quite say that, Brandon. But any interest I would have in you would be very inappropriate, to say the least." Cornelius smiled ruefully.

"Figures." Brandon sighed and shifted on the bed.

Cornelius drew in a slow breath, catching the faintest hint of arousal in the air. He felt the faint answering stir within himself. "Mael would have my hide." The words, spoken under the exhalation of breath, were meant as a warning to himself.

"So would I, but I doubt Mael and I would have the same intentions." Brandon rolled over, and his erection was visible through the denim of his jeans.

Cornelius tried to still the small sound threatening to come out and the urge to feel what he could see. A low growl vibrated his throat, and he was unable to pull his gaze from Brandon's body.

Brandon glanced over at Cornelius as he opened his eyes. "Damn those student-teacher issues."

With the words, Cornelius' attention was drawn away from where it shouldn't be. "You are right, Brandon. Way too many issues." Clearing his throat, he desperately tried to think of a new topic of conversation. "If you think you can handle the Latin, you can try reading the treatise. It's fairly simple, though boring as hell."

"Want it out loud?"

Caught off guard by the question, Cornelius stared at Brandon over the rim of his glasses before the meaning caught up with him. Shaking his head slightly to get his mind of the gutter, he said, "If you want."

Brandon opened the book and began to read. As he read through each sentence, he pronounced the Latin with ease and then worked to translate each one. Although he stumbled over a few words, he managed to get through it. Glancing up, he asked, "How am I doing?"

Cornelius forced his body to more fully relax and his mind to stay centered on listening to the words themselves. "You're doing better than I expected." He found himself pleasantly surprised with Brandon's grasp of Latin.

Smiling, Brandon continued reading, once more switching between Latin and English. Before long, Cornelius caught no mistakes at all, and the Latin seemed to roll off the young vampire's Welsh-accented tongue like it was a native language. When he was done, Brandon closed the book and looked back up.

The slow sweep of Cornelius' gaze continuously ran over the lines of Brandon's body, and when the young vampire stopped reading, it took a few seconds for Cornelius to realize it. Reaching up to readjust his spectacles, he met Brandon's gaze with a smile.

"Very impressive, very impressive indeed." Whether he was talking about Brandon's grasp of Latin or his body, Cornelius wasn't entirely sure himself.

Brandon smiled as he pushed the book back toward him. "Thank you." He rolled onto his back, and Cornelius watched the unconscious slide of Brandon's hand across his chest and belly. "I need to feed soon."

Cornelius' gaze remained on the slow movement of that hand, watching the motion, fascinated. "I suppose you should ask Ben to have a bottle sent to your room." He forced the words out, unsure if he should really risk trying to feed Brandon right now.

"I suppose you're right." There was a vague hint of disappointment in Brandon's words before he sighed. "Although," he said quietly as he stared at the canopy over the bed. "Maybe I could try with a mortal? If anything, I think I'd get more satisfaction out of a warm male body than a bottle."

Cornelius' first thought was that he knew this was going to be hell on him since he would have to supervise that feeding to insure it didn't get out of hand. When he spoke, not one fraction of uncertainty revealed itself. "That shouldn't be a problem. Why don't you head back to your room, and I'll be along shortly with someone for you." Not by the tiniest bit did his inflection change.

Brandon nodded and got up. As he turned, he smiled at Cornelius before walking out the bedroom door.

Chapter Nine

Against his better judgment, Cornelius found himself in front of Brandon's door with Seth beside him. The experienced ghoul wore only a loose pair of cotton pants and a vest that always showed his body off to best advantage. Sighing quietly, Cornelius knocked at the door. When he heard Brandon's answer, he opened the door, let Seth walk in, and then followed behind him.

"Seth will be glad to take care of your feeding needs, Brandon." Moving to the chair nearest the bed, Cornelius settled into it as Seth walked toward the bed with a smile.

Brandon rolled over and met Seth's smile. He bit his lower lip as his gaze traveled slowly up the slender, toned body in front of him. "Thank you," he said quietly.

Cornelius said nothing as he looked between the two; he already knew everything that would likely happen. He folded his hands very neatly in his lap as he carefully maintained the illusion of being relaxed. "Seth knows the ropes, Brandon. You shouldn't have any worries feeding from him. Or anything else."

The look the young vampire gave Seth made clear exactly what he wanted in addition to feeding. Reaching out, Seth offered his hand to help Brandon sit up. A gasp escaped him as the ghoul's body brushed lightly against his, and Seth's hands slid up his arms and across his shoulders. With only a minute amount of pressure, Seth pulled him forward. When their lips touched, Brandon moaned softly before opening his mouth. His arms snaked around the ghoul's waist, pulling their bodies together as Brandon groaned deeply.

Watching silently as the two became quickly entangled in each other, Cornelius shifted uncomfortably in the seat. A silent prayer winged its way to the gods for the fact that the robe and his position would hide any of the effects on him. His gaze traveled slowly over Brandon, and he hoped he remained unnoticed.

Seth's lips moved from Brandon's mouth to his neck, nibbling lightly on his skin. His hands slid down over Brandon's body, following the hard lines and gliding over the smooth flesh. The young vampire tangled his hands in Seth's hair, pushing him to his knees. As he moved lower, Seth pulled the thin lounge pants down over Brandon's hips and legs to pool at his feet.

Cornelius' gaze was fixated on them. The sight of Brandon's cock drew Cornelius' attention, and he stared at the young vampire with fascinated intensity. Oh, how he wanted to taste the boy. That thought flooded his mind along with a slow tingling as Seth wrapped his hand around Brandon's shaft and flicked his tongue over the tip.

When Cornelius lifted his gaze, his eyes widened, becoming caught in a heated gaze as the young vampire stared back at him for a moment. He really was in deep here, but he could not help the fact that he wanted Brandon for himself.

Seconds later, Seth's mouth slid over Brandon's prick, and Brandon's head fell back as he thrust forward between the ghoul's lips. Brandon rocked his hips, his cock sliding in and out of the warm, slick mouth. His grip tightened on

Seth's hair, and he pulled out of Seth's mouth. Slipping his hands under Seth's arms, Brandon pulled him back up and into a hungry kiss. With Seth's body pressing him backward, Brandon fell onto the bed, his pants slipping off his feet. As Brandon spread his legs, Seth shifted, pushing his own pants down before following Brandon down onto the bed.

"Fuck me," Brandon pleaded breathlessly. He arched his body under Seth's, causing their erections to slide over each other. Gasping with the friction, he moved his hands down to grip Seth's ass.

Seth grinned and drew back, spitting in his palm and stroking his cock. "That can be arranged." Not giving Brandon a chance to say another word, he rubbed the head of his cock across the hole and thrust inside. A deep-seated growl erupted from Brandon's throat, and he thrust his hips up, causing Seth's cock to drive deeper inside him.

Cornelius never once looked away from Brandon, watching each change of expression over the young vampire's face as Seth played with him. A soft growl of annoyance vibrated from his throat because he couldn't stop imagining himself doing everything the ghoul was doing. The pulse of that growl changed when he watched Seth take Brandon. In that moment, Cornelius didn't like what he saw. A scowl descended over his face before he could control the wayward burst of emotion. It took him a moment to realize he was jealous, and he had to ruthlessly push away the thoughts and feelings.

Brandon curled his fingers around Seth's biceps as his body rocked with every thrust. He turned his head, and Cornelius stared back at him, the scowl on his features deepening. Holding Cornelius' dark gaze, Brandon reached between his body and Seth's and wrapped his fingers around his cock. He began pumping his hand up and down, matching Seth's rhythm.

"Oh, fuck," Brandon panted. "Don't stop..."

Cornelius watched him, and because the young vampire's gaze still held his so hungrily, he almost knew what was going though Brandon's mind. Brandon wanted him, wanted him watching as his body started to tremble beneath the ghoul.

Seth's thrusts grew hard and quick, and seconds later, he bared his throat. Brandon growled and pulled him down with his other hand, piercing Seth's neck with his fangs. His body jerked then, and he pulled away from Seth's throat as his cock pulsed in his hand, slicking his fingers and stomach with his seed. Seth thrust hard inside him and grunted with his own orgasm. Brandon slid his tongue over his lips, the gaze directed at Cornelius, almost begging.

Cornelius' mouth clamped tightly shut, biting back any sound struggling to be free. His hands moved to the arms of the chair, tightly gripping them to stop himself from dragging Seth off of Brandon. That possessive anger was clear as he held Brandon's gaze. The sound of their releases only made the emotion burn more hotly in Cornelius. He felt the overwhelming need run through his own body, seeing the pleading in Brandon's eyes. A pained sense betrayed him in the tightness of his features as he tried to shut himself out.

Brandon swallowed hard as Seth leaned down to kiss him once more. As the ghoul pulled away and withdrew from him, Brandon opened his eyes. When Seth turned away to dress once more, Brandon mouthed "I need you" to Cornelius.

Cornelius had thought he could control everything he knew he would feel. The jealousy was no surprise to him. What he wanted, he always became insanely jealous over. Barely able to stifle the groan that needed out, he looked over to Seth. "Thank you, Seth," he said quietly.

Brandon watched in silence as Seth left the room. The tension in the air was palpable. Cornelius stood beside the bed, staring down at Brandon. A soft sound finally escaped him as he leaned over, very gently touching Brandon's face. In his eyes, the mixture of dark jealousy and deep desire showed openly. He wanted the young vampire to belong to him, giving him that sole right to possess Brandon. But there wasn't a damn thing he could do about it.

Brandon twined his fingers with Cornelius'. He closed his eyes, a faintly pained expression crossing his face before he whispered, "Thank you."

Cornelius' fingers briefly tightened on Brandon's before he had to let go. The look veiled itself behind a quiet, gentle expression, and he smiled down at Brandon. Turning away, he walked toward the door without saying a word. After shutting it quietly behind him, he leaned against the wood, trying to calm the riot of his own reactions.

The images branded into his brain played out in too loving detail for him to get away from them. He could still feel his own jealous rage as he pushed away from the door. Trying to subdue it didn't do him any good; he wanted Brandon. He walked slowly down the hall to his room a few doors down from Brandon's. Safely inside the room, Cornelius shut the door behind him, wanting to shut out the memories in the same way. Grasping the edge of his robe, he slipped it off over his head before draping it on the back of a chair.

He padded silently to the bathroom and turned on the shower, hoping to get rid of the painful erection. He'd barely managed, through the use of magic, to keep that from showing. Stepping into the tub, he groaned softly as he leaned back against the cool tile of the wall. As he closed his eyes, a hand wrapped around his cock. Brandon's face and body flashed within the internal reverie going through his mind. He'd seen and understood the need that stared at him from the young vampire, even after Seth had been done with him. He'd seen how much Brandon had wanted him.

The slow movement of his hand quickened with the memory, and Cornelius' own desire filled his thoughts. The sight and feel of Brandon beneath him became the center of his focus as he felt his body tightening with his own need for release. He wanted far more than that. In that moment of clarity, Cornelius knew he wanted everything from Brandon, not just his body. His own emotions became entangled within that picture, feeling the instant release as he came.

Once he was spent, he stepped forward into the spray of water to rinse off. Turning off the water, he rested his forehead to the glass of the shower door, closing his eyes. Though the painful excess had faded, everything else still remained, and the temporary release hadn't been what he wanted at all. The sight of a pair of laughing, dark brown eyes haunted him now, and he didn't know what to do. There was no way that Mael would allow that kind of relationship between them. But everything he saw in Brandon was everything he had ever wanted.

* * *

Brandon shifted, rolling from his stomach to his side, and read the first passage in chapter five of his alchemy book...for the third time. Normally, he didn't have any trouble keeping his mind on his studies, but this time was different. Every word became a name, and every illustration became a face. He closed the book with a sigh and stretched out on his back. He stared up at the canopy over his bed, but all he really saw was the face of a raven-haired mage with piercing green eyes.

"Brand, you've gone off the deep end," he muttered to himself. And it was true.

His experience with Seth had been good, but it had been nothing more than a casual fuck. That wasn't what he wanted. What he wanted was to pull Cornelius into his arms and melt into him, confessing his love. And that was the real kicker. He had a sneaking suspicion before that he might be falling for the court mage, but when Cornelius' stare gave away an intense jealousy, Brandon knew the truth. He had already fallen.

He slid his hands down his face and closed his eyes. It was something he simply couldn't deny anymore. Whether Cornelius felt the same or not, Brandon knew his own feelings for the mage had gone well beyond a student-teacher relationship. True, he wanted Cornelius, in every sense of the physical term, but he also wanted more than he feared Cornelius would give him. He wanted the mage's heart.

* * *

Mael stretched slowly before arching upward into the clothed body covering his. His hand combed through the golden hair, wrapping his fingers around its thickness at the nape of Cian's neck. As he released the strands, they spilled over them both. He groaned softly, feeling the tight grind of the sorcerer's body reacting to the arch of his. His hand slipped down through the cascade of hair to settle on the sorcerer's ass, pressing him tighter. A deep, almost feral growl stopped him in the midst of lifting his head to catch a kiss, but he didn't immediately realize the direction of the sound, until he looked over Cian's shoulder.

The sight of another Cian striding toward the bed sent a feeling of pure unadulterated shock through Mael. The determined fingers of the other man wrapped in the blond's hair, jerking him up and away from the prince beneath him. As the second blond swiftly drew his knife, he pressed it to the other man's throat, holding his head back in an iron grip.

"Who the fuck are you?" the second Cian hissed through his teeth. His eyes were pitch black; anger laced with fierce jealousy colored his words.

In a blur, Mael sprang off the bed to the other side. The growl that came from him was a distinct warning.

With an agile twist, the man in the second blond's hand slipped from the grasp, putting distance between them. "What the hell is going on?"

For a span of several seconds, all three of them were rendered speechless as they stared at each other. The second blond finally rushed the other man. He shoved him against the wall, knocking over a small table. The porcelain lamp on it shattered as it hit the floor.

In reaction, the first blond struggled. "Who the hell is he?" he spat out to Mael, nodding toward the man who had hold of him.

A calculating look entered Mael's eyes as he stared at the two men, and he rapidly took in the situation. When he spoke, his voice came out silky smooth. "Who is the assassin?"

The first blond stared wide-eyed at Mael, then shot a terrified look at the man holding him. "Mael," he purred. "Surely you know I would never hurt you." His gaze never left the other man's eyes.

Grabbing for his robe, Mael hastily put it on as he watched both of them. "Get away from him." He growled out the words as he moved slowly around the side of the bed. The shadows nearby him writhed with their master's agitation. The situation was a precarious one. The two men were too damn close together.

With a slow curve of his lips, the first blond ducked out from under the other's grip and then walked slowly around the bed toward Mael. Spinning around, the second blond growled low as he watched Mael's face closely, and when he caught the prince's gaze, he mouthed the word "blood."

The first blond smiled almost sweetly as he approached Mael. "*Cariad*," he said. "Come. Let us expose this imposter and be rid of him." He tilted his head toward the other man.

Growling in warning, a writhing mass of shadows thickened in the air, blocking either of them from getting to Mael. Drawing a slow breath, he caught both scents mingling in the air. He couldn't get close enough to distinguish one scent from another. Shaking his head slightly, the strong unmistakable scent of his own blood tinged the air as his gaze traveled between the two, closely watching them.

As the one closest to him stopped short of the shadows surrounding Mael, the second closed his eyes, catching the unmistakable smell of the blood. It drew a visible shudder out of him as his heart began to race even faster, and when he opened his eyes once more, he pinned a dark, heated, and *hungry* gaze on the prince.

The first blond turned to angrily face the other. "How dare you come into my lover's bedchambers disguised as me!"

A slow smile curled Mael's lips. The darkness in front of him instantly vanished as he launched himself at the assassin before he could get close to Cian again. The force of the impact sent them crashing into the wall, breaking the plaster, and showering them both with it.

The assassin shoved Mael off of him with brute force. Standing, he hurled himself at Cian. He jerked Cian around by a handful of golden hair and pressed the tip of a dagger to Cian's throat.

"Come any fucking closer," he hissed at Mael, "and I'll kill him right now."

A deadly calculating focus was etched on Mael's face as an unseen force gathered within him. Then he unleashed it. The assassin dropped the blade as blood poured from his mouth in a mist. When Mael opened his own mouth, the bloody mass filled it. Cian pulled abruptly away, too visibly shocked to say or do anything.

With a practiced hand, the assassin's hand dug into his own flesh. A bloody stake emerged from his arm. In a blur, he rushed Mael, striking true at his heart. The metal edge protruded from Mael's chest as he stumbled back.

"Mael!" Cian rushed to him.

The prince fell to the floor as the bedroom door burst open and several of his enforcers flooded into the room. The assassin took his chance for flight, running for the balcony. The shocked guards formed a barricade in front of their prone prince, all four of them uncertain of the identical Cians as one bolted for the balcony. Cian took one last look at Mael before he raced off after the assassin.

It took Mael a few moments to reorient himself. A slow inward force pushed against the stake embedded in his chest as he sat up. Jake leaned down and grabbed a hold of his arm to help him up. Since his heart wasn't precisely where it was supposed to be, a stake didn't leave him paralyzed. As he stood up, he gripped the stake and yanked it out. His knees buckled with the sudden pain and rush of energy to heal the wound, and Jake had to support him until he could stand on his own.

Casting a quick glance toward the balcony, Mael didn't bother to hide his worried expression as he explained the situation and issued a quick set of orders to his enforcers.

Quickly, he cleaned the blood from his body and then dressed. No damage marred his skin from the stake. He felt extremely anxious knowing Cian was out there, chasing the assassin. The briefest touch of his mind reached out just to gain a reassuring sense of the sorcerer's thoughts. Leaving his bedroom, he went downstairs to the main hall.

Several minutes after he'd settled in his throne, the doors of the room flew unceremoniously open. Cian stormed into the middle of the room, his hand wrapped tightly in the assassin's hair and a knife at the blond's throat. He stopped before the throne and pressed the dagger into the blond's neck.

"Why don't you tell the prince what you so kindly told me?"

When the assassin didn't speak, Cian twisted his hand tighter in his hair and drew a long but shallow cut across the vampire's throat, making his intentions very clear.

Quickly, the assassin spoke. "I was hired to murder Prince Mael Black."

"That much I had deduced," Mael said. "But who hired you, and why the deception of imitating the sorcerer?"

When the questions didn't get a quick response, Cian pressed the knife harder, drawing a second, deeper line across the assassin's throat. It almost seemed as if Cian was morbidly enjoying it.

"It is well known that Cian Carmichael is free to come and go throughout this palace. Who better to imitate than someone so *close* to the intended target? As for who hired me, I'm sure the sorcerer can tell you all about her. Her name is Rachel Centers. She hoped by killing you in the guise of the sorcerer that the sorcerer would be put to death. Two for the price of one." He maintained an eerie calm, despite having Cian's knife pressed to his neck.

Mael's gaze narrowed on the assassin with the "close" comment. He looked up at Cian, smiling faintly. "Now I wonder how Miss Centers would have gotten the money to pay his fee. I'm fairly sure it was at least an arm and a leg."

"Perhaps two legs," Cian remarked bitterly. His jaw tightened, and he spoke in the assassin's ear, loud enough for all to hear. "For your crime of the attempted assassination of Prince Mael Black of London, I judge you guilty."

With the final word, he plunged the knife into the assassin's throat and drew it across. At the same moment, both of their bodies were engulfed in brilliant blue flames. The assassin shrieked and struggled, but Cian's grip on him was unrelenting as he was burned to ashes before the entire court.

The majority of those present remained silent, no more than witnesses to the death of the assassin. Mael watched without a word, though seeing a form of Cian die troubled him. A flash of that shone in his eyes as he glanced back at his lover. With a negligent wave of his hand, he dismissed the court members to return to their quarters.

Cian brushed his clothes off and waited until the throne room was emptied before speaking. "You scared the hell out of me, Black."

"Why do you say that?" Lazily, Mael uncurled from his position and then moved slowly down the steps toward Cian.

Cian's gaze drifted down to where the stake had pierced his chest not long ago. "I thought I had lost you."

"It's not that easy to get rid of me. I was more frightened for you, my friend. Running after that assassin wasn't necessary." As he stilled in front of Cian, Mael's fingers touched a strand of blond hair, twirling it around his finger.

Cian took a quick glance around and then reached out, pulling Mael to him. "I cannot die easily," he admitted. "But losing you would probably do it."

Mael took a deep breath of Cian's scent. The soft touch of his lips pressed to the hair curled around his finger. "I thought he was you. I could have lost you as well. We were both meant to die."

Cian smiled faintly. "It would take a well-informed assassin to kill me, *cariad*." Cian closed his eyes. "If it hadn't been for the scent of your blood, I don't know what the outcome would have been. He was quite convincing, even to me."

Leaning forward, Mael nuzzled Cian's throat, taking another deep breath of the familiar scent. A soft growl rippled from his throat with the press of his lips to Cian's skin. Each kiss left a butterfly touch of sensation. "I'm thankful that you came when you did."

A soft sigh escaped Cian as he threaded his fingers slowly through the Mael's hair. "As am I," he whispered. "I've never been prone to jealousy before." The gentle pressure of his hand on Mael's head increased as Cian tilted his head to the side in invitation.

Mael's teeth scraped gently over Cian's skin in a light bite, but he didn't break the skin. Drawing his head back, he said quietly, "Not here, Cian."

Cian groaned and tugged Mael roughly against him. "Then where?" He pulled Mael's head back and kissed Mael hard.

Mael slid his hands upward over the front of the sorcerer's shirt. It wasn't until the soft sound of someone clearing their throat interrupted them that they parted, somewhat startled. Sav, with her hands neatly folded in front of her, gazed down at the ground, waiting for their attention.

Cian turned around, and his mouth fell open in a look of shock and recognition. "You. You're the one who's been following me."

As Mael eyed his assassin, he tried not to laugh at her expression. Schooling his features into less amused lines, he said, "Cian, this is Sav. A member of my court."

Raising her eyes, she gave a small smile and a polite nod.

"It's a pleasure to meet you in person finally," Cian said. He looked to Mael and then back to her. "I imagine this looks a bit awkward."

Sav eyed Cian, and a look of distrust passed over him before she nodded slightly. When she spoke, her voice contained a musical softness that didn't do much to match the words. "You are lucky I saw you earlier, or I would have killed you before this moment, just in case you were an imposter." Turning to Mael, she added, "One of his friends, the one you asked me to track, hired an assassin to kill you, Your Excellency. He plans to take on the look of the sorcerer to get to you."

"It's all right, Sav. I know all about it. Thanks to Cian, I'm still here, and the assassin is dead."

"Rachel Centers is anything but a friend," Cian said.

The attitude Sav showed toward Cian eased slightly. It didn't look like she precisely liked Cian, but she was not being as accusatory. "I apologize for thinking you a part of it, Carmichael."

Mael laid his hand on Cian's shoulder, noticing the demeanor of his lover, and Cian relaxed under his touch, but the wariness remained.

"You are most likely not the only one. My brother is intricately involved, as he and Rachel have been lovers for some time. Rachel hasn't cared for me since the day we met her."

"Cian wasn't a part of any of it, Sav, and neither was his brother." Mael's words were a faint warning to head off her mistaking anything. He gently squeezed Cian's shoulder as he glanced over at the sorcerer.

"I understand, Your Excellency, and I will continue overseeing everything else you need." Politely, Sav bowed her head to Cian again before heading back out the throne room doors, deliberately leaving them open.

"Her protectiveness toward you is admirable," Cian said quietly.

Mael chuckled. "She likes to keep me out of trouble, but it never works. Even less so lately."

Cian turned and lifted a golden eyebrow at him. "Are you saying I am trouble, Your Excellency?"

Mael's brow arched upward. When he lowered his voice, his words were a whisper only for his lover: "When you look at me like that, I'm *deeply* in trouble."

Cian raised his right hand, and the throne room doors closed with a soft click. "You were saying?"

Mael squeezed Cian's shoulder and then slid his hand slowly downward over his arm. His fingers curled around the sorcerer's hand, drawing Cian back to him. "Why is it I really don't care at the moment who sees us?"

Cian pulled Mael closer. "Why is it that I cannot think straight with you near? You told me once that you enjoyed playing with fire, prince." He raised his other hand, and a blue flame flickered to life. He blew gently on it, and the flames took shape, forming into two lovers entwined on a bed of blue silk.

"Now that I can answer. I don't *want* you to think straight," Mael said. Before he could say anything else, a hard kiss, tinged with a distinct hunger, silenced him.

Chapter Ten

Cian walked into the alley, letting the door to the bar close quietly behind him. It had been like this for nearly two weeks, and during that time, he had wished many times he was mortal. While he could not get drunk, he could still feel the slow, steady burn of the wine. It was his only solace, his only escape from the pain his heart and mind were in. The incident with the assassin kept playing over and over in his head, and before long, he began to wonder if the prince was safer without him. He was so lost in his thoughts that he didn't notice anyone before it was too late.

A man in a dark green robe stumbled and ran into Cian. "Ah, dammit."

Cian looked down. "Excuse me," he said with a nod. He stepped to the side, but then slumped against the brick wall as another surge of hunger washed through him.

"Oh, my. I never expected to see any of *your* kind in this city. Whatever did you do to get sent here?"

Cian found himself scrutinized by a piercing green gaze. "What?" It was then that he recognized the man as belonging to Mael's court. "What do you mean by 'my kind?'"

The man didn't do so much as blink. "Don't you know what you are? You're an angel, of course, but I would have thought you knew that."

Unable to help it, Cian laughed. It was the first time he'd done so in quite a while. "Of course, I know what I am. But how do you know?"

The man lowered his head slightly, eyeing Cian over the rim of his spectacles. "You *glow*, man. Didn't they ever teach you that in angel school, or wherever it is you learn?"

Cian cocked an eyebrow. "First of all, we aren't taught anything; it is our nature from the moment we are created. Secondly, only a man of magic would see such a...glow," he said with a roll of his eyes. He allowed his gaze to travel briefly over the man, from the hem of the robe to the silky dark length of his hair. But the man's eyes were what held Cian's gaze longer than he knew was safe. Had he not had Mael to think about, he would not have hesitated for a moment with this man. "Who are you?"

"They certainly do grow them quite perfect in heaven, don't they?" The man looked slowly over Cian and smiled cordially as he held out his hand. "I'm Cornelius, magician to the Prince of London. A distinct pleasure to meet you, angel."

Despite the warnings sounding in the back of his mind, Cian took the man's hand in his own. "It's a pleasure," he said, though he stifled the groan at the mere thought of the prince.

"You've been drinking, haven't you?" the mage said with a wrinkle of his nose. "Why would you bother when it has no more effect on you than it does me?" He paused, seeming to think on what he had said. "Well, it has effect if someone drinks it and I drink their blood, but I shouldn't think that would do you much good."

Cian leaned back against the wall again. "I've had my share of experiences with vampires," he muttered, more to himself than to Cornelius. "I drink it because the burn of the alcohol makes me forget everything else."

The brows above the mage's deep green eyes rose in surprise before a thoughtful look settled on his face. "Yes, well, if you've experience with vampires, then that would explain you drinking. Most of them would drive me to drink as well. Useless lot of sycophants. It was a great deal different when I was younger, believe me."

"I wouldn't call them all useless." Cian's gaze traveled down over the mage's body. He cursed himself silently for thinking of such things.

A rather knowing look crept into the mage's eyes. "My, my, you *do* have a problem, don't you? But you are a damn fine angel..." His words trailed off as he shook his head. As he moved toward the back entrance of the bar, he said, "Come, come. Let's go get 'not drunk' together. It's ever so much more fun than getting 'not drunk' by yourself." When he opened the door, it became very obvious he expected to Cian to follow him.

Cian wondered on the wisdom of following. However, with the pulse of another hunger pang, he decided it couldn't hurt. He held the door open and motioned for Cornelius to go in before him. Cornelius walked slowly past him and down the small hallway into the main area. Once he found a quiet, dark table, he settled into a seat.

"Now why don't you tell me why you have a problem? And, by the way, what is your name?" the mage asked as Cian slid into the booth across from him.

Cian wondered if it was wise to tell him who he was. Thinking it might be worse if he didn't, however, he said, "Cian Carmichael."

The mage's brows lifted, and his eyes widened. "Oh, dear. The vampire hunter?"

"One and the same."

Silence reigned at the table for a moment before the mage opened his mouth again. "You realize, of course, a vampire and an angel are a very stupid idea together, don't you?" He fixed an almost stern look on Cian, though it faltered after a moment. "You really are one of the most beautiful beings I have seen in a long time."

Leaning forward, Cian clasped both hands together on the table in front of him. "I'm fully aware of the ramifications of an angel and a vampire together. How do you know who I've been with?"

When the waitress approached, Cornelius ordered a bottle of wine for them and waited for her to wander off before he answered. "Perhaps I shouldn't have to wonder too much." His tone was dry. "First Mael blathers about you, and now I hear you talking about vampire problems."

Cian's pulse sped up as another hunger pain coursed through him. "Mael talked about me?" He held the mage's gaze and settled back against the seat, raising his arms and locking his fingers behind his head.

Cornelius blinked, and it was obvious he was trying to keep his eyes on Cian's face. "Yes, he was going on about you a bit back." He shrugged as his gaze traveled slowly downward over Cian. "No wonder he has such a problem. I mean, really."

Cian's lips curled into a wry grin. "And what problem would that be?"

Cornelius looked toward the waitress as she set the bottle and glasses on the table. Digging under his robe, he withdrew the money to pay her. When she was gone, his gaze returned to Cian. "Perhaps you should ask him that yourself."

"Your prince is stubborn," Cian said dryly.

"Mael Black is an arrogant pain in the ass, but it's such a cute ass. It excuses a lot." A grin flitted across Cornelius' lips.

"You talk like you have a history with him."

"A very, very long time ago, we did. But I'm not the easiest person to have a relationship with."

Cian shifted and stretched out, leaning back against the wall. He rested his head back and turned it slightly to look over at Cornelius. "What about you?"

A questioning look entered the mage's eyes. "What about me?"

"I've seen the way you look at me."

The mage took an inordinate amount of time pouring them both glasses of wine. His gaze remained locked onto the table as if it was the most infinitely fascinating thing he'd ever seen. "As far as looking at you goes, if you weren't so damn gorgeous, I wouldn't have a problem."

Cian chuckled softly. "Is that why you're so enraptured with the tablecloth?" he teased quietly. He dipped a single finger into one of the wine glasses and brought it to his lips. He rolled his tongue slowly around the tip before sucking it into his mouth.

The mage looked up, and his dark green eyes widened slowly. "You, my friend, are positively a danger to anybody walking the face of the earth."

"Why?"

The look that crossed the mage's face was one of disbelief, and his voice lowered to a soft whisper. "There's hunger in you. You are looking at me like I'm the next piece on the plate to devour."

Twisting around, Cian leaned forward, bringing his face closer to Cornelius'. "If I had my way, Mael Black would be the main course for all eternity," he growled, "but as it stands, he knows nothing about my nature, and I am not going to tell him. I have my needs, mage, and you are dangerously tempting yourself."

A quiet, almost startled look settled on the mage's face. "You are hungry. I didn't realize. Shit..."

Cian clenched his hands tightly into fists and closed his eyes, hissing as a sharp twist of hunger bolted through him, stronger than the ones before. "I've been trying to ignore it," he said, his voice nearly a growl as he slowly began to lose his battle with his hunger.

Seconds later, the mage slid into the booth beside Cian, shielding him from any casual onlookers. A cut appeared on Cornelius' wrist and he lifted it toward Cian's mouth. "Drink."

Cian descended on Cornelius' wrist in a blur. He drank deeply and hungrily, not bothering to suppress the soft growls as the mage's blood flowed over his tongue and down his throat. He pulled away from the mage's wrist, sliding his tongue slowly across his lips to lick away a stray drop of blood. "Thank you," he whispered.

Cornelius nodded the slightest bit. He leaned in toward Cian as his hand lifted to Cian's face. "You are too much of a temptation." The words came out in a whisper before his lips molded softly to Cian's.

A startled gasp escaped Cian, yet he opened his mouth, sliding his tongue inside the mage's, moaning softly at the delicious, slick heat. In his mind, all he could think of was Mael's lips on his own. Just as the mage began to return the kiss, a low, angered growl sounded above them, and Cornelius broke away.

Mael towered over them in front of the table.

Cornelius seemed momentarily nonplussed, and a flicker of annoyance showed in his expression as he eyed the prince. "About damn time you showed up." He slid out of the booth and patted Cian's shoulder. "You two really need professional help." He smirked over at Mael before calmly heading for the door.

The mere presence of the prince brought a fresh wave of hunger slithering through Cian. The mage's blood had been little comfort when all Cian wanted was Mael Black. He looked up and watched Mael's expression closely. Mael's gaze followed Cornelius, and he remained silent as he looked back at Cian. The prince held out a hand to him. Cian eyed Mael for a moment before taking the vampire's hand.

The moment their hands touched, the hunger returned with a vengeance. The expression on Mael's face softened slightly, and he led the way out to the back alley. Before the door had a chance to close completely, Cian shoved Mael hard against the opposite wall, flicking his tongue across Mael's throat. His hungry growls filled the otherwise quiet alleyway. Shadows swiftly descended over them, keeping them from view. A cut opened at Mael's throat, and Cian latched onto it quickly. He shuddered against Mael's body, his hunger slowly diminishing with the taste of Mael's blood. It was both the sweetest nectar of heaven and the darkest elixir of hell.

"You belong to me, sorcerer. Never forget that."

The soft sound of Mael's voice surrounded Cian, coming from the darkness all around him. He shuddered as Mael's words settled inside him, and as he drank from Mael's throat, he searched out Mael's hands, lacing his fingers through them tightly. He knew he belonged to Mael, and when he pulled away, he whispered on the prince's lips.

"If I am yours, then I want everything in return, Mael. *Everything.*"

"You already have everything I am. My blood, my body, and my life."

"I want your heart."

The shadows slowly dispersed from around them. "I don't have a heart to give you," Mael said quietly.

Cian pulled away slowly. He closed his eyes and nodded, swallowing the pain of his heart slowly breaking. "I understand." He opened his eyes and looked up at Mael, steeling himself to look into those blue eyes. "You will have the sword within the week."

Mael cupped Cian's face gently. There was an unfathomable darkness to the prince's eyes. "I couldn't even love Cornelius enough to keep him with me." His hand slid back into Cian's hair, drawing him close again, the hard press of his lips claiming Cian's.

Cian returned the kiss, laying his own claim to the vampire. When he pulled away, he brushed his lips across Mael's cheek to whisper in his ear. "Then I'll wait for you, my prince. I have all of eternity, and you are worth the wait."

"I was afraid you would leave me."

"Why would I leave you, my beloved prince? I cannot live without you."

"You would be the first then."

"Then let me be the last," Cian whispered. "I need you."

Resting his head back against the wall, Mael stared unblinkingly at him. "You have that as long as you will remain with me. You will be the only one, Cian. I can give that to you."

Smiling softly, Cian pulled a small knife from his belt. "You have a heart, Mael, and I pray I'm the one who will open it once more." He drew the knife down the side of his throat, creating a small cut. He slid his fingers through the back of Mael's hair, cupping his neck and pulling the prince toward him. Mael growled softly as his mouth covered the wound. Cian held Mael tight against him.

"*Rwy'n dy garu di,*" Cian whispered. "*Duw, rwy'n dy garu, di.*"

Mael's hands slid up into Cian's hair, his fingers slowly combing through the strands as he drank. Cian felt the full relaxation of Mael's body; only when he had taken enough did Mael draw back, resting his head against the wall. When he opened his eyes, one of his hands untangled from Cian's hair to rub his thumb slowly against Cian's neck, his look one of mild curiosity at the absence of a wound.

Cian reached out and stroked his fingers slowly down Mael's cheek, his gaze focused on Mael's eyes, searching for the one thing he wanted more than anything in this world. Mael was capable of love, yet he had no idea of it himself.

"You're more beautiful than you give yourself credit for." He stroked his thumb gently across Mael's lips, a sad smile settling on his own. "You have the most beautiful soul I've ever known."

Mael pressed a soft kiss to Cian's thumb before saying anything. "You know so little of what I am and what I have done, Cian."

Cian opened his mouth to argue, then closed it. Instead, he smiled and leaned forward to brush his lips across Mael's. "I know enough to want you by my side for eternity."

"I'm beginning to think you may care a bit too much for me. That may not be such a good thing."

Sighing out of resignation and frustration, Cian simply shook his head. "Has anyone ever told you how stubborn you are, Mael?"

"Quite often, so you may as well get used to saying it." A grin quirked the prince's lips.

Cian rolled his eyes and rested his forehead to Mael's chest. "Gorgeous and stubborn. *Cariad*, you could make an angel exasperated."

"But I only have the urge to exasperate you, Cian."

Cian closed his eyes, drinking in the delicate touch of Mael's words. He distracted himself by sliding his arms around Mael's waist and placing soft kisses on his chest.

"Most times, I'm not sure I really think straight with you around," Mael whispered. "Just have patience with me, please."

Cian didn't miss the soft, pleading tone to Mael's words, and he continued his kisses, up Mael's chest, across his neck, until he reached the hollow of his throat. He traced a line up with the tip of his tongue, ending at Mael's lips. "I told you: I will wait forever for you."

"And I hope you never grow tired of reminding me."

Cian's tongue delved into the warmth of the prince's mouth, his soft keening moans betraying his hunger for something other than blood. With his arms still tight around Mael's waist, he slipped a leg between Mael's, pressing his thigh against Mael's groin.

Mael groaned and broke away slowly from their kiss. "I need to get back, Cian." The hunger in his eyes matched Cian's, but they both knew he couldn't stay.

Cian nodded as he willed his pulse to slow its furious racing. "As do I. I have a bit of work to get the sword."

"It won't be much longer before I seek you out, wherever you are," Mael said with a distinct touch of frustration. He slipped out from between the wall and Cian slowly.

Cian watched him walk away, painfully aware of the ache in both his heart and his groin.

* * *

Home.

It had been so long.

Cian took a deep, calming breath, feeling his worries drain away, floating on the wind as he exhaled. Mael's presence remained with him, and the hunger was beginning to build once more. He looked around him, taking in the lush green grasses, the brilliant blue of the sky above. He stretched his wings out, feeling a freedom he hadn't known in quite some time.

A well-worn path stretched out across the verdant plains in front of him, and he began to walk, enjoying the soothing feel of the ground beneath his feet and the gentle breeze around him. He could fly, but right now, he needed the time it took to reach Michael's palace to think. The forest behind him stretched on, its depths dark but hardly forbidding. This was the Kingdom of God; nothing was out of place here.

After several moments, which would have seemed a lifetime to a mortal, he arrived at the towering, gilded gates of Michael's palace. Beyond them an enormous building stood, its brilliant white surface gleaming in the midday sun. The gates swung open, and Cian walked through, his old friend's presence surrounding him in a comforting blanket. He made his way up a flight of steps, each one settling his troubled mind a little more. As he neared the top, he spied a familiar face — serene yet strong, golden hair stirring in the breeze. The Archangel's smile did much to settle Cian's thoughts, and as he reached Michael, he knelt slowly to one knee.

"My friend," Michael said. "It is good to see you again." There was laughter in his voice, a sweet, melodic sound like the chimes of a thousand crystals.

Cian stood at Michael's bidding. "It's good to be home."

Michael put an arm around Cian's shoulders as they walked through the ivory doors of his palace. They passed through the first hall and into Michael's throne room. Several others were gathered about, talking amongst themselves, but with a raise of Michael's hand, they quickly dispersed, leaving the two friends alone. Michael sat down on his ivory throne and smiled — softly yet knowingly. Cian took a seat beside him, the seat left vacant when he was not here.

"You are troubled, Cian."

Cian sighed and lowered his gaze. "Yes, I am." He stood and began to pace the floor in front of the dais. "I do not know where to start." He stopped and looked up at Michael. "There's so much."

Michael smiled and waited patiently. Cian resumed his pacing.

"The hunts have been going as well as can be expected," he said, "given the nature of my work. I even managed to corner one of the more elusive ones." He glanced over at Michael and noted the pleased smile gracing the Archangel's lips. "I also was able to rescue a young one, born of a rogue but who had not killed yet. He's safe now, residing under the care of the Prince of London."

"And it is the Prince of London whom you have on your mind now," Michael said.

"Yes." Cian combed the fingers of one hand through his hair. "Michael, I don't know what to do." He looked the Archangel in the eye and knew he needed to say no more.

"You don't know what to do about drinking the prince's blood?" the Archangel asked. "Or what you feel for him?"

His soft smile reflected in his pale blue eyes. "Is it your love that you fear, Cian?"

Cian returned to his seat beside Michael and lowered his head to his hands, cradling it between them. "I don't know. I don't think Mael understands. He thinks it's simply the blood bond between us talking."

"Is it?"

Cian looked up then and found himself caught in a searching gaze. "No." He dropped his head to his hands again and muttered, "I've fallen in love with a vampire, Michael." A soft touch on his head drew it back up.

"Love knows no boundaries, Cian," Michael said calmly. "If you love him, then so be it. Drinking his blood might have been an accident, but it cannot be undone. Do not let him go because of your fears."

Cian found it hard to breathe, and a surge of hunger tried to break the surface of his rather tenuous calm demeanor. "There is something else I need to speak with you about."

"And that would be my sword."

"Yes."

"Are you aware of the dangers of the sword? A single touch will kill a vampire, whether they are good or evil."

"I understand," Cian said. "I talked him out of the Eye of Baal. Once he felt the power of the Eye, he realized he could not give it to Selena."

"Very well," Michael said, rising from his throne. "I will give you the sword, but you must return it to me."

Michael turned away and disappeared through a doorway. Cian remained where he sat. When Michael returned, he carried a length of blue velvet, wrapped with a silver ribbon. Cian didn't need to unwrap it to know what lay within. He took the sword from Michael and closed his eyes as Michael placed a soft kiss on his brow. Like his own similar gesture to others, the kiss helped calm him.

"Be safe," the Archangel said. Adding as an afterthought, he whispered in Cian's ear, "and don't let go of him."

* * *

"I have something for Prince Black, something he requested." Cian waited a few minutes while the servant bustled off. As he looked around at the various suits of armor, Mael's secretary came up to him.

"Good evening," Ben said.

Cian turned and lifted the velvet-wrapped bundle. "Mael asked me to bring this to him."

"His Excellency is holding court," Ben said. "This way, please."

Cian followed him to a set of doors, and when they opened, he saw Mael sitting on his throne, surrounded by several others seated on red cushions around the room. The others were engaged in varied acts of feeding or pleasure. Judging by the expressions on some of their faces, Cian surmised the two acts blended for many. Mael observed them all without much interest. He motioned silently for Ben and Cian. As they walked through the room, Cian felt his pulse quicken at the scent of blood and the sight of the prince. He stopped with Ben as they reached the dais. He gave Mael a slow, graceful bow.

"You can go back to your duties, Ben," Mael said to his secretary before his dark gaze settled on Cian. His voice remained the same quiet, even tenor as he spoke. "Sit, if you will." He politely gestured to the seat to the left of his own.

"Thank you." Cian sat down and placed the sword across his lap. He glanced over at Mael, and his gaze traveled over the prince's body.

"Thank you for coming. I expected it to take longer to get what I needed."

"It wasn't as difficult as I thought. It seems it was already known that I would come looking for it."

"I was afraid you might have to move heaven and hell. Thankfully, it seems you didn't."

"I assure you that I have it through the blessings of the highest authority."

Mael's hungry gaze dropped to Cian's lips. Although the prince's words and tone remained formal, Cian felt Mael's desperate need just as strongly as his own. He barely managed to hide the shudder that ran through him. He sent his own thoughts to Mael, his own desires to feel the prince's possessing touch.

Cian longed to feel those lips on his, those fingers slide through his hair, those fangs piercing his throat. He shook his head, trying desperately to will away the erection forming in his leather pants.

"You delight in teasing me, my sorcerer."

"I delight in everything about you, my prince."

Mael chuckled. He stood and tipped his head toward the doors leading to the garden. "Would you care to take a walk with me?"

"Of course."

Mael pinned him with a hungry look before turning away. A servant opened the doors for them, and a slow grin etched itself across Cian's lips as they stepped out into the garden.

"I had not expected you to be the sentimental type to enjoy garden strolls, Black."

The doors closed silently behind them.

"I wasn't thinking so much of sentimental as I am less well-lit paths." Mael grinned wickedly at Cian as he slowly led him further into the formal gardens. The path was lit by an occasional fairy light at the edges of the walk.

Cian drew a single fingertip down Mael's spine. "I need you."

Mael shivered. "I can feel that in every part of me, Cian. As much as my own need for you."

When he was certain they would not be seen, Cian gripped Mael's arm and turned him around, pushing his tongue between the prince's lips in a hungry kiss. *I want you, in whatever way I can have you right now."*

Mael's arms circle Cian's waist, pulling him close. *"You would have me if I could. I can think of little else."*

Cian growled softly into Mael's mouth and backed him up against the nearest tree. The prince groaned, and his hands fell to Cian's hips, pulling their bodies together. Cian could feel the vampire's hunger and need, the desire that Mael held so strongly for him. He moved his lips over Mael's cheek and whispered in his ear.

"What I wouldn't give to turn you around and bend you over, to bury myself in your body."

Cian moved down in a soft, slow line to the prince's neck. He drew the tip of his tongue along the hollow of Mael's throat, over his chin, and finally back into his mouth. Then he pulled away from their kiss and took Mael's hand in his. He lifted it to his lips and kissed the palm softly.

"Just feel."

He kissed a slow line up Mael's middle finger, and when he reached the tip, he winked before sucking it into his mouth. He rolled his tongue around it, sucking gently as he kept his gaze on Mael. With every move, the sensations were redirected to Mael's cock, as if Cian's lips were wrapped tightly around it. Mael stared steadily back at him, and Cian could feel a distinct hardening as the prince's hips pressed tighter into his. Mael hissed softly, and his eyes darkened to midnight blue, signaling his full arousal.

Cian reached down with his other hand, closing it over the front of Mael's pants. When he squeezed Mael's cock, he sucked harder on the prince's finger. He moaned, knowing the vibration slid through Mael's body. He pulled Mael's finger from his mouth slowly and wrapped his own fingers around it.

"Now imagine this..." He squeezed Mael's finger tightly as he began to stroke it. "Is my ass. With every slide of your finger in mine, your cock slides deeper inside my body."

Mael immediately nudged against Cian's hand and shuddered. "I want you...now."

Cian could hear the prince's desperation, and he chuckled. Should he drive Mael to the point of orgasm this way, there wasn't a soul in his court who would miss the unmistakable scent of spent arousal. Mael's free hand pushed between them, and his fingers brushed slowly to the front of Cian's pants, outlining Cian's cock.

"I'm yours. Do with me what you will."

Mael drew in a slow, deep breath, seeming to clear his thoughts from their haze. "Oh, I will, Cian." The soft, silky purr of his voice held a distinct promise as his fingers rubbed slowly against the leather. "But we're both going to have to wait. Just imagine what I will do to you when I finally *do* have you." His dark eyes reflected the intensity of his words, and Cian shivered.

Cian's fingers tightened over Mael's pants, and he drew in a quick breath as he closed his eyes. Just a few strokes of Mael's fingertips would see him come where he stood. He had never been on such a sharp edge in all his existence. When he was finally able to speak, his voice was low, gruff, and laced with hunger.

"Keep that up, and I won't have to wait."

The tip of Mael's finger slowly smoothed against the hardness straining against Cian's pants before the prince withdrew his hand.

"Happy now?" Mael asked, smiling wickedly.

"Bastard," Cian whispered with tortured amusement. He brushed his lips over Mael's throat, nicking his flesh with his teeth. "Just one taste, my love."

Cian knew Mael could not deny him that much. When a small wound opened on Mael's throat, Cian covered it with his mouth, drinking deeply. Mael's thoughts reached him once more, a sense of wonder within his words.

"You call me your 'love.'"

"That I do."

Cian felt Mael's arm slide around his waist, pulling him closer. He could feel Mael's confusion. Mael couldn't understand how someone could love him, how Cian could love the monster that he was. The prince was still convinced it was the blood lust making Cian feel the way he did. Cian sighed as he pulled away. He kissed Mael softly, and the vampire returned his kiss, telling Cian he was indeed capable of love, if only he would open his heart to the possibility.

"You will understand in time, *cariad*," Cian said quietly.

Mael regarded him with a steady gaze, pain and confusion warring within the dark depths of the prince's eyes. "*Che potrei averlo per sempre.*"

The words were spoken in Italian, and while Cian couldn't readily understand them, he felt the emotion behind them, confirming what he had felt in Mael's kiss. He touched Mael's cheek softly, running his fingers down the side of his face. He rested his forehead to Mael's.

"Will we forever be speaking in tongues to one another?"

Mael cupped his face gently with his palm, lifting Cian's head to meet his soft gaze. "I said that I wanted to have you forever, my sorcerer."

Cian closed his eyes, placing his hand over Mael's. "And why would you want me forever? I am a hunter."

"And I am what you would hunt, except for the law. Something you cannot love. There is nothing about us that makes sense, Cian. But when I am with you, I forget everything else."

"I was sent to hunt the rogues only, Mael." Cian smiled, even though his heart ached. He slipped the fingers of both hands through Mael's hair and tilted Mael's head forward, placing a soft kiss on his forehead. It was a kiss he reserved only for those he loved with all his soul, and the mere touch of his lips would bring serenity to the recipient. "Someone once told me to never let you go."

A single red tear slid down Mael's cheek as his face took on an unfathomable calm. Yet Cian sensed a deeper pain, a deeper regret, within the prince. He took Mael's face softly in his hands and licked the blood tear away with the tip of his tongue. He kissed Mael softly, letting him taste the blood.

"We must get you back to your court, my prince."

There was a quiet reverence to Mael's kiss before his arms dropped from Cian's sides, releasing him. "Thank you from the bottom of what heart I have for bringing the sword to me."

Cian stepped back and picked up the sword from where he had placed it on the path. He handed it to Mael. "Promise me you'll come back to me."

As Mael took the sword, he said quietly, "I'm not even sure hell itself could keep me from you."

Cian cupped the back of Mael's neck. "Make no mistake," he said firmly, "I will walk through hell myself should anyone harm you."

"What makes you think I would allow you to put yourself danger over me?"

"I will do whatever is necessary to keep you by my side for eternity, prince."

"I would argue you with you, but you're not listening very well." Mael chuckled softly, taking it in good humor.

Cian fell in beside him as they walked back toward the doors. "In my lifetime, I've heard that more times than I care to count."

"And I'm sure you'll hear it many more times from me," Mael said, his easy smile reflecting in his eyes.

Cian returned the smile, but muttered under his breath, "That's not what I really want to hear from you."

Mael stopped and grabbed his arm. "And what is it you want to hear? Or should I ask?"

Cian cupped Mael's jaw with his palm. "Nothing. It's nothing." He glanced toward the mansion. "The members of your court will be quite curious as to what has kept us out in the garden this long."

The prince's brow quirked in curiosity. "I'll leave it alone...for now." He turned his head slightly, brushing a soft kiss to the tips of Cian's fingers before he pulled away.

Cian leaned forward to kiss Mael. "Get back to your court," he whispered. "I must be going."

"You keep saying that as if you are trying to get rid of me."

As Cian watched Mael walk away, he closed his eyes and whispered to Mael's mind. *"Never, my love. You know how to find me when you're ready."*

The doors opened, and Mael stepped inside. *"And I will find you."*

When the doors closed behind the vampire, Cian whispered, "I love you, my prince."

Chapter Eleven

Mael deliberately emptied his throne room, knowing Sav and Eric would soon be bringing his expected guest to him. Relaxing, he enjoyed the quiet of the room before the silence was broken by the sound of voices in the doorway. He eyed the young female, his assassin, and his enforcer.

Rachel jerked her arm free from Sav and stood straighter. "After you," she huffed with an indignant wave of her hand toward the room.

Sav folded her arms over her chest. "You go in...alone." Eyeing the woman, Sav waited for her to move as Eric stepped back. The large, burly man didn't even have to act intimidating; his frame and behavior gave that impression all on their own.

"Whatever." Rachel rolled her eyes as she strode into the throne room like she owned it. Stopping at the bottom of the dais, she crossed her arms over her chest as if she were impatient to get on with things.

Mael folded his hands together, two fingers propping up his chin. "So nice of you to join me, Rachel. I've wanted to meet you."

Rachel sighed impatiently. "Spare the pleasantries. Why am I here?"

"You're here to die, of course. If you're in a hurry to do so, I'll be more than happy to oblige you." The faint smile on his lips had an unpleasantness to it.

She took a step back and laughed. "You can't kill me. It's against the law to kill a mortal."

"You are quite right, Rachel. However, you've meddled in affairs that have brought you into my territory, which would be enough on its own for me to rightfully kill you. There's also another little matter that makes it all that much easier. Unfortunately, you're not exactly mortal anymore." The nasty smile widened.

Rachel laughed nervously. "What are you talking about? Of course, I'm mortal!"

Mael shook his head in mock sadness as he stood. "I must tell you, sadly, you aren't. From your reaction, I'm going to assume either Iverson didn't tell you what he did, or that you don't realize what drinking a vampire's blood will do."

The color drained from Rachel's face, and Mael caught the vague memory from her of tasting Iverson's blood one night during sex. She watched him closely, backing up another couple of steps as he advanced on her.

"Merely drinking it won't do anything to me," she countered. A blanket of shadows swiftly covered the doors, leaving her no way to escape.

Mael approached her, his words casual. "I'm afraid it does. It puts you solely under my jurisdiction, with you being a ghoul and all. And you've pissed me off, young lady."

Rachel looked around, her movements becoming frantic as she shook her head. "What have I done to you? Merely dealing with Iverson isn't enough of a crime to kill me."

"Dealing with a prince who creates rogues is a very naughty thing. Hiring an assassin to kill me and lay the blame on Cian Carmichael won't be well received either. It would be enough for the mortal authorities to take care of you, but it would take a bit longer to deal out a death sentence. I'd rather do that myself." A hard grip wrapped around her arm before she could even blink or move.

Denial etched across her paling face before realization set in. "Lee. That son of a bitch told his faggot of a brother!" She struggled to pull free and winced at the crushing pain of Mael's grip.

"My, my, how temperamental you are, Rachel." Mael simply touched her forehead. The power stilled the struggling but left her mind intact. Mael delved deeply into her thoughts, searching swiftly through the fragments to piece together a deeper picture of her and her dealings. "As far as that goes, you were overheard telling Iverson yourself."

Within her mind, Rachel screamed, staring at him with wild, frightened eyes. No matter how much she tried to move, her body was frozen. All she could do was wait for the inevitable.

"Relax and enjoy. At least it's a pleasant way to die, Rachel. Better than what you plotted for me and Cian." Mael sank his fangs into her throat. The fierce, unrestrained pull of his mouth drained not only her blood but her life as well.

The last thought to flicker through her mind was one of sheer, indescribable terror, and he felt the struggle of it within his own. As he drank, her last scream slipped from her lips. When she weakened, he quickly grabbed her to hold her up. Listening to the faltering beat of her heart, he didn't release her until it stopped. Her body dropped to the floor, and he stepped over her as he opened a gateway, touching the crystal at his throat. Before he stepped through, he issued orders to Jake to take care of the body.

Entering the tower once again, he paused, looking toward Cian working at his table. A flood of memories of them both lying in the nearby bed hit him. It had only been a few nights ago, and Mael felt the familiar ache.

Cian stopped, his hand stilling just as he was reaching up for a sprig of rosemary. He turned. "I had not expected to see you so soon."

"I need to talk to you about Rachel."

Cian's gaze narrowed, and he looked back down at the mortar and pestle in front of him. He plucked the rosemary from above without looking up and dropped it into the marble bowl. As he ground the leaves and flowers into powder, he said, "Why do I have the distinct feeling that I'm going to be consoling a distraught brother sometime soon?"

"Because she had her hand way too deep in too many pies, Cian. I took care of her myself."

"It does not surprise me," Cian said, "but I honestly have no idea how I'm going to explain this to Lee." He pushed the bowl away. "What did she have to say?"

Mael leaned against the table. "She didn't have much to say at all, other than to act like she hadn't done anything wrong. I gleaned enough from her mind to warrant her death, more than you might want to tell your brother. She was sleeping with Iverson. She'd even become his ghoul, though she wasn't aware of that. She wouldn't have stopped until we both were dead. I drained and killed her."

Cian began pacing, the agitation radiating from him in waves. "He loved her. He loved her more than anything in this world, and she broke his heart." He paused at the window. Then without any warning, his fist connected with the stone frame. The walls of the tower seemed to shake, while his hand bore no mark of the impact.

The display surprised Mael. He walked over to Cian and took hold of his hand, studying it. He found it hard to believe there wasn't a scratch on him.

"No, I cannot easily be hurt." Cian fell back against the wall, not pulling his hand from Mael's. "What do I tell him, Mael? I don't know what is going to hurt him more: her infidelity or her death."

Mael pushed away his own curious thoughts over the sorcerer's lack of wounds as he tightened his hand on Cian's. "You can tell him that she wanted you dead, Cian. She hated you. She hated everything about you. Her mind was twisted with you, and somehow, she thought you stood in her way."

Cian laughed, the sound bitter. "She's hated me since the two of them got together. She didn't get involved with vampires until after she and my brother started dating.

"She wanted more than what she had. She played right into Iverson's hands. He had more of what she wanted than anybody else."

Cian pushed away from the wall, pulling Mael over to the table. He released Mael's hand and reached for the bottle of wine and two glasses. Straddling the other chair, he poured them both some wine. "We met Rachel not long after coming to London. Lee insisted on dragging me into one of the local gothic clubs, even though I much preferred a club of a different sort." He pushed one of the glasses to Mael. "Rachel was a waitress. The moment she came to our table, I knew my brother had lost his heart. I, however, was more cautious. Something about her bothered me." He took a sip of wine and continued.

"It ate away at me for quite some time. When I finally went to Lee, he threw a beer bottle at me. He wouldn't listen then, and I'm not sure he'd understand now." He sighed and downed the entire glass of wine in one swallow. "He's as stubborn as you are."

"You were wiser than your brother. She was a greedy little soul. Which, I'm assuming, is why she apparently hooked up with Iverson to begin with. She had no problem turning you over to him for a very nice sum of money. That part was witnessed by one of my spies in Iverson's camp. Would you want me to talk to your brother? I'm not sure how much good it would do but hearing the facts from a third party might help."

Cian shot Mael a look that clearly said that would be horrible idea. "No offense, *cariad*, but Lee isn't exactly fond of vampires. I'd rather not put either one of you through that. I'll talk to him. If all else fails..." He paused for a moment, as if unsure of what to say. "Well, either way, I'll get it through his thick skull somehow."

Reaching across the table, Mael covered Cian's hand with his. "If I thought that she would've walked away from everything and leave it all alone, I wouldn't have killed her. Both she and Iverson used each other: one to get to me, the other to get to you. If I had let her live, she would have found another method against you."

Cian tipped the bottle up and drank the wine straight out it. "I know," he said as he set the emptied bottle down.

He waved his hand over the top and then poured himself another glass. "Did she put up much of a fight?"

"No, but then, I didn't give her much of a chance to put up a fight."

Cian drank the glass of wine and started to pour himself some more, but he stopped with the bottle half-tipped. "Iverson will find out quickly she's gone. Perhaps I need to make *him* my next target."

"I take it you already know we didn't catch him in the attack. He slipped out of Seymour's fingers and hasn't been seen since. As far as I could tell, Rachel didn't know where he was holed up. My enforcers are already looking for him, and chances are, he already knows Rachel was taken. There was no big secrecy around bringing her in, and it's probably already spreading like wildfire through the grapevine."

Cian eyed Mael dubiously. "You're taking this in stride. Or perhaps it is just my nature to worry about you."

"I've been through too many battles to lose my head or my ability to rule, Cian." Mael regarded him steadily. "The only time I seem to lose that is with you."

Lifting a pale eyebrow at him, Cian chuckled. "Why is that?"

"I haven't a blessed clue."

Cian smiled and leaned forward, slipping his fingers through Mael's hair. "I have done nothing to you but take you to bed, my prince. Surely that is not enough to scramble your brain."

A soft growl rippled through Mael with the touch of Cian's tongue to his lips, and he rested his hand on Cian's thigh. "I want to be back in that bed."

"I am yours, *cariad*."

Those words were all it took. Mael ran his hand slowly upward over Cian's thigh as his other hand went for the sorcerer's hair. His lips brushed in a lingering kiss to Cian's before he deepened it into a hungry invasion of the man's mouth. A wayward caress of his fingers drew Cian's legs apart. Cian gripped the back of Mael's neck, moaning possessively as he deepened their kiss. Then Cian pulled away and slid out of his chair.

When Cian straddled him, Mael pushed his hands up underneath Cian's shirt, playing over his skin as he felt the downward grind of Cian's hips. His sorcerer's response delighted him completely. "As soon as our clothes are off, I'm going to fuck you until you can't see straight."

"Is that a promise, my dark prince?" Cian slipped his hands between them and began unbuttoning Mael's shirt. He pushed the shirt off of Mael's shoulders and stood, holding out his hand in invitation.

"Why don't you undress for me, and then you'll find out."

The sorcerer's darkening gaze reflected his own smile as he pulled his shirt over his head. He tossed it onto the floor and slid his hand over his chest, watching Mael closely as his fingertips drifted over his torso. His fingers glided to his left nipple, and he twisted it slightly, closing his eyes for the briefest moment, a hiss of sweet pain escaping his lips.

Mael's gaze remained pinned on Cian with a deepening intensity. A low growl started in his throat in appreciation. "It has become my favorite thing to see your body revealed to me, the desire and need lighting your eyes."

"It is your body to touch." Cian's hand slid down his stomach, and with nothing more than a wave of his hand, his leather pants fell to the floor. He took his shaft in his hand and began to stroke himself slowly. "Fair is fair."

Mael's gaze dropped to Cian's hand as he stood up. Unfastening his pants, he slipped off his shoes. Careful to maintain that small distance between them, he took of his pants. "I think you want to feel something other than that hand, don't you?"

Cian crooked a finger and beckoned him over. "To feel your lips surrounding me, to slide into the moist warmth of your mouth, is heaven on earth to me." He continued to stroke his cock from base to tip. "Touch me," he whispered. "Show me that I am yours."

The sorcerer couldn't have picked a better way to raise the possessive beast in Mael. Mael brushed Cian's hand away and his own took its place. He pushed Cian toward the bed as his fingers curled to stroke over him. "You *do* belong to me, and when this night is through, you'll remember that."

"Then prove it." The backs of his legs touched the bed, and Cian fell back, slipping from Mael's grasp. His golden hair lay splayed over the blue silk of the blanket, and his legs parted.

Mael remained standing and stared hungrily at the body stretched out on the bed for him. The eagerness and need shone in Cian's eyes, and Mael reveled in that. He crawled onto the bed between Cian's legs. His hand caressed over Cian's thigh and then gently grasped the base of his cock. Then he took Cian in his mouth, lips encircling Cian's cock fully.

"Mael..." The name was nothing more than a breathy whisper as Cian arched, burying himself in Mael's throat. His hands tangled in Mael's hair, and he began thrusting slowly in and out. "Please, don't stop."

Mael followed the rhythm of Cian's thrusts, taking him in with each one. With each partial withdrawal, the tip of Mael's tongue rapidly flicked from side to side just beneath the head. Then he lifted his head, not allowing Cian to come that way.

"Isn't there anything you want, my sorcerer?" A slow glide of his nails ran over both of Cian's thighs.

Cian groaned in frustration and raised his head to meet Mael's gaze. "You. I need *you*. I need to feel you inside me, possessing me. I need to feel the richness of your blood, flowing over my tongue as I come beneath you. I need to feel you claim me as you feed."

Smiling slowly, Mael settled on his knees between Cian's legs. He enjoyed having Cian right where he wanted him and to hear him begging. "You do have lubrication, don't you?" He went back to idly rubbing over the sorcerer's cock as he waited patiently.

Cian leaned over to the bedside table and pulled open the drawer. He reached inside and pulled out a bottle of clear gel. "Olive oil worked well long ago, but this works just as well." He closed his eyes and rocked his hips, drawing his legs up to allow Mael to settle further between them.

Mael didn't take the bottle and instead leaned forward, hovering over Cian. Placing one hand on the bed for support, his other continued the slow teasing strokes on the sorcerer's cock. "Why don't you do that?"

Holding Mael's gaze, Cian opened the bottle. He squeezed some of the gel in his palm and reached down. He began stroking Mael's cock slowly, applying increasing pressure from base to tip. Mael growled softly, and his hips nudged in against the touch repeatedly before he was released. Cian then slipped his hand between his own legs. He bit his lower lip as he slid two fingers deep inside himself. He struggled to keep his eyes open and added a third finger, pushing all three deeper inside.

"Is that what you wanted, prince?"

Looking down, Mael watched those fingers disappear inside Cian's body. He brushed Cian's hand aside and grasped the base of his own cock. Positioning it, he rubbed the head slowly over Cian's hole. He pushed slightly inward before drawing back.

"Mael, please..." Cian groaned and rocked his hips. "I need you." His gaze locked onto Mael's, a desperate plea within his eyes. "Show me how much I belong to you."

Mael drank in Cian's features, listening to the words he loved to hear. A smoldering flare lit within him, burning into Cian, and Mael never looked away as he slowly pushed back inside. A quick inward thrust buried him deeply into the tight confines of Cian's body. A fierce growl wrapped within the words as Mael's hips drew back, only to repeatedly thrust back into Cian with each word spoken.

"You are mine. You will *always* be mine."

Cian gasped and rocked his hips to meet every thrust. "Always yours, my prince," he breathed. His back arched, and his breathing became more labored. "Mael...please..." He tilted his head, baring his throat.

Mael kept control of his own swiftly rising need to come. He lowered his head and swiftly sank his fangs into Cian's flesh. A greedy hunger pulled at Cian's throat as the pace of his body kept to the relentless hard claiming of what belonged fully to him.

"Mael!" Cian shuddered repeatedly beneath him, and the sorcerer's fingers tangled in Mael's hair. He cried out again as another bolt of pleasure shot through him as Mael fed.

Only after he savored the sweetness flooding Cian's blood did Mael unleash his own control. He grabbed Cian's hip, and with one last hard push, he came, buried deeply inside, a hard shudder rocking his body with the release of the unbearable tension. A wound instantly opened to the sorcerer, and Cian latched onto the cut. With the connection between them wide open, Mael's mind was overwhelmed with the massive waves that crashed over him, feeling the rush that hit him from Cian. An uncontrollable shiver took over his body as he lost sense of everything but what Cian felt and gave to him.

When Cian stopped feeding, he pulled away from Mael's throat and drew him down into a searing kiss. He cried out into Mael's mouth as his body arched with a burst of brilliance. Barely capable of reacting to anything outside of them, Mael could only ride what took him over until it began to fade. When the light and waves of pleasure finally subsided, Cian's head fell back onto the pillow as he struggled to catch his breath. Mael collapsed heavily on top of him, totally unable to move. He buried his face in golden hair.

"That was not expected," Cian murmured.

Mael could only cling to his sorcerer. All he could do was shake his head. Internally, his mind sought the comfort of being within Cian's to help bring him down.

"I am yours, *cariad*. Everything I am."

Those words soothed over Mael as he carefully rolled off of Cian and onto his side. He drew Cian up against him. "Let me stay the day with you. Please don't let me go until I wake again."

"If it were up to me," Cian said as he stroked Mael's face gently, "I would *never* let you go. You are welcome here, whenever you wish." He kissed Mael's forehead, releasing a gentle, soothing wave to surround them. "Sleep, my prince. When you wake, it will be in my arms. Where you belong."

Mael understood he needed Cian the moment the words formed in his mind. A whisper of growing contentment filled him with the soft kiss, quieting his mind and keeping him safely within it. When the darkness of sleep took him, all he felt was the peace Cian gave him.

* * *

The next evening when he awoke, Mael propped himself up on his elbow to watch his sleeping lover. He smiled as his gaze traveled slowly over the golden hair spread out over the sheets. The peaceful, relaxed lines of Cian's features beckoned Mael's touch, but it was time for him to go. Tonight, he needed to take care of Selena. Cornelius had already taken the sword to perform his own ritual over it, and it would soon be ready.

Very carefully, Mael shifted to the edge of the bed, not wanting to awaken the sorcerer. Glancing at Cian over his shoulder, he really wanted more than anything to simply stay here and forget everything else. Knowing he couldn't, he stood and quickly dressed.

After stepping through the portal, Mael headed for the bathroom for a quick shower. Once dressed, he went down to the library. He needed something to occupy his mind while he waited for Cornelius to finish with the sword. In the library, it took him no more than a moment to find a book to distract himself before he settled in a leather wing chair with it.

The attempt to calm a sense of increasing agitation really wasn't working. He poured a glass of brandy from the decanter and took a sip before turning another page. All he had to do was wait until Cornelius finished the ritual. Unfortunately, he also had to return the sword to Cian later tonight. His thoughts turned to what if he didn't return. Sighing, Mael closed the book and set it on the stand.

A few moments later, Brandon opened the door, "I'm sorry," he said. "It's time for my studies."

Mael gave him a warm smile. "Come on in, Brandon. Ben left a note on the desk of the books he wanted to you to get."

Brandon smiled back at him and closed the door. After picking up the note, he began browsing the shelves for the books.

"I'm sure Ben left a great deal of work for your studies. Just let him know if it gets to be too much." Mael chuckled.

He knew his secretary all too well, and Brandon had one hell of a list in his hand.

Laughing, Brandon pulled a book from a shelf. "In all honesty, I miss stuff like this. I loved school."

"Then you should have no problem at all. Although some of those books are very dry and dusty, at times too hard to get through, as I recall." Mael took a sip of his brandy, watching Brandon.

Brandon turned to look at him, a look of genuine surprise on his youthful face. "You had to do this, too?"

"Ben enjoys his prince being well educated and well rounded, unfortunately," Mael said dryly. "So, yes, I have."

"Ah." Brandon turned back to hunt for another book. "Do you like to read otherwise?"

"I enjoy reading more than I have time to do so."

The door opened, and Ben stepped in, then immediately tried to make a hasty retreat.

"Ben."

Ben paused in his tracks.

"Have you been avoiding me lately?" Mael eyed his secretary. The question was mild, though his expression was not.

"No, of course not, Your Excellency."

"Then that means you've found what I wanted." Since he'd been hounding his secretary for the same thing over the last few weeks, Mael received only a long-suffering look from Ben.

"No, I haven't, Your Excellency. I told you that earlier this evening."

"How hard is it to find a Welsh translator? The damn country isn't that far away."

"You're looking for a Welsh translator?" Brandon asked.

"Well, Your Excellency, the mortal ones I've applied to don't seem too willing to..."

Directing a less than pleased look at Ben, Mael turned to face Brandon. "I have been looking for one for a while now. Not that anybody has had much luck, as you can tell."

"It's my native language."

"Well, there you go, Your Excellency," Ben said. "You have your translator. Now if you will excuse me, I have more important business to attend to." Turning on his heel, he disappeared down the hall.

"Forgive me, Brandon. I'm not angry. I've wanted the translation of a particular phrase that has been nagging me. Ben didn't believe it to be important, and I have been unmercifully hounding the poor man over it."

"Understandable. Might I ask what phrase?"

Mael took a small drink of the brandy still in his hand before he turned back toward the chair he'd vacated earlier. "Do you know the meaning of 'ruin di gara dee?'" The words were spoken very carefully, reproducing the phonetics as best as he could.

Brandon blinked several times. "It was the last thing my mom said to me before my dad kicked me out."

Stilling abruptly, Mael frowned; that didn't sound too promising. "Kicked you out? What the hell does it mean then?"

Brandon shrugged. "It means 'I love you.' Why?"

The glass in Mael's hand slipped from his fingers, shattering as it hit the floor. He wasn't entirely sure he heard Brandon right. "I love you?" He knew he sounded rather like a parrot.

Brandon lifted an eyebrow and eyed him curiously. "Mael? You okay?"

"That's not possible. How could he love me? Why *would* he?" Mael's thoughts were outracing his own ability to process them. Given that Cian had said that to him the first time they were together, he tried to take in the ramifications. The restless agitation was akin to a caged tiger, heedless of the crunch of glass beneath his shoes. "Even *my* blood doesn't work that fast."

"Who loves—" Brandon's eyes widened. His next word was a breathless whisper. "Cian."

Mael stilled, and a dark gaze settled on Brandon. The young vampire froze, and he began backing away toward the door. Mael realized from the way Brandon stared at him that he was probably scaring him. He held his hand out. "Please, Brandon. I don't want to frighten you away."

"I'm afraid I might have said too much," Brandon said quietly. He stopped his retreat and took Mael's hand.

Mael tugged Brandon gently toward him. Although he was distracted, he still smiled warmly at the young vampire. "He's been trying to tell me over and over again. I think he's done everything but hit me upside the head with it."

Laughing, Brandon looked up to meet his gaze. "He does, you know."

"I had thought it was because my blood bound him to me." He felt the spark of confusion, couldn't see any reason for Cian to love him. "I am nothing to love."

Brandon rolled his eyes, but his smile remained. "You don't give yourself enough credit, Mael. Cian loves you. Accept it for what it is. It's not often someone loves us despite our faults and vices."

"And I'm starting to think you are both giving me too much credit." Mael's hand tightened on Brandon's. "You are right, it doesn't happen often. Still, for me, it is a very hard thing to take in. You sound like you might have a touch too much experience."

Brandon turned his head away, but not before Mael saw the tears forming in his eyes. When the young vampire spoke, his voice was wavered. "I was kicked out of my house by my father when I was fifteen. He found out I liked guys, and he was afraid that I would do something with my brother. I haven't seen or heard from anyone in my family in seven years. Cian was the first person to show me real kindness."

Mael sighed heavily. It was a story he'd heard too many times in his years. He gently grasped Brandon's chin, drawing his face back to look at him. The words and tone he used were as gentle as the brush of his thumb, caressing the line of Brandon's jaw. "Your father was an ass for not wanting a son like you. Cian was the first, but he won't be the last."

"Thank you," Brandon whispered. "Don't let him go, Mael."

"I can't let him go." The admission came out in a soft whisper. "Nor am I going to let you go. You're stuck with a stubborn, pig-headed prince looking out for you now. You realize that, don't you?"

"Cian's made that same distinction about you a few times. Do you love him?"

"I don't know. I don't even know if I'm capable of that."

"On another note, I think I've made my decision finally on a Father. I just don't know if he's available. If he's not, it's okay."

"There's no hurry for you to decide, but I would like to know who you are thinking of," Mael said. He planned on grilling any prospective choices, just to make certain that Brandon would be taken care of properly.

"Cornelius," Brandon said tentatively. "If that isn't possible, it's okay. I understand."

Mael blinked in surprise. "Cornelius? You mean my magician?"

"I've been sitting in the workroom and helping him for a while." Brandon looked nervous for a brief moment before continuing. "I've never met anyone like him. It feels like I've finally found where I belong when I'm in the workroom with him. I've never had a friend like him before."

Mael was confused. Normally, Cornelius had his nose buried in a book and rarely paid attention to anything or anyone outside of that. "There's nothing to disqualify him from being your Father, Brandon, but he does tend not to pay attention to much outside of his magic."

"He pays attention to me. We love talking to each other. It's almost like we've been friends for years." Brandon shrugged. "Besides, when we're working, it's not unusual for both of us to get lost in whatever we're doing. I do it, too."

"I didn't realize you had an interest in magic as well. I suppose it explains the attachment. Though Cornelius does have a serious tendency to get lost in his work. That said, I see no reason why he can't stand as your Father, if that's what you want, and he agrees to it."

"I've always loved science, alchemy, and the like. I've wanted to get into magic, but never met anyone I got along well enough with to even think about trying it. In all honesty, Mael, he and I aren't much different from each other."

"I'm glad you've found someone who fits so well with you. Though I'm surprised it's Cornelius. Still, I'll go ahead and let you discuss everything with him, unless you already have."

Brandon shook his head. "Not yet. I wanted to talk to you first."

"Ah, then I won't offer him my congratulations until after you've spoken with him."

Brandon set his books down and put his arms around Mael, hugging him tight. "Thank you."

Mael returned the hug. "I take it I have a budding magician on my hands. I really hope you won't be as much of a trial as Cornelius."

The young vampire pulled away with a laugh and gathered his books. "I hope I become as good as he is," he said with a hopeful grin. "And I promise I won't drive you nuts."

Mael ruffled Brandon's hair affectionately. "I don't think you will. I'm more likely to think everybody will drive you nuts with all the books you'll be reading."

"Are you kidding? I'd die if I didn't have books!"

"You are going to fit right in."

"I already do," Brandon said as he started out the door. "Oh, and Mael, if you ever want to give Cian any sort of gift, give him a bottle of red wine." With that, he walked out the door, closing it behind him.

Mael's gaze followed Brandon, wondering about that remark. He'd received more than one shock during their conversation, yet he had little time to dwell on anything. A whisper of words formed in his mind, letting him know the sword was ready for him. He made his way to Cornelius' third-floor workroom. Without even bothering to knock, he opened the door and stepped inside.

"I'm just finishing up, Mael."

The magician gave him a quick smile before returning to the bowl in front of him. He took a pinch of the powder and sprinkled it over the material covering the sword. His lips moved in a silent chant as he passed his hand slowly over it. Mael watched him as he walked toward the table. The velvet took on an iridescent sheen, sparkling brightly in the light before it slowly faded.

"There, all done now. You can have it back." Cornelius started to clean the mess on his table. "The sword will automatically return here after it's used. I'll make sure Cian gets it back if anything happens to you."

Mael rested his hand on his magician's shoulder in silent gratitude. Turning to face him, Cornelius took one look at his face and smiled.

"None of that, Mael. Everything will be fine."

"Cornelius, if it isn't, make sure Cian gets that sword back. Then take Brandon and get the hell out of here." If he died, London would become hell on earth. Not even Selena would be able to fully control the others who would descend on the city to fight for a suddenly empty throne.

"I will, I promise, but I'm not going to need to." Cornelius seemed far more confident about things than Mael did.

Mael picked up the sword. As he left the room, he forced himself to settle the frenetic tenor of his thoughts. It wouldn't do him any good to face Selena in this state.

* * *

As he entered Selena's throne room, the weight of the sword was a reassurance to Mael. With a wave of her hand, Selena dismissed everyone. Stilling in front of the dais, Mael bowed to her.

"That seems to be larger than what I am expecting, Mael. Please don't tell me you weren't successful in getting what I wanted."

"It is no more than a gift until I have what you want, Selena."

"Set it on the table."

She seemed bored, eyeing him as he set the bundle down. He untied the silver cord and brushed back the velvet to reveal the sword. Its highly polished steel blade reflected the light of the chandelier above. Unlike most swords, it had two sharp points on each side near the hilt, pointing downward. The finely wrought gold hilt included, at midpoint, a pair of half-spread wings with a single blue diamond the size of Mael's thumb embedded between them.

The impressive sight was fit for an angel. Aware he couldn't touch it, Mael very carefully drew back his hands and straightened.

Selena's gaze flicked over it. "Very pretty." She dismissed it, looking back over at him.

When Mael stepped back, a pair of gold cuffs appeared on his wrists and ankles, embedding into his skin. The chains attached to them winked into sight before their tug at his arms forced him to raise them above his head. He felt the rapidly spreading taint of the gold as it invaded his body, setting his blood on fire, but he refused to give her the satisfaction of hearing his pain. Two of her servants slipped around from the back of her throne. They moved toward him and cut off his clothes, stripping them from his body. Stepping back once they were done, the two servants silently disappeared back behind the throne.

"Yes, my pet, I know your little secret," Selena purred. "Your allergy is convenient. You are lucky it will only weaken you; that's not the way I want to see you die. I do appreciate your little gift, though, and I will be using it soon on you."

Selena slowly stood from her throne and approached him. Several cuts sliced across his body without her touching him, an ability she shared with her Father, Memnet. As each cut healed itself, two more took its place. She slowly circled Mael, watching her handiwork as the small seeps of blood became trickles from the growing number of cuts appearing all over him.

"The Romanorum will have your head for this, Selena." The burn of the poisonous gold flooded Mael's system, increasing the stinging pain of the cuts tenfold. He could escape this if he wanted to, but he already realized it would be the price he paid, waiting for her to touch the sword. His body tried to heal each wound as it formed. It was a battle, however, that he was rapidly losing; he couldn't keep up. Selena's hand drifted along his chest, her fingers stained with his blood.

"No, they won't, dearest Mael. You are the one in league with the sorcerer, not I. And you are the one behind this terrible rash of rogues. After I've taken care of you, I will deal with the sorcerer." Shaking her head in mock sadness, Selena continued. "Where did I go wrong with you?"

"You lie! The sorcerer has no nothing to do with this! Leave him be, Selena." His words were heated as fear rose up sharply in him. Even after he deliberately stopped the healing nature of his own body, new cuts continuously formed. The blood dripping from him became a pool at his feet. He could feel himself weakening.

"It doesn't matter. I will have your full confession for the Romanorum anyway." Pausing, she eyed him, and her fingers traced through the blood before lowering to his cock. "You are trying to protect the sorcerer. That surprises me. You aren't normally so concerned about others when your own neck is in the noose."

A jolt of forced pleasure rushed through the pain, causing him to cry out.

Her soft laughter was a throaty purr. "I've always loved your responses, Mael. It really is a pity that I have to kill you. I suppose the least I can do is let you have some pleasure before you're truly dead. Perhaps I will do the same for the sorcerer when his time comes."

Mael growled sharply at her, staring back at her with a mix of rage and fear.

"You are already possessively jealous of Cian Carmichael and afraid for him as well. How amusingly delicious, my pet."

Mael tried to get away from her, but the next burst of sensation that rode him caused his hips to jerk into her hand. His head tipped back as he cried out again with the agonizing pain ravaging his body and the almost mind-blowing pleasure. When the sound faded, he struggled against his bonds, trying to get to her. He knew he had to kill her first; he couldn't let her touch Cian. There was no doubt in him that she would twist the sorcerer's soul, shattering the beautiful innocence. He cast a quick glance at the sword. Even knowing it would kill him, he measured the potential chance of being able to kill her first before the sword destroyed him as well.

Selena's nails ran over his thigh slowly. The sudden stabbing pain as she gouged into his skin, tearing it to ribbons, barely registered. It was the excruciating flood of power from the contact that made him scream. All thought scattered from his mind as it was enveloped in a sea of hellfire that left him in unending flames. He could feel it consuming him whole, unable to escape the hellish nightmare.

Chapter Twelve

Cian knew before the door ever opened that some sort of news had reached Lee. Lee glared at him. Cian walked past him, and Lee closed the door.

"We need to talk."

Lee crossed his arms angrily, and the feathers on his wings bristled. "Damn right we do." He twisted around and headed for the kitchen, then jerked a bottle of beer from the refrigerator and opened it. Cian knew he had heard something; Lee never drank unless he was upset.

Cian sighed and leaned up against the wall. "What have you heard?"

Lee's icy glare didn't leave Cian as he took another drink. "Rachel's missing. I know your prince has something to do with it."

"There is a lot you didn't know about Rachel, Lee. She was working against Mael Black, working with the rogues. She was cheating on you with Iverson."

"What?" The pain in Lee's voice was tangible.

"She was overheard by one of Mael's spies in Iverson's court. She had been sleeping with Iverson for some time, I fear. She was a vital link in the plot to kill Mael." Cian took a deep breath. "And for that she was taken directly to him. Her sentence was death, which Prince Black carried out himself."

Cian had no time to duck. The bottle shattered on the wall by his head, raining green shards of glass down on him. He moved quickly out of the way before Lee could reach him. Lee's fist connected with the wall, shaking it and probably the entire building on its foundation.

"Lee, stop!" Cian ducked another swing and caught Lee's arm. His brother's face was wet with tears. "Lee! She was plotting to have me killed as well!" That seemed to hit a nerve. Lee's arm went limp, and Cian released him cautiously.

Lee sank to his knees on the floor. "Why? Why her?"

Cian knelt down and brushed Lee's blond hair from his face. "I'm sorry."

"Just go," Lee muttered. "Please, just go, Cian. I'll talk to you later."

Cian nodded and kissed Lee's forehead softly before standing. He looked back at Lee one last time before walking out, closing the door behind him. As he stepped outside into the cooling night air, he had one thing on his mind. Iverson had become enough of a thorn in everyone's side and one that had to be dealt with accordingly. With that single thought, he waited and watched as groups of people walked by. After nearly two hours he began to wonder if the vampires of the city had all simply vanished, but then a group of five men caught his eye. He trailed them in silence, keeping a safe distance to avoid being detected but close enough to catch snippets of their conversations. Before long, he knew he had his man.

Iverson was flanked by several others, all of them rogues. Cian's brow furrowed in thought. This was going to take some strategy on his part to avoid getting himself into more than he could handle. While he couldn't be killed by ordinary means, he could be overwhelmed. As he watched from the shadows, a familiar presence made itself known. He turned his head the slightest bit and peered down at Brandon.

"What are you doing here?"

Brandon looked up at him. "I was hoping to talk to you, but it looks like you're busy." He nodded to the group of rogues that had turned down another street but still remained in sight.

"Yes, I am. What did you want to talk about?"

"Cornelius."

The mention of Mael's court mage surprised Cian, and he looked down at Brandon. The look on the young vampire's face said enough. "Oh, no," Cian said with a groan. "You realize Mael isn't going to take too kindly to it. He's incredibly protective of you, Brandon."

"So are you."

Cian nodded. "I'm not the Prince of London."

"But you're in love with him," Brandon countered.

Cian shot a look down at him. "That has nothing to do with it." He snapped his attention back to the rogues. The streets were blessedly empty, free from mortals and vampires alike, save for the group he was watching. "Stay here."

He left before Brandon could say anything in protest and moved through the shadows. There were two on either side of Iverson. They were within sight of Mael's palace, a fact that didn't settle well with Cian in the least. He stepped out into the street in front of them, his wings stretching out to their full span of nearly twice his height. The looks on the rogues' faces were a combination of confusion and rage.

"What the fuck is that?" one of the rogues said as they all pulled knives. They began to advance on Cian.

"No idea, but I bet he bleeds." Another rogue twirled his knife in his fingers, reminding Cian of Ashton Carter for a brief moment.

Only when they moved within a few yards of Cian did recognition show on Iverson's face. The prince sneered as he started toward Cian. Cian's feathers bristled, but he did not move.

"Well, well," Iverson said. "If it isn't the infamous hunter. And wings? Now that's an interesting touch. What are you supposed to be? Some queer-as-fuck angel or something?"

Cian raised his right hand, and a ball of swirling blue fire grew in his palm. "Something like that."

He watched as the fear crossed over the faces of the rogues behind Iverson. The prince himself seemed unmoved. Cian brought his hand to his lips and blew. The fire fanned out, circling him and the rogues. The others tried to retreat, but when they neared the flames, one of them shrieked. The vampire slapped his leg to put out the fire, but the flames spread, quickly engulfing his body. Iverson looked back with only mild interest before turning back to Cian.

"Impressive, sorcerer."

Cian moved forward, and the fire began to close in around them. The closer he got to the prince, the tighter the circle of fire drew in. The others looked around nervously, realizing escape was no longer an option. Terror painted the faces of two more as flames crawled over their bodies.

Iverson glanced at them and then back at Cian. "You do enjoy your work, don't you?"

The last rogue tried to run through the ring of fire but didn't make it far beyond the perimeter before the ashes drifted to the street. Iverson finally snapped. He growled and hurled himself at Cian. Cian dodged the knife aimed at his chest and spun around, a new fire cradled between his palms.

"For your crimes against humanity," he said with an even, authoritative calm, "for your plot to assassinate Mael Black, Prince of London..." The flame between his hands grew and pulsed. "...And for the unlawful creation of rogue vampires, you have been sentenced to death."

Before Iverson had a chance to react, Cian hurled the fire toward him. The prince's eyes widened in fear for only a brief moment before the flames made contact with his flesh. Cian stepped up to him, coaxing the fires to kill him slowly. He reached out and gripped Iverson's throat. He pulled his knife from his belt and drew it across the prince's neck.

"And that is for breaking my brother's heart."

The fire hissed as it made contact with the prince's blood. Seconds later, the Prince of Bristol was nothing more than a pile of smoldering ashes at Cian's feet. He looked up toward Mael's palace. There was only one left to deal with: Selena. A flicker of thought, of his conversation with Michael, came back to him. With a crushing feeling, Cian realized he hadn't told Mael about the sword's ability to destroy a vampire. Without wasting a single moment, he started for the palace, his heart in his throat.

Once he reached the front door, Cian forced himself to calm down and ring the doorbell, instead of pounding on the door as he wanted to. He rang the bell again and was nearly to the point of pacing when the door opened. The servant on the other side bowed his head.

"May I help you, Master Carmichael?"

"I must speak with Prince Black."

"I'm sorry, but he's not here right now. His secretary is here, however, if you would like to speak with him."

"What about the court mage?"

"He is up in his workroom," the servant said as he stepped to the side, allowing Cian to enter. "If you'd like to follow me, I'll take you to him."

"Thank you."

The door closed quietly behind him before the servant turned to lead the way up the stairs. In silence, they went up to the third floor, then branched off down one of the hallways. As they approached Cornelius' workroom, the servant gestured toward the door before he turned on his heel, heading back the way they came. Cian knocked none-too-calmly on the door, his heart racing. The door opened a few seconds later.

Cornelius was seated at his workbench, and all of a sudden he bellowed, "Aristotle, if I don't get that bottle back, I'll stuff you in a bottle of cheap French perfume! You hear me?"

Cian walked in and closed the door behind him, giving them privacy. The shadow form of a man deliberately whizzed over Cornelius' head, seeming to egg Cornelius on. A dark hand ruffled the mage's hair, causing his curls to bounce.

"Dammit, Aristotle, stop it," Cornelius muttered gruffly at the damn spirit. As he turned his head, he said, "Oh, hello there, Cian."

Cian stood stock still for a moment, unsure if what he was seeing was real. "I've seen many things in my lifetime, but what exactly is he?" He nodded toward the shadowed form.

"Who? Aristotle? He's the spirit of my crystal ball. And a damn sorry excuse for one, let me tell you. He thinks he's the real Aristotle. You know, the philosopher. Most delusional spirit, I've ever met."

"Where is Mael?"

Cornelius blinked at Cian over the rim of his spectacles. "Mael left for Selena's. To kill her, you know."

Cian stepped back, his eyes widening. "Fuck."

"Such language. And from an angel, no less." Cornelius made a tsking sound at Cian, taking him to task.

Cian scowled. "How do I get there?"

One of the mage's brows rose nearly above his hairline. "Two miles south. Right straight down the road from here. Whatever is your problem, Cian?"

"I gave him the Sword of Michael, but I hadn't thought he'd try to use it himself. I failed to mention that one touch would kill a vampire, good or evil."

"I know that, Cian, though it's not referred to in the book." Cornelius shrugged slightly, looking back at his work.

Cian couldn't believe what he was seeing or hearing. The mage didn't seem to care either way.

"I don't know if he knows that, though," Cornelius continued. "I really never expected him to get it anyway. You might want to go tell him."

"Yeah," Cian said with a distinct touch of sarcasm. Damnable mage. "Thank you." He opened the door and started down the hallway, letting the door close behind him.

Once outside, he took to the air. Several minutes later, Cian was pounding on the front door of Selena's palace. When a servant opened it, Cian opened his mouth to speak, but then a shrill cry of pain came from within. Cian knew that voice like no other. For the span of several seconds, he was frozen in place as the cry echoed through the palace. He burst through the doorway, nearly knocking the servant to the ground.

He followed the sound of Mael's tortured cries until he found the door he was looking for. He kicked it open, and the sight that greeted him drove him to rage. His wings unfurled behind him. His gaze shifted from the woman to Mael, and his anger flared, causing his wings to curl downward in a position to attack.

Selena whirled around, and an amused smile curved her red lips. Mael, on the other hand, hung from the golden chains that kept him suspended. Cian tore his gaze from Mael's slumped form to lock onto Selena.

"Release him." A fire erupted around his body, the blue and white flames licking at his clothing but catching nothing on fire.

"Why ever would I do that when he is so much fun?" Her hand brushed slowly over Mael's cock, sending another shock of pleasure with its underlying pain. The prince's body shuddered as another sharp cry was torn from him. Selena turned her head toward Cian, smirking faintly. She withdrew her hand and brought it to her lips to lick delicately at the blood. "Care to join me?"

The fire flared around Cian, and he let out a deafening roar. He beat his wings furiously, fanning the flames. He raised his hands, and a ball of blue fire and swirling smoke formed between them. "He's mine," he growled as he hurled the flaming ball at Selena.

In one split second, it seemed as if Selena was at Mael's side, but in less than a blink of an eye, she sidestepped the flaming ball. She reappeared directly in front of the prince. "Do be careful, Cian Carmichael, lest your next blast hit the wrong target." Her voice had an almost sing-song quality to it as she mocked Cian.

Mael managed to lift his head, and it seemed as if he recognized Cian's voice but couldn't focus on him.

Cian glared at her, never taking his eyes off of her or Mael. While his fire might not have had much effect, he had other means at his disposal. He closed his eyes for the briefest second, then opened them. His dark gaze turned brilliant white, and he advanced on Selena, chanting the names of God with force. This time when Selena opened her mouth, a bizarre, keening wail came from her. At the same moment, three distinct voices spoke to Cian.

"Do not waste your time, sorcerer."

"What cannot hear you, cannot obey."

"You will lose your love. Forever banished from you by his own will."

Cian shook his head, forcing the whispers from his mind. His chanting faltered and stopped altogether as Mael suddenly disappeared, his body becoming nothing but shadows. The insubstantial shape slipped from its bonds to the floor.

"No," Cian whispered breathlessly.

Selena smiled almost sweetly at him as she took a step toward him. The triumph in her eyes mocked him. "Such a beautiful creature, you are." As she stepped to his side, her fingers very slowly caressed his wing before she deliberately plucked one of its feathers. Cian hissed in pain. "Would you like a last taste of your lover, Cian?"

The flames erupted around Cian and engulfed Selena, but none could find purchase on the marble texture her skin had taken on. Cian's eyes widened in shock, and his pulse began to race. From the white flow of her hair, to the entire white of her eyes, and even to her dress, Selena seemed to be made from marble itself. The only color to her was the blue feather in her hand as she stepped back from him. She lifted the feather and brushed it slowly across her lips, her colorless gaze holding his with an amused look. As she moved, it was like a statue given life for a brief moment before it slowly faded from her skin.

"If we're done with the foreplay now, why don't you and I talk?" The feather in her hand ran slowly down the front of Cian's shirt as she tilted her face upward, smiling at him.

"What do you want?"

"So nice of you to realize you do have something I want, Cian. I want the Eye of Baal. It's been terribly bothersome getting it, but I really do want it." The feather continued its slow drift back and forth across his chest.

Cian closed his eyes as the combination of his name and the feather slipped through him like wayward caresses. "And what makes you think I have it?" he asked, his breathlessness betraying him.

"I really hope you're not going to be a bothersome creature and try to deny that you *do* have it. I can taste your attempt at a lie." Her hand rested against his chest, replacing the feather.

A distinct tingling sensation fluttered through Cian at her touch. His breath left him, and his heart skipped a beat. "You will not have the Eye."

Mock sadness colored her voice. "That is not what I wanted to hear, my lovely angel."

Selena lifted her hand to his face to touch him, and a painful rush of electric fire raced through his body. Before Cian could utter a word, he fell to knees, a strangled cry escaping him. His body shook as he attempted to remain at least on his hands and knees.

"I really hate to be disappointed. Especially since I believe you and I could work so very well together."

Cian rocked back on his knees and glared up at her. "What makes you think I would work with you?"

"You are disappointing me, Cian. Such a shame really."

Cian stood, straightening himself to full height. He reached out, cupping her delicate face with his hands as he chanted the names of God in rapid succession. His body glowed for the briefest second before the divine light flooded through Selena's body. The swift current caused her to shudder with the heat. She stumbled back and shook her head to clear its effects.

"Can we try that again without the light? Never mind, it would do me no good anyway."

When he realized pain was her game, Cian decided to try a different approach. He moved slowly toward Selena, reaching out to cup the back of her neck. Before she could react, he pulled her swiftly to him, sliding his tongue into her mouth and projecting the intensity of his pleasure with Mael into his kiss. Selena's mouth opened in protest, but she was silenced by the invasion. Her body shuddered with pleasure as her arms quickly snaked around his neck for support. The intensity buckled her knees with something he knew she could barely take in.

He slid a hand around her waist and jerked her hard against him as he conjured up images of Mael stroking his cock. His own cock hardened in response to his fantasies, and he ground his hips against Selena, growling into her mouth. Her hands slid back down and pushed sharply at his chest. She stumbled back from him, hissing at him in warning. A mixture of wariness and something indefinable shone in her eyes. Cian regained his footing and narrowed his gaze, waiting for another opportunity. He watched her closely, waiting to see what her next move would be.

"You would mock me, angel. Pleasure isn't mine to feel; it never has been." Fear and anger were visible in her eyes as she backed away from him.

Cian began to advance once more, slowly, as he watched her. He knew enough now not to assume she was cowed. "It's a shame."

In her anger, the temperature of the room began to drop rapidly, surrounding them in its chill. A slow, unpleasant smile curled the corner of her lips. "Yes, do come closer, Cian."

Cian stopped abruptly, a chill rushing through him. His wings enfolded his body, shielding him from the cold. Yet it still seeped through, settling inside him somehow. He shook his head, forcing himself to see Mael before him. It was enough to warm him, yet his wings remained curled.

"Or don't come closer. It doesn't matter." She suddenly disappeared from his view. Seconds later, her lengthened talons, hard as steel, slashed across one of his wings before she jumped back away from him.

Cian whirled around, wincing at the stinging bolt of pain. He rushed at her and gripped her head, pressing his lips to her forehead. A brilliant white light surrounded her body and pulsed through her. She completely stiffened as the powerful sense of tranquility filled her. She cried out softly as blood tears spilled over her cheeks.

Completely dazed, she stared at him. In that moment, Cian felt the pain well up inside both of them. He felt something within her reach out, grasping at the salvation he presented. Yet just as it had appeared, it began to retreat, its brilliance fading within the blackness of her soul. His mind cried out, struggling to stop her from retreating, but the words refused to fall from his lips. He smoothed his thumb across her porcelain-delicate cheek, the paleness shining through the red of her tears. As he backed away, he realized his own cheeks are wet.

"I cannot help you now," he whispered.

The pool of darkness on the floor slowly took shape, and Mael's naked body appeared on hands and knees. "Cian...the sword...it will kill her..." He struggled to stand and took several swaying steps toward Selena's throne, reaching for the sword.

Cian's gaze snapped in Mael's direction, and his heart nearly stopped. "Mael! Stop!"

Selena's gaze darted rapidly between Cian and Mael. Fear of dying in her damned state seemed to overcome her and was visible in the twist of her features. Her terror left an acrid scent in her wake as a sudden burst of energy sent her racing in a blur to reach the sword before Mael could. She grabbed it, clutching it against her chest as she backed away from them and into the wall behind her.

Cian rushed to catch Mael before the prince could fall, and his gaze widened as Selena stood, the Sword of Michael held tightly in her hands. Her hands began to lose their color, becoming an ashen gray. It quickly spread to cover her entire body, leaving her frozen and silent, staring at them with wide eyes before the dust dissolved. The sound of the sword clattering to the ground echoed through the room.

Cian's heartbeat slowed down. He couldn't save her. He *didn't* save her. The sharp pain of regret began to settle within him. Mael went limp in his arms, and Cian's wings folded protectively around them. He cradled Mael, his tears wetting the prince's hair. He drew his knife and made a cut in his throat, then pressed Mael to it, praying he had the strength to feed.

"Please don't leave me." Cian closed his eyes and began to chant, a soothing rhythm designed to aid healing. He knew it would take time. "I'll wait forever for you, my love."

The coldness of Mael's body was shocking, but Cian forced his fears from his mind, concentrating on his continued whispers and prayers. He stood up slowly, gently cradling Mael's body. As soon as they were out of the palace, his wings stretched out, and he took to the air, Mael's body held tightly to his. He prayed Mael's mage could help.

Knowing the prince's palace was the last place they could go right now, Cian descended to a dark street and opened a portal. He stepped through and into his tower. He placed Mael's body on the bed and brushed his fingers over the prince's face. He wanted nothing more than to stay with him, but he had no idea how to heal the damage. He leaned forward and kissed Mael's forehead softly before standing once more. He quickly changed his clothes and washed Mael's blood from his face and hands before stepping through another portal. As he stepped back out, he was outside the mage's door. He forced himself to calm down enough to knock. The door opened, and Cornelius turned around. The deep concern etched on his features did not lessen when he saw that Cian was alone.

"Get in here quickly and shut the door."

Cian walked in and closed the door behind him. "I need you. Mael needs your help, Cornelius."

The mage hurried toward his workbench. "I'm assuming so since you are here and he's not. I've already prepared for that. At least I know he's not dead." He began placing several capped vials into a small velvet bag.

"He's not dead, but I don't know for how much longer. I left him somewhere safe to come find you."

"If he's not dead now, then he won't die. How badly was he damaged? The worse it was, the longer it will take him to heal."

"When I got to Selena's, he was bound in gold chains, with cuts all over his body. He was standing in a pool of his own blood. Once Selena was gone, I tried to get him to drink. Although there was a minute reaction, it wasn't enough. He's been unconscious since. He's in my tower, where no others can find him."

Cornelius stared in shock at Cian. The furrow between his eyebrows deepened in agitation. "Gold, you say? Damn, that will make it more difficult." Quickly grabbing one of the small jars on another shelf, he shoved it into the bag as well. He picked up the velvet bag and handed it to Cian. "These are vials of my blood. You're going to need them. In fact, you may have to come and visit me here to be fed." He paused for a moment, a serious expression on his face. "He can't feed you right now, and you're going to have to feed him as much as you can. That small jar should help. It contains a salve you can rub on his lips. That'll get him to feed."

Cian took the bag and gave the mage a questioning look. "Why gold?

"He's allergic to it. It acts like a poison in his system. How she knew to use it on him, I'll never know. I did know that either you would show up needing help or he would. Either way, I was prepared. Just not for the gold part. Damn." There was a frenetic energy to Cornelius as he grabbed a nearby bowl, dragging it closer to him. He moved slowly down the table, reaching up to pluck several ingredients from the shelf. "He needs something to counteract that, or his body will only waste energy trying to heal."

Cian's heart nearly stopped, and he closed his eyes, forcing the thought of losing Mael out of his mind. "What do I need to do, Cornelius? I'm an angel, not a vampire. I know nothing about the biology of a vampire."

As he quickly measured and mixed the necessary ingredients, the mage said, "What you need to do is make sure you keep yourself strong enough to feed him. Plenty of juice, particularly orange juice, will be good for you. Whenever you are hungry, drink one of those vials. You're going to have feed him every night, Cian, but you're not going to be able to feed from him. He needs to rebuild his own blood supply too much." Expert movements mashed the mess in the bowl into a paste before Cornelius grabbed a small blue jar above his head. When he opened it, he used a spoon to scrape the paste from the bowl, putting it into the jar.

"I understand." Cian watched Cornelius intently. "Will there be any lasting effects of the gold after the poison has been countered?"

Once he was done, Cornelius sealed the jar and handed it to Cian. "Not once the poison is cleansed from him. Use this once a night for the next week. Just rub a small amount into his skin. His body will absorb it, and it'll slow the poison in him and get rid of it."

Cian took the jar. "Is there anything else I should know?"

Cornelius turned a piercing green gaze on him. "You're in for a rough time. It wouldn't hurt if you direct a few prayers to you know who."

"I'm sure Michael is getting tired of hearing me." Cian opened a portal in the middle of Cornelius' workroom. "If I need you, I'll be back."

"Don't mix up the salves. The blue jar is for his skin, and the red one is for his lips. Confuse them, and you'll undo all my hard work."

"You underestimate me, sorcerer," Cian called back as the portal closed behind him.

Once back in the warmth of his chambers, Cian set the velvet bag Cornelius had given him on the table and picked up a bowl of warm water. As he passed by the mantle, he grabbed a handful of linen rags and sat down on the edge of the bed. He set the bowl and rags down on the bedside table and leaned over, pressing his lips to Mael's. There was no response, and in truth, he hadn't expected one. As he pulled away slowly, a tear slipped down his cheek to pool between Mael's lips. Cian turned away, swallowing the crushing pain before it could overwhelm him.

He wet a rag in the water and began to clean the dried blood from Mael's body. He followed every line, every muscle, remembering the effect his touch had on the prince. He would give up eternity just to see Mael's smile. The prince's skin was cool, despite the warmth of the water, but Cian held onto Cornelius' words.

"If he is not already dead, then he will not die."

It didn't make much sense to Cian, but he trusted the mage. He had to; Mael was his life.

When all the blood had been washed away, Cian went back to the table to get both jars of salve. He returned to Mael's side and opened the blue jar. The scent of violets wafted up around him, curling around his senses and giving him an odd sense of calm...and hope. He slid his fingers through the paste and began rubbing it onto Mael's chest.

He massaged the salve into his prince's skin and prayed it would work. He recapped the jar and wiped his hands off. Then he stretched out on the bed and picked up the red jar.

After rubbing the oily substance on Mael's lips, he used his knife to make an inch-long cut on his wrist. He pressed it to Mael's lips and pulled the vampire's body close, trying to ignore the coldness of his lover's flesh and the purely mechanical sucking at his wrist. He closed his eyes, praying once more to help them get through this.

* * *

When next he awoke, Cian realized the entire day had passed, and night was beginning to fall once more. He looked over at Mael, noting the line of dried blood that ran down Mael's face to disappear under his neck. Cian got out of bed and stretched, a bit disoriented at having slept the entire day away. He picked up a rag and wet it, wiping away the line of blood on Mael's face and neck. When he sat back, he realized it might be quite a while before he ever saw another smile.

Time seemed to go by in a blur to Cian, and by the start of the third day, he was beyond exhausted. He found that he couldn't sleep, even with Mael in his arms. It wasn't the chill of Mael's flesh but the uncertainty of what would happen when Mael did recover. And then he had the fight itself to reflect on.

Selena's death had been inevitable, yet Cian felt as if he'd failed somehow. Something within Selena — something within the blackness of her soul — reached out to him, calling desperately for help, to save her from the darkness. But before Cian had been able to react, the tiny spark of light within her began to fade, retreating out of his reach. He sat on the edge of the bed and cradled his head in his hands. He could have saved her. He *should* have saved her.

As he sat there, brooding about his failure, Cian felt the bed move. Or, more specifically, he felt Mael move. He jumped up and turned around, daring to smile in hopes of seeing his lover's eyes focus on him. Yet Mael's eyes were closed, and a small bead of blood slowly appeared on his forehead. As Cian moved closer to wipe it away, Mael moved again. Cian froze.

Mael's body began to shake as if he were having a seizure. A blood sweat broke out over his skin, turning his pale flesh a dark red as the blood began to thin out. Then the red became black, and Cian backed away in horror as the unmistakable smell of rot permeated the area. He bumped into one of his tables and stood in place as Mael began to thrash around on the bed. Cornelius had not told him about this.

By midday, Mael's thrashing had become worse, and Cian was forced to tie him to the bed. He stepped back when he was done and looked over Mael's body as it twisted and pulled against the binds holding his wrists and ankles with every violent spasm. The bed was covered in blood and a thick black substance, and the stench in the room was nauseating. He had to see Cornelius; this couldn't possibly be right.

Chapter Thirteen

"Due to injuries incurred during a fight with Selena, our second formula Romanorum leader, Prince Mael Black, is unable to hold court sessions. While the injuries have not proven to be fatal, he will be away from the court for a number of days. As far as I am aware, Selena herself has been killed. I have already informed Diocourides of the events and will publicly announce any messages from him. In the meantime, I will be maintaining Prince Black's throne until such time as he returns."

Brandon didn't need to hear anymore. He left the room, forcing all emotion from his face until his bedroom door closed behind him. He collapsed into a chair, not believing what the mage had said. When he heard a light knock at his door, he stood up. Before he could answer it, however, the door opened, and Cornelius stepped inside, shutting the door behind him.

Brandon turned and fell back onto his bed, covering his face with his arm. "Hi."

"There's no need for that. I realize what's bothering you."

Lowering his arm, Brandon took a deep breath. He rolled his head to the side to look at Cornelius. "Is he going to be okay?"

"Of course, he is. He just needs to remain safely away from here while he heals. If he was going to die, he'd be dead already." Cornelius' expression gave no hint of dismay or upset, and a look of understanding crossed over his face as he fixed his gaze on Brandon.

"Where is he?"

"With Cian. Unfortunately, Cian couldn't bring him back here. It would have caused a frenzy in some of our more ambitious fellow creatures."

"Then I know he's safe. How is Cian handling it? He loves Mael, you know."

Cornelius remained silent for a few minutes before answering him. "He was in rather a rush the last time I saw him, but I'm sure he'll hold up under it all."

"They're both strong. I know they'll be fine. It's just..." Brandon trailed off, taking a steadying breath.

A sympathetic light glimmered in the mage's eyes. "It's understandable, Brandon. It's hard when you're not there to know exactly what is happening. But there's absolutely no reason to worry. You know Mael is completely safe with Cian, and he'll return as soon as he can."

"I know. Cian will take good care of him."

"If I had not told the others right away, rumors would have started flying from Selena's palace. My mind was half dozen of the one and six of the other. Or however it is you say that." Cornelius chuckled, and Brandon eyed him, amused. He loved the way the mage laughed.

"I guess you're right. Rumors like that could turn bad quicker than you can blink."

"Oh, good heavens, yes. They would have had Mael dead most definitely, and we'd be facing a war for Mael's position. That doesn't even bear thinking on. Since he's fine, for the next few days, you will need to be with me during the court sessions. I have the annoying task of keeping this worthless lot in line, and you get to be right next to me. Won't that be fun?" He gave Brandon an almost gleeful grin that very distinctly said "no, you won't enjoy it either."

Brandon cocked an eyebrow. "A pleasure," he said with a smirk.

Cornelius chuckled. "Get used to it, my boy. The pleasures are never ending in this place." Reaching over, Cornelius ruffled his hand through Brandon's hair. "I'll have to show you the places to hide around here. You're going to need them as much as I do."

"Dare I ask what happens in the hiding places?"

"One hides, of course. What else would one do?"

Brandon struggled to suppress the grin and shrugged. "Whatever comes to mind."

The mage stared at him. "Work comes to mind. But then, most don't have my mind."

Settling back in his chair, Cornelius smiled. It was the kind of smile that lit up his face, bringing out the delicate lines and the deep green of his eyes. That smile twisted Brandon from the inside out every time he saw it. He bit the corner of his bottom lip.

"Did anyone tell you that you have a wonderful smile?"

Cornelius peered over the rim of his glasses. "No. Generally, they either want to fuck me or completely ignore me."

"Can't blame them."

Cornelius pursed his lips slightly before a smile edged at the corner of his mouth, threatening to come out. "They usually go away after a while, but a few can get quite devious. It's those who generally annoy the hell out of Mael."

"So, do you?" Brandon asked him.

"Do I what?" Cornelius adjusted his glasses.

"Do you fuck them?" Brandon asked him. He cocked his head to the side. "You know, you're really sexy with glasses on."

"Oh, um, yes, sometimes, but they never stay very long." Cornelius blinked almost owlishly at Brandon. The smile finally came out again. "Thank you," he said quietly, his voice softening over the words.

Brandon sat up and turned, sliding his legs off of the edge of the bed. He leaned back, propping himself up on his hands. "Why don't they stay very long?"

The mage's thoughtful look deepened. "I suppose because I don't give them the attention they think I should. I get lost in my books and my potions, and they simply go away."

"That's no reason for someone to walk away from something so good, and there's definitely nothing wrong with getting lost in books and potions. I lost a few boyfriends in school because they thought I spent too much time with my nose stuck in a book or tinkering with my chem set. They simply didn't understand."

"There is nothing wrong with walking away either. It can be the very devil putting up with me. But you're right: I've never met any who had the patience. Though some have tried."

Brandon leaned back on his elbows. "I still can't believe anyone would walk away, Cornelius."

Cornelius' gaze traveled slowly over Brandon. "After I've missed the twelfth dozen attempt to get my attention because I'm in the middle of an extremely important potion, a person can get the feeling my magic is more important to me than they are. Though it's not necessarily true, it's very hard to see that it's not for most."

Brandon smiled. "What would you do if someone came along who could understand?"

"What would I do?" After echoing the question, Cornelius stopped to think about it. "If I really wanted them to stay, I would hope, as I always do, that they would. But I would understand if they didn't."

* * *

Cornelius watched in silence as Brandon stood. The young vampire stepped in front of him, put his hands on each arm of the chair, and leaned down to press a soft kiss to Cornelius' lips. In the back of his mind, an alarm bell sounded.

Mael will fucking kill you if you touch this one.

There was a definite hesitation to the return pressure against the lips touching his. Cornelius reached up, catching his hands in Brandon's hair. Brandon opened his mouth and slid his tongue along Cornelius' bottom lip, and a soft groan caught in Cornelius' throat with the touch. His lips parted, giving Brandon access to him before he could even think about the action. Brandon took the invitation and released the chair, sliding his fingers through the curls of Cornelius' hair as he deepened the kiss. He moaned softly into Cornelius' mouth, and when he pulled away, he licked Cornelius' lips.

"God, I want you."

Cornelius slowly opened his eyes. "I think I need to get back to my potions, Brandon." He gave the young vampire a shrewd look. "And I think you need to come and help me, just to keep your mind busy."

Brandon grumbled. "Fine."

Cornelius went to the door, expecting to be followed. "Then come along and don't dawdle. We have work to do."

* * *

Cian stepped out of the portal and spotted the mage near a table. "What's wrong with him?"

Turning to him in surprise, Cornelius said, "What do you mean what's wrong with him?"

Brandon looked up from his work, watching both of them but saying nothing.

"My lover is thrashing around on my bed like he's possessed. My entire tower reeks of rot. What is wrong with him? Or did you fail to mention that little tidbit?"

The mage smiled, his expression taking on a gleefully pleased look. "That is excellent, most excellent." He paused for a moment, seeming to finally take notice of Cian's distress. "Well, I *did* tell you that you were in for a rough time. That's just the poison being forced from his body. As long as it doesn't stop too fast, he should be waking up soon."

"Excellent?" Cian said, shocked to the core at the mage's reaction. "You call watching the man you love bleed and convulse 'excellent?' What do you mean 'as long as it doesn't stop too fast'?"

Cornelius frowned heavily. "Well, where would you expect the poison to go? At least it isn't remaining in his body. And, yes, that is excellent news. If it stops too fast, it means some of the poison will be left."

Cian sighed and fell back against the nearest wall, closing his eyes. "I'm sorry," he said quietly. "I know it may appear as if I'm not grateful, but believe me, I am."

Cornelius' hands settled on Cian's shoulders. "Cian, I know it's hard for you, but everything is fine right now, no matter how it appears. I'm not sure how long it will take for the poison to completely leave him. It all depends on how long he was in contact with the gold. If it does stop too soon, you'll know when he doesn't wake up after at least an hour or two. Once it stops, just clean him up and pray for the best."

"I didn't expect this to be easy, not by a long shot. I just wasn't expecting to see him like that. I don't want to lose him, Cornelius. No matter how arrogant and hard-headed he is, I still love him." Cian pushed away from the wall and ran his fingers through his hair. "I'd give anything to just see him smile again."

"You're not going to lose him. If he doesn't wake up, come get me. It just means we have to begin the process again. He'll be annoying the hell out of us again sooner or later."

Cian smiled for the first time in a while. "Thank you." He opened a portal and paused before stepping through. "I couldn't get through this without your help."

The magician chuckled and waved him away. "Just go back to him and wait it out. If you need me, you know where to find me."

Cian nodded and entered the portal. Upon stepping back into the tower, he forced himself to remain calm. He went to the window and stared out, looking at the dark mountains beyond. During the day, he kept a blanket over the window to shield Mael from the sun, but now it was hanging from one corner, as downcast as his wings were in his current state.

An hour passed, and the convulsions stopped. Cian was exhausted, having had little sleep at all since this had started. He leaned his head up against the stone of the wall, completely lost in his thoughts. Another hour passed, barely noticed, before he heard a pained groan coming from the bed behind him. Cian spun around, his heart thundering in his chest.

"Mael." He hurried to the bed and smoothed his fingers over Mael's forehead as he sat down, brushing away a lock of dark hair. He stroked his thumb gently over Mael's lips.

Mael's gaze seemed to fix somewhere near his face, clearly trying to bring him into focus. "Cian?" Another moment later, the prince's eyes widened as he smiled slowly.

"I've tried to heal you. If it hadn't been for Cornelius, I'm afraid I wouldn't have known what to do."

"She's dead." The words were spoken with uncertainty. "The last thing I remember is seeing you and her, and I was..." Mael's words trailed off as if something else occurred to him. "You have wings."

Cian stood and stretched his wings out slowly. The silver sheen in their azure feathers shimmered in the light from the fire in the hearth.

"I thought I was dreaming." Mael's expression was one of confusion and awe. Lifting his hand, he reached out to Cian.

Cian smiled as he sat down again. Sliding his hand over Mael's, he laced their fingers together. He leaned down and pressed his lips to his prince's forehead in a kiss. Mael drew their joined hands to his chest.

"You are an angel in truth, not just one of my imagination."

"That I am, my prince," Cian whispered. He moved his lips down to brush them over Mael's in a soft, chaste kiss.

The blue eyes opened, and Cian caught Mael's gaze, holding it as Mael whispered, "You are *my* angel, Cian." No matter his state, the words had a possessive tenor.

"More than you realize, I think. *Rwy'n dy garu di*, my prince."

"I know your words, my beautiful angel. Even if I didn't understand before, I do now." Mael gently touched Cian's face, brushing back a stray strand of his hair.

Cian blinked as realization set in and opened his mouth but shut it once more. "I love you."

"I still don't know why you love you me, but I know that you do. Something in me wants that."

Cian kissed the prince's palm. "I don't know what I would have done had you..." He stopped, unable to finish. "I cannot live without you, Mael. As God is my witness, I cannot live without you."

"Nor can I live without you, Cian. I need your love and your heart. You took care of me, I know you did, and I can see what it did to you." A great deal of understanding shone in Mael's gaze as it traveled slowly over Cian's face.

Cian pulled Mael's hand to his lips and kissed his knuckles. "I've wanted to hear that," he said quietly. "I needed to hear that." He leaned over and brushed the backs of his fingers down Mael's cheek. "I would do it all over again, although I pray I never have to. To have you in my arms is worth any price."

"I don't understand why, Cian. I think you love too selflessly, but I can't question it. I don't want to lose it." Mael's gaze remained on Cian's face even as his face tipped slightly into the touch.

"I've been around for longer than I care to admit at times. I've never once found someone whose soul shines like yours. To me, you are a beacon in a tempest, Mael. I would walk through the fires of hell again if I had to, just to prove what you mean to me."

Mael shook his head. "You don't need to prove anything, Cian. I can see it in your eyes and feel it in your touch. You'll just have to forgive me for not understanding the why of it."

Cian laughed softly. "It's enough for me that you know. I'm glad I listened to Michael."

"It took Brandon translating those words for me. I think he tried to smack it upside my head as well." Mael eyed him for a moment. "Michael? What did he say?"

"I was so worried about how my love for you would be received, but Michael told me to not let you go. I guess you could say we have the blessing of Heaven."

A startled look passed over Mael's face. "I'm starting to wonder about everybody's sanity now." The soft sound of his laughter had a note of rich warmth in it that drenched over

Cian. "I need to feed, and after I rest, I want to show you how much I appreciate your love."

Cian could barely contain his joy at having his prince returned to him. He stood and undressed, then pulled the blanket back to lie down beside Mael. As he reached for his knife to make the cut in his wrist, Mael caught his hand. The prince's gaze never left his as Mael drew Cian's wrist to his lips. A swift pain accompanied the bite before the prince's mouth tightened on Cian's wrist.

Cian gasped and slid his other arm under Mael, pulling his prince close. The prince's dark gaze drank him in just as Mael's mouth drank in his blood. The vampire's hand remained curled on his arm as the other lifted to his face, a finger smoothing in a tender gesture along his lower lip.

When he pulled away from Cian's wrist, Mael whispered, "Stay beside me until I wake up again. I'll know you are with me. Please stay with me."

"I would never leave your side, love." Cian kissed Mael's fingertip and settled, pulling Mael to him as his right wing enveloped them.

As he closed his eyes, a more peaceful cast descended over Mael's features. A quiet tendril of thought connected them, sharing that peace, before the prince slipped downward into sleep.

Chapter Fourteen

For the last several nights, Cornelius hadn't been able to spend as much as he had liked in his workroom. Too much nonsense dealing with the rest of the court had seriously tried his patience. It had gotten to the point where he had to sneak around, hoping to get to his workroom before somebody stopped him. He'd also sent a note to Brandon, telling him to join him.

Every time the young vampire worked with him, Cornelius had gotten the feeling that Brandon greatly enjoyed the work. He really wanted to ask Mael what family Brandon was, and he couldn't help the feeling that Brandon might be Magi.

Hearing a light knock, he hurriedly moved to the door and opened it. Already knowing it was Brandon, he reached out and grabbed his arm. He pulled him inside before hastily shutting the door.

"Let's see how much time we can squeeze in tonight. Damn morons aren't leaving me alone at all." When he released Brandon's arm, Cornelius adjusted his spectacles as he went back to his stool in front of his table.

Brandon chuckled. "What are we working on tonight?"

"An old potion I am trying to tweak. The silly thing isn't worth much as it is. It only allows you to use the shadows for short distances." Cornelius was acutely aware of the close proximity between them. Aristotle, hovering above them, reached down to tug playfully at Brandon's hair.

Laughing, Brandon brushed the spirit away. When he turned back around, his lips came dangerously close to Cornelius'. The young vampire bit his lower lip before moving back just a few inches. "So...what is my job?"

Clearing his throat, Cornelius motioned further down the table. "You can get that beaker for me."

Brandon got the beaker and handed it to Cornelius. He leaned his hip against the table and crossed his arms, waiting for further instructions.

Cornelius took the beaker and set it on the table. "I also need you to grab a stool and sit down here next to me. Then carefully measure out each of the ingredients in the bottles next to the bowl. The list is there too; follow it carefully, please."

Pulling up a stool, Brandon straddled it, locking his feet around the legs. He pulled the bowl and the list over and began working, meticulously measuring out the ingredients to the exact amounts.

When Brandon finished each one, Cornelius added the dry ingredients to another bowl, and the liquids to the beaker. Before adding another liquid, he carefully swirled the beaker around, watching the changing colors. Reaching for one of the spoons, his hand accidentally brushed Brandon's. He turned his head and smiled, very much enjoying having a companion in his space.

Brandon returned the smile before turning his attention back to his measurements. "Have you ever had someone work with you before?"

"Sadly, no. Nobody else has ever shared my love of doing this. You're the first one who's shown any interest in being in here with me. I must admit: I am enjoying it. Maybe I can even talk you into letting me experiment on you."

"I'm grateful you allow me to help you. I love my books, but I'm more of a hands-on man."

As he glanced quickly over at Brandon, it was somewhat hard for Cornelius to miss the grin, and the double meaning of Brandon's words was very clear. "I see," he said quietly. He cleared his throat again, refocusing on the work at hand. "I'm grateful you're so willing to learn. Since I'm of the Magi family, normally I would only teach my own children. But I never had any, so I've worked alone."

"Understandable."

Cornelius opened his mouth to continue, but Brandon's lips were suddenly on his, tongue sliding into Cornelius' mouth in a slow, searing kiss. Whatever Cornelius was going to say was lost to that kiss, and he couldn't help but respond to it.

After a moment, Brandon pulled away slowly and released him. "You were going to say?"

Cornelius could only stare at him, trying to find his voice again. "I...um...normally, once a magician reaches his full potential and is accepted into a prince's court, it isn't allowed for more than one magician to remain in a court."

"You're rambling, Cornelius." Brandon chuckled and sat back on his stool. He locked his feet around the legs, which left his legs spread the slightest bit.

Cornelius' gaze roamed over Brandon and stilled at his crotch before flying back up to his eyes. He really wasn't used to having somebody flirt with him while he worked.

While he was very deft at avoiding it in any other situation, Brandon definitely unnerved him. "Yes, well, I do that."

Brandon licked his bottom lip. "I noticed. Your potion," he said with a sideways nod toward the table.

"Oh, yes, that." Blinking rapidly, Cornelius frowned before reaching for the next ingredient, only to discover it hadn't been measured out yet. "As soon as you get the Blessed Thistle for me, I'll add it."

Brandon measured it out and sat back.

"Last one that I need." Cornelius flashed a quick smile at Brandon before taking the last ingredient and adding it.

"What's next?"

Cornelius was too damn aware of Brandon beside him, and he shifted on the stool. The young man didn't have to do a damn thing. "Now I just have to carefully add the liquid extracts to the dry ingredients. Then I'll seal it in its own jar overnight. Hopefully, tomorrow night, the paste will be ready for use."

"What can I do?"

Standing, Cornelius reached up to the shelf above and took down several new jars and bottles. "I want you to clean up the mess and put those bottles away up on the shelves. Everything is labeled and in alphabetical order."

"Gotcha." Brandon stood and bent slightly over the table as he began to clean everything up. When he'd finished, he put away the bottles on the shelves, taking special care to make sure all labels were turned perfectly to the front and aligned in a straight row.

Cornelius surreptitiously watched Brandon while finishing his own work. "Once you're done, take the pink, blue, gold, and green bottles to the cauldron in the fireplace. The water should be boiling by now. Add the pink first, then stir it exactly twenty times; next the blue, stir the same way; then the gold; then the green."

Without a word, Brandon gathered the bottles and went to the fireplace. He began adding them as instructed, counting quietly with every stir. "And when I'm done?"

"Use the potholder to take the cauldron off its hook and set it over on the table where you were sitting." Turning on his seat, Cornelius allowed his gaze to drift over Brandon's backside, admiring the smooth movement of muscle beneath skin.

"What's this for, anyway?" Brandon asked as he grabbed the potholder and lifted the cauldron.

Cornelius scraped the paste he had made into the appropriate jar. "One of those damnable favors I owe that I wish I didn't. It's a love — or, better called, a lust potion. Seems Erikson is having a problem gaining the attention of somebody he wants. But that goes no further than you and me."

Brandon chuckled as he set the cauldron down on the table. "Lust potion, huh? All someone would need to do is take one look at you."

Turning to look at him, Cornelius said, "I turned Erikson down when he did. The fool had damn well better know not to use one on me." If Erikson even tried, once he came down from the effects, Cornelius would kill the bastard. "Just let it cool for now, and then it can be poured into bottles in a little while."

Brandon nodded and tossed the potholder beside the cauldron. He stood behind Cornelius and snaked an arm around his waist as the other hand tangled in Cornelius' hair, pulling his head back. Brandon flicked his tongue over Cornelius' ear and whispered, "I won't say a word."

Cornelius shivered. He didn't draw away, though he knew he should, and there was a barely noticeable trembling to his hand as he set the jar back on the table. Brandon's body was pressed up against him, the hard ridge of the young vampire's erection digging into his ass. Brandon slid his hand down the front of Cornelius' robe, caressing him. Then Brandon let him go.

Cornelius remained utterly still, biting at his lower lip and trying to stifle any sound from escaping. "Brandon..."

"Yes?" Brandon sat on his own stool with an almost angelic, innocent look on his face.

Cornelius' brow arched. "If I told you to stop, would you?"

Brandon grinned, completely unashamed. "You'd have to handcuff me to the bed to keep me from touching you."

"I can't tie you to the bed, Brandon." Cornelius tried for serious, but it was rather difficult when his body betrayed him.

"We can always try it the other way around."

Closing his eyes, Cornelius cupped his hand over his face as he propped his elbow on the table. "You can't tie me to the bed either," he muttered.

"Damn, so I guess I can't tie you down and lick your body from head to toe, huh?" One thing was for certain: Brandon was persistent, if nothing else.

A small, pained sound escaped Cornelius. He stood. "No, you can't do that either. Or kiss me. Or lick me." His voice totally failed him as he suddenly found himself pinned against Brandon's body. The feeling sent an instant reaction through him, and the sound of Brandon's moan caused a tightening deep down.

"Why?"

"Mael would *kill* me if I so much as look at you wrong." The words were more of a reminder for himself, and no truer words were spoken. Mael would flay his skin from his body and nail his hide to the workroom wall. Cornelius' hips instinctively pressed tighter before the young vampire let go of him. He stepped further back, trying to calm the rush of lust.

"I'm patient."

"Mael would take exception to it, Brandon. You don't understand."

"He controls who I want to have sex with? "

Cornelius backed away, and Brandon followed him. "No, not exactly. He doesn't control who you sleep with. But when it comes to me, he will be very upset. He'll skin me alive." When he felt the press of the wall against his backside, he couldn't move any further. "I'm not a fit companion for you, Brandon."

"Don't fucking move." Brandon dropped to his knees and lifted the robe. He wrapped his fingers around the length of Cornelius' shaft and quickly took him halfway into his mouth.

Cornelius inhaled sharply, and a startled gasp escaped him. He gripped Brandon's shoulder to push him away, but found himself thrusting forward, trying bury himself in Brandon's mouth.

Brandon pulled off slowly and looked up. "Just enjoy it." He lowered his mouth back over Cornelius' cock and began to milk it with his fist as he rolled his tongue around the head.

Cornelius' head banged against the stone wall behind him. It took an enormous amount of his will to move his hand from Brandon's shoulder to his head. His fingers caught in the brown hair, and he pulled Brandon gently back as he shifted enough to get away. Before Brandon could react, Cornelius reached down and pulled him up. When his arms encircled Brandon's waist, he captured Brandon's lips in a kiss to still any potential protests. The young vampire let out a surprised gasp before melting into him.

"Damn, you taste good."

Cornelius had the sinking feeling Brandon didn't understand at all, and he knew the kiss had been a mistake on his part, just one he couldn't resist. "Brandon, I'm not a fit companion for you. You're going to have to get that through your head." Shaking his head, Cornelius went back to the table. "Go ahead and start pouring that potion into the bottles."

Brandon followed him, but before he started to do what he'd been instructed to do, he leaned over to whisper in Cornelius' ear. "I'll find a way to make you come, even if I have to do it without touching you."

"No, you will not." Cornelius' voice took on a stern edge as he deliberately returned to his own work. The only thing he could do was ignore the deliberate enticements of the young vampire as best he could.

"You don't share the desire?"

Pausing, Cornelius turned his head to look at Brandon. "If I didn't, I wouldn't have kissed you, and you wouldn't be here now. But you have to understand that, no matter how much I want you, I can't act on what I feel."

Brandon picked up another bottle. "What if Cian were to speak with Mael?"

"I don't think that has anything to do with it, Brandon. Mael has his reasons."

"Cian's persuasive, especially with Mael." Brandon set the last full bottle down and sat down on the stool.

"Persuasive doesn't work when somebody is right." Even Cornelius knew his own nature. Eventually, Brandon would probably get hurt by it all. Sighing quietly, he busied himself with cleaning up.

"What do you need me to do?"

"We'll just finish cleaning up here before I have to return to the throne room." Cornelius frowned slightly when he looked up to see the look of disappointment on Brandon's face. "I'm not rejecting you, Brandon. If anything, I wish that we could."

Brandon smiled at him. "You do?"

Cornelius just shook his head. "Have you looked at yourself lately?"

"Not since I got kicked out by my dad. That was seven years ago. I've never had a big opinion of myself. I was a nerd in school."

Cornelius was more than a little surprised. "I see lack of some brain material might run in the family." He took Brandon by the shoulder, leading him toward the mirror on the far wall. He stood behind Brandon. "Tell me what you see."

Brandon stared at himself and didn't seem to be overly impressed. "I guess I look okay, like an average guy."

"Then I will tell you what I see," Cornelius whispered. "You have what I call bedroom eyes: eyes I *know* would darken with a loving touch. And your hair is very hard to resist touching, just to see if it's as soft as it looks."

A pink stain flushed Brandon's cheeks before he looked away from the mirror. "I've never had anyone say anything like that."

Chuckling softly, Cornelius continued. "I already know how your lips feel, but when you smile, there's the sweetest little upturning at the corners. I don't think I can even go into what I think about your body. Just suffice to say: you are one hell of an attractive man."

Brandon stared at Cornelius in the mirror, speechless for a moment, and then he pulled away slowly. "So, what all needs to be cleaned up?"

Cornelius could tell Brandon wasn't used to someone saying things like that and that he honestly didn't know how to react when someone paid him a compliment. "Except for what I was working on, everything is done for now."

"Okay," Brandon said quietly. He looked around for a moment, as if he didn't want to leave the workroom. "Anything else you need from me?"

"If you want to stay, there are several lists over there on the table that need to be worked on. I really could use a serious organization of this place." Cornelius sighed quietly before adding, "I don't want you unhappy here."

"Then please don't send me away." Brandon turned away from him. "I haven't felt at home anywhere else since Cian brought me than when I stepped foot in here."

"I'm not going to send you away. Whatever gave you that idea?" Cornelius couldn't recall anything he had said that would have given Brandon that impression.

Brandon shrugged. "Guess I'm used to it. You'd think after so many years, I'd get over it." He laughed, although the sound wasn't an entirely happy one. He fingered the edge of the table absently. "I'm sorry if I made you uncomfortable."

There was no way in hell Cornelius could let that pass. Slowly, he moved up behind Brandon, laying a hand on his shoulder. "You haven't made me uncomfortable. Not at all. I enjoy having you with me in my workroom too much. You are always welcome here, whenever you want. You're the only one besides Mael who has my full permission to be here."

Turning around, Brandon leaned back up against the table, giving him a wistful smile. "Thank you." He reached out, slipping his arms around Cornelius' neck. "Just one more kiss? Please?"

Cornelius was at a loss for words as he stared at the young vampire. His head slowly lowered to Brandon's, and he kissed him softly. Feeling the slow parting welcome from Brandon, a soft growl sounded low in Cornelius' throat. Even though he knew he shouldn't, his tongue darted out, slowly probing Brandon's mouth, taking his own taste.

Brandon moaned, opening fully as his arms tightened around Cornelius' neck. The slow caress of his tongue devoured Brandon before Cornelius had to pull away. He wanted too much and knew all too well Mael would make him pay if he did anything.

Brandon released him, albeit reluctantly. "I know, I know," he said with wry laugh. "You can't do anything."

"A lesson of life is that you can't always have what you want." Turning away, Cornelius headed for the door. "I need to make sure the morons downstairs are behaving themselves. Don't work too hard in here." Brandon's laugh followed him out.

Chapter Fifteen

Waking up to the soft light from the fireplace dancing over the room, Mael was aware of Cian fast asleep beside him. The quiet feeling within the room washed over him as he carefully rolled to his side to watch his angel sleeping. Propping up on his elbow, he smiled and tenderly brushed back a lock of golden hair. For the first time in his existence, his own mind was at peace. Even though he didn't fully understand Cian's love for him, he couldn't imagine living without it. He knew how barren his own soul would be without its light.

Hunger began to nag at him, and he realized it had taken just about everything out of him to heal. He had the feeling it had devastated Cian as well. He'd been barely aware of anything when Cian had brought him here. The only thing that stuck in his mind was that he was safe in the tower with his sorcerer. He'd also been shocked by the realization that the wings he thought he'd imagined were *very* real.

He smiled, realizing the blue feather he'd found near his bedroom balcony had been his lover's. He'd known that the sorcerer had spied on him, but the feather told him what had been seen.

Sighing with the incessant need to feed that constantly rolled through him, he stared down at Cian's face. He couldn't feed from Cian since he already had the feeling that Cian had probably fed him for however long he'd been out of commission. Being very careful not to awaken him, Mael got up. Even without a stitch of clothing on his body, he had no qualms about appearing to Cornelius. He touched the crystal hanging around his neck, and when a portal opened for him, he stepped through. Emerging on the other side into Cornelius' workroom, he silently summoned both the mage and Seth to him. He would need both of them because the low amount of blood in his system was only enough to allow him movement.

Several moments passed before the door opened, and Cornelius entered with a beaming smile as he looked Mael over. "Good to see you back on your feet. You gave us a bit of a worry there, but I see Cian took excellent care of you these last four days."

Mael frowned; he hadn't expected it took that long. "I left Cian sleeping so I could feed."

Seth opened the door and stepped inside, shutting it behind him. Without a word, he walked over to Mael and, with a tilt of his head, presented himself. Mael drew him close and lowered his head to Seth's throat, sinking his fangs in quickly.

"You'll probably need more, Mael," Cornelius said offhandedly.

A soft growl from Mael answered the mage as he continued drinking the hot crimson nourishment he needed. Seth nudged closer to him, wrapping his arms around Mael's neck, moaning. The only sound within the room was the crackling of the fire and Seth before Mael released him. He still needed more but didn't want to take the chance of weakening his ghoul too much. He silenced the soft protest from Seth with a light press of his lips.

"You know better, little one." Smiling slowly, he drew back, running an affectionate touch to the side of Seth's face.

"It never hurts to try, Your Excellency." Thoroughly unashamed, Seth grinned back at him. "When will you be returning home?"

"I'll be back tomorrow night." Turning his head to look at his mage, Mael said, "Think you can handle the fort until then?"

Rolling his eyes, Cornelius muttered, "They are absolutely driving me to drink, Mael. Not a one of them seems to be able to do anything without a whip." He paused, then sighed. "Oh, all right. Just one more night won't hurt. But no more than that, you hear me?"

"Thank you, Cornelius. I just wanted one more night—"

Sliding from his stool, Cornelius interrupted him before he could finish. "Yes, I know, I know. You have it. Give him a kiss for me." Cornelius' smile was positively wicked as he stopped in front of Mael. "Now feed and get back to him. I think he's been through hell trying to take care of you."

Closing the small distance between them, Mael burrowed against the mage's throat before biting him. The spurt of blood filled his mouth before he swallowed, and he tightened his mouth to take another. The more powerful richness would be all he needed for his system to return to normal. He felt Cornelius' arms encircle his waist and the slow, comforting sway of their bodies as he feed more deeply.

It took several hard draughts before Mael could even slow down. The familiar fire warmed through his body as his lips and tongue nuzzled over the wounds. Cornelius held him, letting him take what he needed, the soft cadence of his murmur rising and falling while Mael drank. When Mael knew he'd had enough, he healed the marks and drew back.

"Feeling better now, are we?" Chuckling, the mage grinned at him before reaching up and gently smacking his cheek.

The door opened again, and Brandon came into the room. Upon seeing them, however, he stopped in his tracks. He abruptly turned on his heel to leave, but Cornelius stopped him.

"Don't go, Brandon. I've finally managed to sneak back in here, and we've got a bit of work to do."

Mael caught the confused look on Brandon's face before he touched the crystal at his throat once again. "I'll be back tomorrow night. I know you two can keep things calm here until then."

When he stepped back into the tower, he returned to the bed, taking his place beside Cian again. He was thankful the sorcerer hadn't woken up while he was gone. As he stretched out, his mind marveled at the thought that struck him. He had a place beside the most beautiful creature he had ever seen. Settling on his side, his fingers drifted slowly to the outline of Cian's features. He didn't want to wake him up, yet he longed to see the beautiful blue eyes open and see him.

* * *

Cian opened his eyes slowly, only to meet the entrancing gaze of his prince. *His prince.* He smiled and reached out to caress his fingers down Mael's cheek.

"I wanted to wake up beside you," Mael said quietly.

"And you did. I never dreamed this could happen to me. You're so beautiful." Cian slipped his hand around to cup the back of Mael's neck, pulling him in for a kiss.

"I was thinking the same thing."

Moaning softly into Mael's mouth, Cian found himself lost in the prince's touch and their kiss. He felt the prince's acceptance, and it spoke volumes about Mael's soul. Mael pulled away and studied Cian for a moment.

"I had to leave here before you woke, but only to feed so that I could come back to you as I wanted. Cornelius told me you went through hell, Cian. You seem somewhat lost in thought. A penny?"

Cian caressed Mael's face, and his gaze settled on Mael's eyes, those deep blue windows to the prince's soul. "I've seen many beautiful beings in my lifetime," he said quietly. "The angels of Heaven hold nothing to you."

"I see the same in you. So beautifully pure it almost hurts. If I let myself go, I could fall into you forever."

"I want so badly to touch you, to feel you," Cian said with a hint of hesitation, "but I know you must still be weak. I miss feeling you inside me, the way you taste."

A soft touch from Mael's hand trailed slowly downward over Cian's chest. "I might be able to accommodate that." A faintly wicked tinge showed in the prince's smile as he lowered his face to Cian's. Leaning forward, Mael gave him a quick kiss, and his teeth caught at Cian's lower lip, nicking the skin with one fang. He licked the tiny wound.

Cian whimpered softly and fought the faintest touch of his own hunger. He knew Mael couldn't feed him, but it didn't lessen the burning ache.

"Oh, but I can, sorcerer. I *can* feed you, and so much more." The prince's fingers casually descended toward Cian's stomach.

Cian's breath caught in his throat, and a slow tremor moved through him. "Mael...please..."

"You'll be saying that many times before I am done with you." The soft sound of Mael's laughter wrapped around Cian's senses. He shifted position and lowered his head to Cian's chest. He tasted Cian's skin in slow flicks before pausing at his left nipple, drawing it into his mouth. The edge of his teeth bit gently at Cian's skin.

Cian drew in a sharp breath, and his fingers tangled in Mael's hair. His heart thundered, and his body arched, desperate for more. Mael's name became a whispered prayer. His flesh burned sweetly at every point their bodies touched. Then the prince moved down, and his fingers circled the base of Cian's cock as his tongue slowly swirled around the head.

Cian thrust his hips up, wanting to feel those lips around him. "Mael..."

The flat of Mael's tongue rubbed against the sensitive underside, ignoring, for the moment, the sudden thrust wanting deeper into his mouth. Finally, his mouth enveloped Cian. Cian's grip tightened as he began to move in and out of the velvet heat of the prince's mouth. Welsh and English mingled until the words began to sound like a chant. His body tightened, but he fought it off, not wanting to climax yet.

The teasing brush of Mael's hand barely drifted over Cian's balls, then further back. A ghost of a touch ran over Cian's skin, and the tight cavern of Mael's mouth pulled

Cian in more deeply with each instinctive thrust. One of Mael's hands reached for Cian's, twining their fingers together.

"Come for me, my angel. Don't hold back from me."

"Mael."

The whisper became a deep growl as Cian's body tightened, then released. He cried out Mael's name as he buried himself in the prince's mouth, his cock pulsing as he came. Mael's throat contracted around Cian, drinking his release. A pulsing vibration sent ripples of additional pleasure through Cian, and he tightened his grip on Mael's hand. Taking advantage of their connection, he sent a flood of his pleasure to the prince. With a deeper vibration of Mael's throat, Cian's body rocked as another wave hit him.

* * *

Mael shuddered hard with the unexpected sensations that flooded him. Unable to fully react, he ran the flat of his tongue upward, cleaning Cian's cock before finally letting him go. Mael moved to his knees between Cian's legs and stared down at him, drinking in his angel's reaction.

"I'm not done with you yet." It was a serious wonder he could even get his own thoughts back together after that completely unexpected sharing of Cian's orgasm.

Cian's eyes widened for a moment. "Are you trying to give me a heart attack?" he asked with a playful smirk.

"No, but I'm fairly sure after this one, you'll be begging for me. Or I will be begging for you. Whichever one comes first."

Tendrils of shadows formed from the darkness at the corners of the bed. They slithered slowly across the corners and wrapped around Cian's wrists and ankles. The other ends curled tightly to the four posters of the bed.

Cian tried to move, and his gaze narrowed as he looked at Mael. "What are you doing?"

"Just making sure you don't touch for now." Mael chuckled softly as he rose slightly on his knees, just enough for Cian to get a very clear view of him. His fingers brushed slowly over his own chest, lingering in slow circles around each of his nipples, his gaze never leaving Cian's.

An intent gaze locked onto Mael's fingers and followed their every move. Cian's breathing became labored once more, and he strained against the bonds with his arms. "This isn't fair, Mael," he pleaded, although the look in his eyes told Mael that he was enjoying himself.

"It's not meant to be fair. Tonight, you're in my power, and I'm going to enjoy that to its fullest." The downward path of his hand already had Mael's cock hardening before he'd even touched it. The combination of the intensity of Cian's stare and his own thoughts aroused him more than he thought possible.

"This is torture. I want to touch you so bad."

"But this isn't the half of it, Cian." A soft, purring tone caressed to his angel's name as Mael raised his own hands above his head. Shadows shot out from underneath the canopy, wrapping tightly to his wrists. Darkness formed, in the shape of hands, at Mael's chest and above Cian's. Feeling like velvet, the shadows ran slowly over their skin in twin movements. "I think the shadows want to play with us, too."

"Oh, God..."

As he felt the velvety texture close around his cock, Mael groaned softly, closing his eyes. "Next it will be you, my angel." He tipped his head back as his hips jerked forward. The touch of two other shadows began probing inside them both.

Mael parted his legs further, feeling the slow push of the darkness that slid into his ass, expanding to fill him. A low sound of deeper need accompanied the friction of the darkness moving within him and over his cock. More ragged moans fell from his lips as the shadows increased rapidly over his cock. His body tightened for a moment, and he struggled against the ties that held him as he opened his eyes.

"I need you to fuck me, Cian." They were the only words Mael could get out before his body strained forward as he came, the spill of liquid contained with the shadows.

"Mael!" Cian's hips rose as he groaned. He bucked his hips against the shadows that impaled his body and stroked his cock. His eyes turned pitch black, and he growled in frustration.

The tendrils released Cian but left Mael suspended. Mael bowed his head, trying to regain his scattered senses. Within his mind, the need that was spoken before he came remained overwhelming.

Cian tangled his fingers in Mael's hair and jerked his head back, crushing their mouths together in a possessive kiss. His other hand reached around to Mael's ass, and he buried two fingers deep inside Mael's body roughly. As he felt Cian's need and desire wash over him, Mael's low groan was drowned by the roughness of Cian's kiss. Hungrily, he returned the kiss and pushed back against the angel's fingers.

Pulling abruptly away, Cian stared down into Mael's eyes, drawing Mael deeper into him. The only thought within Mael's mind was the acceptance of Cian's possessiveness. Without removing his fingers, Cian pulled him down and shoved him onto his back on the bed. He drove his fingers deeper inside Mael's body. A soft cry escaped Mael, and he pushed back almost desperately against Cian's fingers.

"Fuck me, my angel. I need you to fuck me."

Cian pulled his fingers out and rolled Mael over, pulling him onto his hands and knees. He rubbed the head of his cock over Mael's hole and wrapped a hand in Mael's hair, jerking him up and his head back. The second their bodies were pressed together, Cian thrust forward, impaling Mael on the entire length of his cock. The sudden pain of the brutal entry rocked through Mael, translating within it the need to *feel*. He cried out with the mixture of pain and pleasure that engulfed his body. The hold in his hair kept his head back toward Cian, his hips grinding back into the movement.

"I want to hear you beg, prince. I want to hear you screaming my name in desperation." Cian thrust even harder, the move taking both of their breaths away.

Mael reached back desperately, fingers clawing into Cian's hip, relishing the hard movement pounding into him. "Cian, please, let me feel how much I belong to you." He rasped out the words, barely able to speak.

The muscles of his body tightened as he turned his head to look at Cian. Then Mael tilted his head slowly. A wound appeared at the side of his throat, a trickle of blood spilling from it. The sense that he would let Cian drain him and take all of him filled through their connection.

Cian swiftly descended, sucking hungrily as he drove deeper in Mael with hard, quick thrusts. The sound of his growl settled deep inside Mael's mind, curling around his soul as the words slipped from Cian's mind to his.

"You. Are. Mine."

Mael shuddered uncontrollably as Cian fed from him. "Cian. Cian, I am yours." The words broke from him and echoed in the corridors of his mind. The nails at Cian's hip dug harder, drawing blood as Mael's other hand tangled in the golden hair, holding Cian to his throat before his entire world exploded in a bright flash of pure, exquisite pleasure.

With blinding force, Cian came. He pulled away from Mael's throat and turned Mael's head roughly, shoving his tongue into the prince's mouth. The tendrils of their connection flooded with the exploding rush of pleasure. Cian's love and soul wrapped around Mael's in a tight, divine embrace. There were no more words, only the joining of their souls in that moment, merging them as one.

As their bodies began to still, Cian pulled away from their kiss and out of Mael. He collapsed onto his back on the bed and urged Mael down with him, cradling the prince in his arms tightly as his wings folded around them. Mael curled in against him, and Cian kissed the prince's hair softly.

"I hope I didn't do any damage."

"No, but I know exactly who I belong to now." Mael tipped his head back to look at Cian.

"Likewise." Cian pressed his lips to Mael's forehead, and a soft, soothing, gentle pulse radiated from the kiss. The quiet warmth settled over them both.

"You can prove that later. When I can move again."

Chuckling, Cian tilted Mael's head up to kiss him. "Would it be a stupid question to ask how you're feeling?"

"Does saying I feel like I'm in heaven make any sense?"

"Would it make sense if I were to tell you that you are heaven to me?"

"That makes complete sense to me now, Cian."

Cian held his gaze. "Do you believe in soul mates?"

"Not until now."

Cian brushed his thumb along Mael's bottom lip. "We're bound, Mael. I felt it the first time I saw you, but I didn't want to believe it. Now I know that I could never live without you." He paused for a moment. "I love you. I hope you never get tired of hearing that."

"We're bound beyond even what you understand. My life and death are yours for our eternity. I'll never tire of hearing that or feeling it take me over."

"Then I will guard your life with mine," Cian whispered. He closed his eyes and pulled Mael closer, tightening his right wing over them.

Mael's arms slid up, encircling Cian's neck as his tongue slipped between his lips in a deeply passionate kiss.

Chapter Sixteen

Cornelius had dealt with enough nonsense for the night, particularly when it became obvious that a few wanted to include him in their particular feeding games. Sighing quietly, he glanced over at Brandon sitting near him. "Think it's about time we sneak out of here?"

Brandon shrugged. "Sure."

Cornelius stepped off the dais and carefully made his way past the reclining bodies. Before he managed to make it to the door, Erikson reached up, catching at his robe. With no more than annoyed glance downward, he tugged the material free and continued on his way. Once outside the door, he waited patiently for Brandon to catch up. He noticed that the young vampire seemed preoccupied lately, but he hadn't probed for any reason.

Shoving his hands in his pockets, Brandon looked off to the side. "What's the plan for tonight?"

"Did you want to join me in getting some work done, or should we just relax tonight?" As he ascended the stairs, Cornelius' hand smoothed over the wood of banister. He cast several side glances at Brandon, very curious as to what was bothering him.

The young vampire sighed and fell in beside him. "Pick one."

Vaguely surprised, Cornelius drew his spectacles down slightly. "I guess I'm in the mood for a bit of relaxation. Would you like to join me?"

"Sure," Brandon said with a shrug. "What did you have in mind?"

"A 'not get drunk' night." Cornelius chuckled as he walked down the second-floor corridor to his chambers. "The last time I had one with Cian, neither of us got drunk."

"Cian?"

"Yes. The first time I met him, he wanted to get drunk, and for an angel, that's impossible. For us as well, but there are ways around that." He opened his bedroom door and stepped inside, leaving it open for Brandon.

Stopping abruptly in the door, Brandon watched him. "Why would an angel want to get drunk?"

"He was brooding. Over what I wasn't sure about at the time, but then it came out that he was hungry and probably moody over Mael. Well, come in and shut the door behind you before somebody passes by and sees where we've gotten to."

Walking in, Brandon closed the door. "So how does a vampire get drunk?"

Cornelius retrieved two glasses from a small cabinet before he reached for one of the bottles. "There's absinthe and mead, but if you don't have either, you can always drink the blood of somebody who's been drinking. Hope you like whiskey; it's always been one of my favorites." Gathering up the bottle and glasses, he sat down next to Brandon, handing him one of the empty glasses.

Looking down at the bottle and then up at Cornelius, Brandon said, "I thought you said absinthe and mead would get a vampire drunk?"

"Yes, I did say that, but I also said this is a 'not drunk' night, didn't I? Why? Would you like to try some of the other stuff?"

The young vampire looked more than confused. "Not drunk?"

Cornelius patted Brandon's knee. "Sorry, Brandon. It's a joke of mine. If I'm drinking whiskey or any other alcohol that doesn't get us drink, I refer to it as a 'not drunk' night."

"Ah. What's the point of drinking then?"

"Why, one enjoys the taste, of course. Did you want some whiskey or not?"

Brandon laughed and held up his glass. "Sure. I haven't had anything in a few years."

Cornelius poured a generous measure into both glasses. "Perhaps some time we'll try the absinthe. I'm assuming you've never had any."

"No. I've heard of it, but never had any." Brandon swirled the liquid in his glass before taking a sip.

"We definitely need to expand your education a bit." Cornelius eyed the bottle in his hand with a rather thoughtful look before continuing. "I've never been quite sure if it's a good thing or not that most alcohol has no real effect on us."

"Why would it be bad if it did have an effect?"

Taking a small sip, Cornelius swallowed, feeling the familiar burn that he enjoyed. "You've seen the silly lot that comprises this court and can still ask that?" He chuckled again. "I really do need to educate you."

"Then can we start by settling something that's been on my mind?"

As he set the bottle on the nightstand, Cornelius glanced over at him. "Certainly."

"Is there more of a relationship between you and Mael than just a prince and his mage?"

One of his eyebrows lifted slightly, yet Cornelius wasn't dismayed or upset by the question. "A very long time ago, there was. Why are you asking?"

"Because when he fed from you in the workroom, it just looked like there was much more going on."

"Ah." The one word conveyed a great deal of understanding. "I see." Cornelius shook his head. "We separated a very, very long time ago, Brandon. All you saw was me feeding him. He needed my blood to regain his own strength. That's not something I would deny him."

"That makes sense." Brandon nodded as he took another drink. He laughed after a moment. "I wish this stuff did get us drunk."

"Is that why you've been so quiet lately? Because you thought there was still something between me and Mael?"

Brandon sighed. "Yeah."

Though he knew he shouldn't, Cornelius couldn't help feeling flattered by an obvious display of jealousy. "There's no reason for it to bother you, Brandon," he said softly. "Anything between me and Mael died many centuries ago. More my fault than his, though I don't think he ever saw it that way."

"I didn't say it bothered me," Brandon countered. "It just surprised me."

Cornelius finished his drink in one swallow before pouring himself another. "Then I take it I've misinterpreted the situation, and you weren't jealous."

Brandon groaned and leaned over, cradling his glass between his hands. "Fine. Yes, I was jealous."

"There's nothing wrong with admitting your feelings," Cornelius said. "And I'd never encourage you to hide what you do feel."

"I really need to get drunk," Brandon muttered under his breath.

"If you want to get drunk that much, I suppose I could feed you, though it would be helpful to get more whiskey into me."

Brandon stood up without a word and picked up the whiskey bottle, pouring himself some more. Then he took a drink, leaned forward, and pressed his closed lips to Cornelius'. Momentarily startled but unable to pull back, the feel of the young vampire's lips had Cornelius opening to him, his tongue taking a taste of the whiskey clinging to Brandon's mouth. Brandon opened his mouth fully, and warm whiskey flowed into the kiss. Then he pulled away and grinned.

"Drink."

Cornelius shook his head as he took the bottle from Brandon's hand. "That is not what I meant, and you know it."

The grin on Brandon's lips widened as he sat back down on the bed. "You can't blame me for trying, Cornelius."

Cornelius drank several swigs straight from the bottle. "No, to be honest I never blame you for trying, Brandon. It's more knowing I can't respond as I would like to."

"Do you really want me to stop? I mean, *really* want me to?"

Cornelius had to continue drinking to avoid the gaze directed at him. He wished at this point he could get *very* drunk. Finally, he quietly answered, "I can't lie, Brandon. No, I don't want you to stop. I wish..." He trailed off, shaking his head because he couldn't say what he most wanted to.

"What do you wish?"

"That I could lay you back on this bed, Brandon, and taste every inch of you that I want." Lowering his gaze to the bottle, Cornelius stared at the label as he picked at the edge of it. "And I really shouldn't say that to you either."

Brandon knelt down in front of him. He slipped his hand under Cornelius' chin, lifting his head up. "Now it's my turn to say what I wish. I wish I could make you and everyone else understand that I finally have a place to call my own. I wish I could express how it feels to be in your workroom, working side by side with you."

"I think I understand how you feel about that. It's the same as I feel having you beside me. And it is *our* workroom now, as much mine as yours. I wouldn't lose that for that world."

Shaking his head, Brandon stood, resuming his almost-frantic pacing. "I'm not so sure you do understand what I mean, Cornelius."

Cornelius set the bottle back on the stand. "Then explain it to me so that I can."

Stopping again, Brandon leaned his forehead against the wall. "I'm afraid it goes well beyond attraction...for me, anyway."

Though he felt dismay listening to Brandon, it was something Cornelius effectively hid. Standing from the bed, he silently moved toward Brandon and gently turned the young vampire around to face him.

Brandon shook his head and put his hand on Cornelius' chest to put some distance between them. "I'm sorry, Cornelius. I know that wasn't something you wanted to hear, but you asked. I don't want your sympathy; I want you."

Cornelius' hands dropped slowly back to his sides. "That's not what I was giving you. You have somebody who wants very badly to answer your need." Sighing quietly, he turned from away and headed for the balcony doors.

Brandon followed him. "What do you mean?"

Curling his hands to the railing, Cornelius tipped his head back and stared up into the night sky. "You know very well what I mean. Every time you do something, I can never push you away."

Brandon's arms slid around his waist, and Brandon rested his head on Cornelius' shoulder. "I'm sorry. Goddamn it, Cornelius, I can't help it. I've been watching and wanting you since the first time I saw you. When we're working together in the workroom, I feel like I'm wanted, like someone finally cares enough about me to have me around."

Cornelius' hand lifted to cover Brandon's. "No, don't be sorry. You're right. You have a place where you are very much wanted, in more ways than one. And somebody who cares a great deal more about you than he should. I don't think either of us can help it."

"If I tell you something, will you promise not to freak out on me?"

Cornelius turned around. "What?"

"I'm starting to fall for you."

Staring down at him, Cornelius gazed searchingly into Brandon's eyes.

Brandon cocked his head to the side. "What? You're not freaked out?"

"Do I look freaked out?"

"Not exactly." Brandon tightened his hold around Cornelius' waist. "I'd give anything to touch you, to feel you inside me." He leaned his forehead on Cornelius' shoulder and whispered, "To love you."

Cornelius turned his head slightly, the soft touch of his lips brushing to Brandon's hair. Each of Brandon's words tugged at him, even if he couldn't answer them as he wanted to. "It would be a lie to tell you that I don't want the same."

"Great. I finally find the man of my dreams, and I can't have him," Brandon grumbled. Then he stilled and looked up into Cornelius' eyes. "If I can't have you as a companion, then can I ask you to be my Father?"

Cornelius stilled, and it took him a minute to recover. "Are you sure you want me as your Father?"

Brandon laughed. "Why would I not?"

"I've never had a child, Brandon. I'm not even sure what kind of a Father I would make for you. There are a hundred reasons why not, but I'm not really sure I give a damn about any of them. I would love to teach you and have you with me all of the time."

Brandon's expression turned serious, and he slid his fingers down one side of Cornelius' face, stroking his cheek softly. "I can think of the best reason to have you as my Father."

Lifting his hand to Brandon's, Cornelius cupped the young vampire's hand against his cheek. "You might have to tell me. I really can't think of a good reason."

"Because I already love you."

Instead of the dismay that should have filled him, Cornelius could only feel the lightness in his heart. "The only relationship I can have with you is that of your Father. And only that of your teacher, but at least I will be able to love you in that."

Brandon closed his eyes. "I understand. Just know that you've stolen my heart."

Incapable of resisting, Cornelius touched his lips to Brandon's as his eyes closed, taking that whisper as his own.

* * *

Mael stepped through the open portal into his chambers. His hand tugged at Cian's, drawing him into the room. The night and day spent in his lover's embrace had already become too much a part of his thoughts. Sighing quietly, he glanced around the familiar room, an odd sense of displacement momentarily disconcerting him. He turned to face Cian and released his hand, only to slide his arms around his angel. Parting was proving much more difficult than he thought possible.

When Cian buried in against him, Mael lifted his hand, smoothing over the golden curls. "I don't want to let you go, but we both have things that we have to take care of."

"I know. Your court will not wait, and the rogues are still a problem, so my work is far from done." Cian angled his head the slightest bit and brushed his lips softly over Mael's. "All you need to do is call me when you need me."

"As soon as I get everything settled here, it will be the first thing I do." Mael found the words very hard to say when all he wanted was to wake up once again beside Cian. The smallest thing was now the most precious to him. As his fingers combed slowly through Cian's hair, they tangled within it. The slight pressure of his hand held his angel close as he molded his lips more tightly to Cian's.

They both had many things that stood in their way, in addition to everything else that needed to be done. The only place they had been free in the last few days and nights was Cian's tower, and neither of them wanted to lose that.

Cian pulled away. "Nothing truly separates us, my prince. Nothing ever will. Though I'd venture to say that Cornelius will be relieved to have you back home."

"I know, but letting you go scares me somehow. And I'd venture to say he's the only one that will be."

"Do not be afraid," Cian whispered. He placed his hand on Mael's chest. "I'm here. When I'm in London, rest assured we will see one another." He slid his arms around Mael's neck slowly. "And don't be surprised if you feel a presence watching you."

Mael grinned. "I suppose I should warn you of the same."

Cian lifted an eyebrow at him. "Is there something I should know about?"

Mael shook his head, not saying anything.

Cian brushed his lips across Mael's. "Very well, don't tell me. But next time Seth comes to feed you, by all means, do not turn down the chance to touch him. He's quite a cute one."

"Cian..." The low rumble of Mael's laughter echoed in the room. "All right. Next time you decide to pleasure yourself, I'd rather do more than just watch from the shadows. Oh, and never leave proof behind when you leave." He glanced over at the blue feather lying on one of the tables.

"Watching you feed was nearly my undoing."

"Watching you come and being unable to join was mine. I've wanted nothing more than to have you since."

"In all my existence," Cian murmured, "your name is the only one that has ever fallen from my lips in such a way."

"Do you know what it does to me when you tell me such things, my angel?"

Cian pulled back with a look of feigned innocence. "No. Do tell."

A low warning growl sounded from Mael. "I would rather show you." His arms tightened around Cian, and he walked them backwards toward the bed.

Cian's tongue slid across Mael's lips slowly. "*Fwcia fi.*"

"I don't speak Welsh."

"Fuck. Me."